"Mr. O'Neal, are you ready to order?"

Teresa asked reporter Riley O'Neal, a regular at the Rainbow Café.

"How about a date with you?" Riley answered, a boyish grin resting on his lips.

It was hard to resist him, but Teresa had two kids and too many bills. Besides, this gray-eyed charmer might be the sexiest man that she'd ever seen, but she wasn't interested in his reckless attitude and irresponsible fun.

"The answer is no. I'm not on the menu, Mr. O'Neal."

"Teresa, one day I will come in here and you will offer me more than just eggs."

—A conversation between reporter Riley O'Neal and waitress Teresa Scott at the Rainbow Café

Dear Reader,

"It was a high like no other," says Elaine Nichols. She's speaking, of course, about getting "the call." After numerous submissions, Elaine sold her first manuscript to Silhouette Special Edition and we're pleased to publish *Cowgirl Be Mine* this month—a reunion romance between a heroine whose body needs healing and a hero whose wounds are hidden inside. Elaine has many more Special Edition books planned, so keep an eye out for this fresh new voice.

And be sure to pick up all the novels Special Edition has to offer. Marrying the Bravo fortune heir granted the heroine custody of her son, but once the two are under the same roof, they're *unable* to sleep in separate beds, in Christine Rimmer's *The Marriage Conspiracy*. Then a hungry reporter wishes his tempting waitress would offer him a tasty dish of *her* each morning, in *Dateline Matrimony* by reader favorite Gina Wilkins.

What's *The Truth About Tate?* Marilyn Pappano tells you when her journalist heroine threatens to expose the illegitimate brother of the hero, a man who would do anything to protect his family. She hadn't giggled since her mother died, so *His Little Girl's Laughter* by Karen Rose Smith is music to Rafe Pierson's ears. And in Tori Carrington's *The Woman for Dusty Conrad*, a firefighter hero has returned to divorce his wife, but discovers a still-burning flame.

We hope you enjoy this month's exciting selections, and if you have a dream of being published, like Elaine Nichols, please send a self-addressed stamped query letter to my attention at: Silhouette Books, 300 East 42nd St, 6th floor, New York, NY 10017.

Best,

Karen Taylor Richman
Senior Editor

Please address questions and book requests to:
Silhouette Reader Service
U.S.: 3010 Walden Ave., P.O. Box 1325, Buffalo, NY 14269
Canadian: P.O. Box 609, Fort Erie, Ont. L2A 5X3

Dateline Matrimony

GINA WILKINS

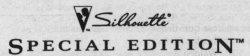

SPECIAL EDITION™

Published by Silhouette Books

America's Publisher of Contemporary Romance

If you purchased this book without a cover you should be aware
that this book is stolen property. It was reported as "unsold and
destroyed" to the publisher, and neither the author nor the
publisher has received any payment for this "stripped book."

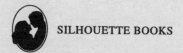 SILHOUETTE BOOKS

ISBN 0-373-24424-X

DATELINE MATRIMONY

Copyright © 2001 by Gina Wilkins

All rights reserved. Except for use in any review, the reproduction
or utilization of this work in whole or in part in any form by any
electronic, mechanical or other means, now known or hereafter
invented, including xerography, photocopying and recording, or in
any information storage or retrieval system, is forbidden without
the written permission of the editorial office, Silhouette Books,
300 East 42nd Street, New York, NY 10017 U.S.A.

All characters in this book have no existence outside the imagination of
the author and have no relation whatsoever to anyone bearing the same
name or names. They are not even distantly inspired by any individual
known or unknown to the author, and all incidents are pure invention.

This edition published by arrangement with Harlequin Books S.A.

® and TM are trademarks of Harlequin Books S.A., used under license.
Trademarks indicated with ® are registered in the United States Patent
and Trademark Office, the Canadian Trade Marks Office and in other
countries.

Visit Silhouette at www.eHarlequin.com

Printed in U.S.A.

Books by Gina Wilkins

Silhouette Special Edition

The Father Next Door #1082
It Could Happen to You #1119
Valentine Baby #1153
†*Her Very Own Family* #1243
†*That First Special Kiss* #1269
Surprise Partners #1318
**The Stranger in Room 205* #1399
**Bachelor Cop Finally
    Caught?* #1413
**Dateline Matrimony* #1424

§Family Found
†Family Found: Sons &
Daughters
**Hot Off The Press
‡The Family Way

**Previously published
as Gina Ferris:**

Silhouette Special Edition

Healing Sympathy #496
Lady Beware #549
In from the Rain #677
Prodigal Father #711
§*Full of Grace* #793
§*Hardworking Man* #806
§*Fair and Wise* #819
§*Far To Go* #862
§*Loving and Giving* #879
Babies on Board #913

**Previously published
as Gina Ferris Wilkins:**

Silhouette Special Edition

‡ *A Man for Mom* #955
‡*A Match for Celia* #967
‡*A Home for Adam* #980
‡*Cody's Fiancée* #1006

Silhouette Books

Mother's Day Collection 1995
Three Mothers and a Cradle
"Beginnings"

GINA WILKINS

is a bestselling and award-winning author who has written more than fifty novels for Harlequin and Silhouette Books. She credits her successful career in romance to her long, happy marriage and her three extraordinary children.

A lifelong resident of central Arkansas, Ms. Wilkins sold her first book to Harlequin in 1987 and has been writing full-time since. She has appeared on the Waldenbooks, B. Dalton and *USA Today* bestseller lists. She is a three-time recipient of the Maggie Award for Excellence, sponsored by Georgia Romance Writers, and has won several awards from the reviewers of *Romantic Times Magazine*.

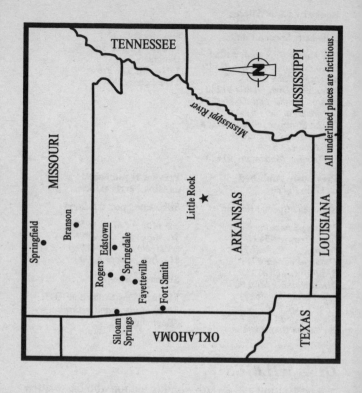

All underlined places are fictitious.

Chapter One

The man with the sharp gray eyes was back for breakfast. It was Friday morning, and it was the third time he'd come in during Teresa's first week on the job in the Rainbow Café. Still she hadn't gotten any more comfortable with him. On each occasion he had been reasonably well behaved, but there was something about him that made her nervous.

He flirted with her—not overtly, but with an underlying impudence that made her wonder if he was mocking her. What was it he found amusing about her? Was he one of those smug and superior types who thought everyone else was slightly beneath his intellectual level, especially a waitress in a small-town diner? He looked the type, she decided, then chided herself for making judgments about a man she didn't even know.

"What can I get you this morning?" she asked him.

She had never seen him open the menu, but he always

had his order ready when she asked. "Denver omelette with a side order of salsa. And coffee. Black."

"Biscuits or toast?"

"Toast. Has anyone ever mentioned that you look a bit like Grace Kelly?"

"Oh, sure. I get compared to dead movie-star princesses all the time," she answered airily. She'd decided the first time she met him that he enjoyed disconcerting people with off-the-wall comments, and she'd quickly decided that the best way to respond was in kind and without making it personal. She figured this guy didn't need any encouragement. "I'll be right back with your coffee."

She made another couple of stops on the return trip with the coffee carafe. Two elderly gentlemen, old friends who met in the diner every morning for breakfast, flirted outrageously with her when she refilled their coffee cups. She deflected their teasing easily, comfortable with them as she couldn't seem to be with the gray-eyed man watching her from the back table.

Though most of the customers were pleasant enough, there'd been a few who were rude, one or two whose innuendos went a little over the line, even a couple who were downright obnoxious. Having worked as a waitress before, she handled them all skillfully. The man who'd introduced himself to her only as Riley didn't fit any of those descriptions. He just made her...nervous.

"You aren't letting those guys turn your head with their flattery, are you?" he asked when she approached his table again to fill his cup. "Old Ernie thinks he's a real Romeo. He's probably proposed to you two or three times already."

She poured his coffee and answered blandly, "They seem quite nice."

It appeared to her that his smile turned faintly mocking again. "Do you say that about everyone you serve here?"

"Not *everyone*." With that subtle zinger, she stepped away from the table. "I'll go check on your food."

She didn't hurry to the kitchen, stopping twice on the way to refill coffee cups and check on customers. Letting the kitchen door swing closed behind her, she set the carafe down with a thump. "That guy is just strange," she muttered.

Shameka Cooper looked up from the pancakes and sausage links sizzling on a large griddle in front of her. "Which guy is that, hon?"

"Around thirty, brown hair sort of falling in his face, silvery gray eyes. Attitude."

Shameka didn't even have to glance toward the pass-through window that gave her a view of the dining room. "Sounds like Riley O'Neal."

"Yes, he said his name is Riley. Is he a jerk, or have I gotten a bad first impression?"

Shameka responded with the deep chuckle that had drawn Teresa to her from the beginning. "Oh, Riley's a sweetie who comes across as a jerk. Usually you just want to hug him, even though there are times you'd really like to whomp him a good one."

Teresa couldn't imagine actually hugging the guy, though she could picture herself wanting to whomp him. "He acts so smug," she said. "As if he knows something I don't. Something he finds amusing."

"That's Riley. And that's exactly why some folks don't care much for him. Myself, I've always gotten a kick out of him. He's not half as cynical as he pretends to be. He just thinks it goes with his image—you know, hard-nosed reporter."

"He's a reporter?" Teresa curled her lip. No wonder he acted so bored and worldly.

"Sure. He works for the *Evening Star*. That sort of makes him a co-worker of ours, I guess, since the family that owns this diner also owns the newspaper. Marjorie's daughter and son-in-law run the paper, while Marjorie keeps the diner going."

"Great," Teresa muttered. It was Marjorie—the mother of her college roommate—who had given Teresa this job. Marjorie Schaffer was one of the nicest people Teresa had ever met, and she'd bet the older woman had a soft spot for the carelessly charming reporter.

"You'll like him once you get to know him," Shameka assured her with a broad smile. "Nearly everyone does. Just don't let him give you any guff. Here's his breakfast."

Even as she accepted the well-filled plate, Teresa found herself doubting that she and Riley O'Neal would ever be friends.

Riley considered himself one of the most misunderstood men in his small Arkansas town. He knew who and what he was—but many people tended to get mistaken ideas about him.

There were some who deemed him lazy. He wasn't, of course—it was just that he did most of his work in his head. Others thought his pointed humor was evidence of a sarcastic and cynical nature. He thought of himself more as a droll observer of human foibles. Some called him blunt and tactless, but he just tried to be honest.

Dubbed a loner by many, he simply valued his privacy. He needed peace and quiet for his writing, something he couldn't get with a bunch of people around all the time. On those occasions when he was in the mood for company, he found it. That hardly made him a loner—did it?

Because he could savor a cup of coffee in peace there, he had decided to have breakfast at the Rainbow Café last Monday morning. He'd known the owner, Marjorie Schaffer, for a long time and was almost as comfortable in her diner as he was in his own kitchen. There were always plenty of greetings, of course, when he arrived. Edstown wasn't very big, and he'd lived there most of his life. Because of that and his job as a reporter for the Edstown *Evening Star,* he knew many of the local citizens. They also knew him well enough to leave him alone while he read his newspaper and ate his breakfast.

He had opened the paper as soon as he settled into his seat, burying his face in the pages. It was an effective deterrent to conversational overtures—and besides, he really enjoyed reading the newspaper. He had an appreciation for the little local paper that paid his salary—the few real news stories on the front page, the local gossip and trivia on the inside pages, the cooking section edited by a retired, eighty-year-old former home-ec teacher, the sports pages written by rotating high school sportscaster wannabes. The Edstown *Evening Star* had its own charm, its own place in this town, but it was the state-wide morning paper Riley perused to stay connected with the rest of the world.

He'd been surprised when someone new had taken his order that morning—and even more surprised that the new server was a real knockout. Shoulder-length dark blond hair streaked with gold was neatly secured at the back of her neck. Clear blue eyes framed with long, skillfully darkened lashes dominated her heart-shaped face. Her nose was straight and perfectly proportioned, and she needed no cosmetic enhancement to make the most of naturally rosy, sweetly curved lips. Her chin was a little pointed, he had decided, trying to be objective—but he liked the shallow dimple there.

Maybe it had been that enticing dimple that had brought him back two more times in the past week, even though he usually visited the diner for breakfast no more than once or twice a month.

His newspaper forgotten for a moment, Riley watched her walk away after taking his order Friday morning. Nice figure, he noted, not for the first time. Not too thin—he'd never been drawn to the bony supermodel type. As befitted the ultra-casual atmosphere of the place, she wore jeans with a long-sleeved white cotton shirt and sneakers. The jeans fit very well, he observed, his gaze lingering for a moment on her shapely derriere.

He guessed that she was close to his own age, thirty. She didn't wear a wedding ring—no jewelry at all, actually, except for a no-frills wristwatch. She was new in town and probably didn't know many people yet. He'd decided to give her a call some time when he was in the mood to go out, though she hadn't given him much encouragement so far.

She returned quickly with his breakfast. "Is there anything else I can get for you?"

A half dozen flip responses leaped into his mind. Casual flirting had always come easily to him, and there were plenty of women who'd reciprocated. Because she seemed to be braced for just such a remark, he bit back the innuendos and answered circumspectly. "Not right now, thank you."

"All right. I'll be back soon to refill your coffee."

"Thanks. By the way, what's your last name, Teresa?" He should know that by now, he thought, having met her three times so far. He must be getting slow.

"Scott," she answered without elaboration. "Excuse me, one of my other customers is signaling for me."

He wouldn't exactly call her friendly, he mused as she turned to leave. Polite enough—but only to the point that her job required. Could be a challenge.

He smiled. When it didn't require too much effort on his part, Riley enjoyed the occasional challenge.

"So, have you gotten a good look at that pretty new waitress over at the Rainbow Café yet?" Bud O'Neal asked his nephew Sunday afternoon.

Riley nodded toward the television screen in front of him. "I'm trying to watch the race, Bud."

"They're running under a caution flag now. You're not going to miss anything by answering my question. Have you seen the new waitress yet?"

Dragging his gaze from the NASCAR race, Riley shoved a hand through his shaggy hair. "I've seen her."

Bud gave a cackle. "So I've heard."

Riley shook his head in exasperation. "Then why did you ask?"

"I hear you've suddenly become a regular at the diner. Some folks that say you've been having trouble taking your eyes off the pretty waitress."

"Yeah, well, we both know there's nothing folks in this town like better than fabricating gossip out of thin air." Riley turned pointedly toward the television and lifted a can of soda to his lips to signal that he considered the subject closed.

He knew, of course, that Bud wouldn't cooperate. He was right. "You always did like leggy, big-eyed blondes," Bud drawled, obviously having a fine time needling his only nephew.

Riley heaved an exaggerated sigh. "What do you

want me to say? I'll admit she's nice to look at. And maybe I've flirted with her a couple of times. But when I did, she nearly gave me frostbite with those big, cold blue eyes of hers. So, if you're finished making fun of me, let's get back to watching the race.''

There were few people Riley would have allowed such leeway, but he was fond of his uncle. Besides, Bud was still recovering from the tragic death of one of his two closest friends earlier that year. It was good to see him smile again, even if it *was* at Riley's expense.

Bud's smile turned to a scowl. "She shot you down? What's wrong with the girl?"

"Nothing's wrong with her, as far as I can tell. She's just not interested. Not everyone is, you know. I'm not quite the lady-killer you seem to think I am.''

Bud snorted. "I've never seen a woman yet who didn't come around when you gave it your best shot. So, only thing I can figure is, either you've decided the pretty waitress ain't worth the effort—or you're just taking your time about going after her.''

"Would you stop calling her the pretty waitress? She has a name. Teresa.''

Bud's bushy, steel-gray eyebrows shot upward in response to his nephew's testy tone. "Not that you're interested, of course,'' he murmured.

Riley looked pointedly at the big-screen TV. "Watch the race. They're going green again.''

Knowing when he'd pushed hard enough, Bud crossed his hands over his beer-swollen belly and leaned back against the couch. His feet, like Riley's, were crossed on the scarred coffee table in front of them. They sat in the living room of Bud's double-wide mobile home, salvaged from his second divorce five years ago, after dining on a Sunday lunch of chili dogs and Tater Tots.

Riley and Bud tried to get together like this often, since they were the only members of their family still living in Edstown. Sixty-five-year-old Bud had never had children, so he'd always taken a rather fatherly interest in his only brother's only son, especially after Riley's parents had retired to Florida almost ten years ago while Riley was a senior in college.

Watching the brightly painted advertising-covered stock cars whizzing past the cameras, Riley changed the subject by asking, "How's R.L. these days? I haven't seen him much since he retired from the insurance business."

"We're going fishing Wednesday morning. Meeting here at a quarter till six. You want to go with us?"

"No, thanks. I'll pass. I'm planning on sleeping in that morning."

"Wuss," Bud muttered with a chuckle.

"Hey, it's chilly out on a lake at dawn in the middle of September. There are some parts of my body I don't want to risk freezing off, okay? I'm not quite finished with them yet."

Bud laughed, then shook his head. "I keep telling you, you don't get cold if you dress right. And come mid-morning, it still gets downright hot this time of year."

"No, really, Bud. Thanks, but it's just not my thing. You and R.L. go and have a good time, okay?"

"I'm sure we will. 'Course, we'll miss Truman."

Riley nodded somberly, never knowing quite what to say when his uncle brought up Truman's name.

Truman Kellogg, who'd been practically inseparable from Bud O'Neal and R. L. Hightower for nearly fifty years, had died in a house fire almost eight months ago.

The remaining two buddies had taken the death hard. Bud hadn't really been the same since.

Had his pal's death forced him to confront his own mortality? Or was it simply that he'd never imagined a time when the three of them wouldn't all be together? The friendship had lasted through their school years, Bud's and R.L.'s marriages and divorces, the death of Truman's wife several years ago, good and bad economic turns—it was only natural, Riley supposed, that Bud and R.L. were having a hard time dealing with their loss.

"Good grief, will you look at that?" Bud shook his head in dismay as several cars in the race crashed into the wall and each other. "That wreck'll put a bunch of 'em behind the wall, I bet."

"Damn. Martin didn't have a chance to avoid the mess," Riley muttered, looking morosely at the formerly sleek race car that was now smashed on both ends from the chain-reaction collisions. The Arkansas-native driver Riley usually rooted for was unharmed, but there was no chance he'd finish the race. "He's had a hell of a season, hasn't he? One thing right after another."

"I know the feeling," Bud said morosely. And then, before Riley could comment, he asked, "You sure you don't want me to talk to that pretty little waitress for you? I bet I could convince her you're not as bad as you've probably come across to her."

"Stay out of my love life."

Bud snorted, making a visible effort to cheer up. "*What* love life? Looks to me like you could use all the help you can get. You want another drink?"

"No. And I'm serious, Bud. Don't you say a word to Teresa."

His uncle grinned as he headed for the kitchen, leaving Riley feeling decidedly wary.

Riley was on his way to the newspaper office after a routine interview with the mayor Monday afternoon when he spotted Teresa Scott stranded on the side of the road. She was standing beside an aging sedan, looking at a flat tire on the right rear, her pretty face darkened by a frown. He promptly pulled his classic two-seater to the side of the road behind her car.

"Looks like you've got a problem," he said, climbing out of his car.

He could tell that she recognized him immediately. He would have described her expression as resigned. He could almost hear her thinking, "Of *course* he would be the one to show up now."

"I can handle it," she said instead. "It's only a flat."

He shoved his hands in the pockets of his jeans while he studied the problem. The tire was deflated down to the rim. "Have you ever changed a flat before?"

"Once," she replied, probably unaware of the touch of uncertainty in her voice.

"Pop the trunk," he said, pulling off his thin leather jacket and tossing it into his car. He didn't want to risk getting it dirty, and it was too warm a day for it, anyway. He just liked wearing it. "I hope you've got a jack and a spare."

"I have both—but I'm quite capable of changing the flat myself."

"I'm sure you are, but since I'm here, and since I'm hoping to impress you with my efficiency—not to mention my gallantry—I'd be happy to volunteer my services."

"But I—"

"No strings," he added. "You don't even have to thank me, if you don't want to. Open the trunk, will you?"

She sighed and shoved her key into the trunk lock. "I don't mean to sound ungrateful for your help. I'm just accustomed to taking care of my own problems."

"No, really?" He bent into the neat-as-a-pin trunk, thinking she must vacuum it twice a week. He could have a picnic in there, it was so clean.

"Yes. It's…easier that way."

"I agree. Hmm. Full-size spare. You don't see those very often any more. Note the way my muscles flex as I lift it effortlessly from the trunk."

From the corner of his eye, he watched her struggle against a smile. "Very impressive," she said dryly.

"Do anything for you?"

"Yes. It makes me glad you're the one lifting it and not me."

"Not exactly the reaction I was hoping for," he replied in a pseudo-grumble, kneeling beside the flat. She stood out of his way as he went to work.

"There's your problem." He pointed to a large metal screw gleaming from within the tread. "Looks like you ran over it recently and the air's been escaping ever since."

"A screw? That's what caused the flat?"

He lifted an eyebrow. "You were expecting me to say that someone slashed your tires?"

"Of course not," she said, looking more annoyed than amused by his teasing.

He often seemed to have that effect on her.

After a few moments Teresa conceded almost reluctantly, "You do that very well. You'll have it finished a lot more quickly than I would have."

He spun the lug wrench, unable to resist adding a bit of flair to the movement. "When I was a kid, I wanted to be on the pit crew of a NASCAR team."

"What changed your mind?"

"I found out it was hard work. Involved sweat and dirt and stuff like that. Not for me. I'm content now to just watch the races on TV."

She looked at him as if she weren't quite sure whether he was joking. "So you gave up your boyhood dream because of laziness?"

"Exactly," he answered readily. "Writing's a lot easier. I hardly ever break a sweat doing that."

"I would think that being a reporter for the local newspaper is a fairly demanding career."

Without pausing at his task, he gave a bark of laughter. "Working for the *Evening Star*? Have you actually seen the local newspaper?"

"Well, no. I just moved here a couple of weeks ago and I..."

"Take my word for it. Real news happens maybe once a month during an exciting year in this town, and there are two of us on staff to cover it. Basically it's a parttime job for me—which leaves me free to pursue other interests."

"Yes, I heard you're writing a novel."

Riley looked over his shoulder. Had she been asking about him? He rather liked that idea. "Did you?"

"Marjorie told me," she said with a shrug that instantly deflated his swelling ego. "She tells me about nearly everyone who comes into the diner. She didn't seem to think you'd mind."

"Harmless gossip is one of Marjorie's favorite pastimes. I wouldn't dream of depriving her of it." He tightened the last lug nut, then lowered and removed the jack. "Ready to roll."

"I really do appreciate this, Mr. O'Neal. Thank you."

"Riley," he corrected her. "And you're welcome."

He loaded the jack and flat in her trunk and closed it with a snap. And then, because he could tell she was expecting him to make another attempt to flirt with her, he moved toward his own car. "Drive carefully, Teresa. See you around."

She was still blinking in surprise when he closed his door and started his engine. He found himself grinning as he drove away after lingering only long enough to make sure she was safely in her own vehicle.

He had never liked being overly predictable. But he *would* be flirting with her again eventually. It was too much fun to resist.

Chapter Two

Riley had never dealt well with rejection. It was a facet of his personality that he freely acknowledged and accepted as unalterable. He would even go so far as to admit that he was rather spoiled to having his own way.

An indulged only child of older parents and the only grandson on either side of his family, he'd never had to compete for attention or affection. Grades and friends had come easily to him in school, and he had enough trust money from his late grandparents to allow him to live comfortably, if not lavishly.

His job with the Edstown *Evening Star* was hardly lucrative, but he enjoyed it for the most part. It forced him to interact with other people on a regular basis, counteracting his natural inclination to hole up alone with his books, his music and his imagination. And yet the undemanding structure of the job gave him plenty of freedom to do just that when he wanted. He'd been known to disappear into the duplex apartment he owned for days at a time without making an appearance unless he was truly needed at the newspaper.

It was probably his aversion to rejection that had kept him from submitting one of his fantasy novels to a publisher. While characteristically confident about his talent, he was realistic enough to accept that most aspiring writers had to deal with at least a few rejections along the road to publication. He wasn't sure how he would react to anyone turning down his submission. Until he was ready to find out, he told himself he was content writing for his own pleasure.

He'd rarely encountered rejection from women, either. Maybe it was because he didn't issue invitations without being fairly confident they would be accepted, but his success rate in that area—as in the other parts of his life—was quite high. He had definitely become spoiled.

Teresa Scott was threatening to ruin his impressive record.

Emboldened by their amiable encounter on the side of the road, he'd asked her out three times during the past two weeks. Though she'd been friendlier to him since he'd changed her tire for her, she'd turned him down every time. Politely, even amusingly, but very firmly. She'd made it clear enough that there was no reason for him to keep asking, but that hadn't stopped him.

So far, he'd asked her to dinner, to a movie and to a high school football game that he had to cover for the paper. Rather than becoming annoyed or discouraged by her consistent rebuffs, he was beginning to see them as a form of entertainment. He figured he might as well keep asking—just to watch her reactions. And who knew, she might change her mind if he was persistent enough.

She filled his coffee cup on the Friday morning almost three weeks after their first meeting. ''What would you like today?'' she asked.

''A date with you,'' he replied promptly. ''How about tonight?''

''I'm painting my fingernails tonight. What do you want for breakfast?''

Chuckling at her rejection, he replied, ''I'm in the mood for oatmeal today. With fruit, toast and coffee. How's your schedule for tomorrow night? Are you free then?''

''No, that's when I paint my toenails to match my fingernails. I'll go turn in your order now.''

She'd shot him down again, but he was pretty sure he'd seen a fleeting glimmer of amusement in her blue eyes. Maybe he hadn't won her over yet—but she found him somewhat entertaining. It was a start.

Okay, so he was reaching, he admitted with a wry smile as he lifted his coffee cup. But still, there was always a chance....

''Hey, Riley.''

Glancing up, Riley smiled. ''Hey, Chief. What's up?''

Chief of Police Dan Meadows slid into a chair on the other side of Riley's table without waiting for an invitation—but then, he knew he didn't need one. ''Lindsey's covering some sort of early meeting this morning, so I'm on my own for breakfast.''

Riley shuddered dramatically. ''It's the annual PTA breakfast at the middle school. Some bigwig from the state department of education is there to make a speech, and a bunch of sixth graders are putting on a musical production. Lindsey offered me the assignment, but I let her take it—I knew she'd hate to miss a program like that.''

Dan chuckled. "Very noble of you."

"I thought so. I'm sure glad you married Lindsey and convinced her to stay in Edstown instead of taking a job with one of the big newspapers. If she'd left, I'd be the one listening to a bunch of moppets warbling off-key at this hour in the morning."

"Happy to oblige."

Riley found his friend's drawled response amusing—as if Dan had only wed Lindsey a few weeks ago to keep her from leaving the *Evening Star*. Lindsey had been in love with Dan for years—but Dan had been a bit slower to acknowledge his feelings. He'd made up for that by losing no time marrying her. Dan wasn't one to put his emotions on display, but Riley had noticed a new glow of contentment in his friend's eyes since the wedding.

Teresa returned to set Riley's breakfast in front of him. She glanced at Dan, who was studying her curiously. "Good morning. Would you like a menu?"

"No, that's not necessary. I'll have scrambled eggs, ham and grits."

"Toast or biscuits?"

"Toast."

Riley looked from one to the other. "Have you two been introduced? No? Teresa Scott, this is Dan Meadows."

"It's nice to meet you, Ms. Scott."

"You, too, Mr. Meadows."

"Chief Meadows," Riley corrected her. "Dan's chief of police here in Edstown."

Teresa looked momentarily surprised, but she recovered quickly. "Is that right?"

"Yes, ma'am," Dan drawled. "You be sure and let me know if there's anything I can do for you, you hear?"

While Riley grinned at his friend's old-west-lawman imitation, Teresa nodded. "Well, actually, I *have* encountered one suspicious character since I moved here."

"Who's that, ma'am? Someone I should keep an eye on?"

"Looks like you already are," she replied, glancing pointedly toward Riley. "I'll be right back with your coffee, Chief."

Dan was smiling when Teresa walked away. "I think she just zinged you, pal."

"Trust me, it's not the first time she's done so."

"She seems nice."

Riley nodded and dug into his cooling breakfast.

"Pretty, too," Dan added, glancing across the room.

"I noticed."

"Have you asked her out?"

"Yep."

"And…"

"Crashed and burned. Every time."

Dan chuckled. "Pretty *and* intelligent."

Teresa returned to set a mug of coffee in front of Dan. "Your breakfast will be ready soon."

"Hey, Teresa, there's a symphony concert in Little Rock next weekend. Want to go with me?" Riley asked.

"Sorry. I'm washing my hair that night," she answered pleasantly.

"I didn't tell you which night the concert's being held," he reminded her.

She didn't miss a beat. "I didn't say which night I'm washing my hair."

"Oh, man." Dan shook his head as Teresa moved away. "You went down in flames, buddy."

"Yeah, but did you see her eyes? She said no, but what she wanted to say was—"

"*Hell,* no."

Riley snorted in response to Dan's droll interruption. "Scoff if you like—but I'm getting to her. She won't be able to resist my charms much longer."

"Is that right?" Dan glanced up when Teresa set his breakfast on the table. "Riley thinks he's getting to you," he said gravely.

"He's right," she murmured, refilling their coffee cups. "He's definitely getting on my nerves."

"You know, we should talk about that. How about over dinner tonight?" Riley suggested.

"Sorry. I'm going to be ill tonight. Excuse me, I have orders to serve."

"I think I like her," Dan murmured appreciatively.

"Just help me pull this knife out of my chest, will you?" Riley pantomimed the motion as he spoke.

"A knife?" Dan asked blandly. "Or is that one of Cupid's arrows?"

"Very funny. Eat your breakfast."

Dan obligingly picked up his fork, though his brown eyes still gleamed with amusement that was most definitely at Riley's expense.

Okay, so the guy was amusing. Teresa had found herself looking forward to the days when Riley O'Neal had breakfast in the diner.

She wasn't particularly flattered by his frequent invitations for dates. She suspected that he was the type who'd make a play for any reasonably attractive new woman who entered his life. But it was still nice to see a look of appreciation in an attractive man's eyes. It gave her a glimmer of hope that someday...maybe...she'd meet someone to share her life with again. Someday far in the future.

"I think he's got a thing for you." Marjorie Schaffer winked at Teresa as she whispered her revelation.

Looking up from the table she was wiping with a damp cloth, Teresa wrinkled her nose. "Old Ernie? I think he proposes to every woman who crosses his path."

"Of course he does. Ernie even proposes to me at least twice a week. But I was talking about Riley O'Neal. Everyone has noticed the way he's been coming in here almost every day to flirt with you."

"Riley's as much of a habitual flirt as old Ernie. I don't take either of them seriously."

"He sure has been coming around a lot since you started working here. Used to be he'd only eat here once or twice a month, tops. Now it's three or four times a week."

"Really?" Teresa was a bit surprised by that. She'd assumed Riley had always been a regular. She found it hard to believe he'd changed his daily schedule just because she was serving coffee here.

Maybe it was a *little* flattering....

She hefted a tray of dishes and moved toward the doorway. "I'll leave you to your romantic fantasizing," she teased her friend and employer lightly. "I have customers waiting."

Teresa was still thinking about Marjorie's words as she approached Riley's table with the coffee carafe a few minutes later. Maybe he really *was* interested in taking her out. Not that she was in a position to get involved with anyone, but it gave her something to daydream about.

She stopped at the table next to the one where Riley and his friend were conversing as they finished their breakfasts. As she refilled the cups of the middle-aged couple sitting there, she couldn't help overhearing a snatch of Riley's conversation.

"I hope your wife's enjoying the middle school program," Riley was saying to the police chief. "I'd rather eat mud pies myself than listen to that bunch of kids mangling Disney movie songs."

Dan chuckled. "You know you don't really dislike kids as much as you pretend."

"Nah, they're okay. As long as I don't actually have to listen to them sing, or watch them dance or act in school plays. Or share a plane ride with them. Or a movie theater. Or a restaurant. Or—"

Dan was laughing quietly when he cut in. "Okay, I get the picture."

So did Teresa.

She wasn't really disappointed, she assured herself. She hadn't seriously considered accepting a date with him. She wasn't interested in dating *anyone* right now. Especially a man who'd just made it crystal clear how entirely wrong he was for her.

She filled the police chief's cup first, and then Riley's. "Is there anything else I can get for you gentlemen?"

"I'll take the check," Riley said. "I like to stay on the chief's good side—just in case I ever need a ticket fixed or anything."

"I wish you'd stop saying things like that," Dan said, sounding rather exasperated. "People who don't know better might think there's some truth in what you've implied."

Teresa smiled faintly. "Don't worry, Chief. I take very little of what he says seriously."

"I *said* she was intelligent," Dan said to Riley, who was giving Teresa an exaggeratedly aggrieved look.

"If there's nothing else you need, I'll get your check," she said, taking a step back from the table.

"You're sure you won't reconsider my dinner invitation for tonight?" Riley asked enticingly.

"I'm quite sure," she said in a tone cool enough to freeze the smile from his face. No teasing this time—no humorous rejoinders or implied maybes. This was a flat-out no, and she wanted him to recognize it as such.

There was no need for either of them to harbor the delusion that there would ever be a date—or anything else—between them.

Riley didn't make a habit of talking to kids. For one thing, he never knew quite what to say to them. And parents frowned on strangers approaching their offspring—rightly so, of course. So, all in all, it seemed safer to just stay away from the tykes.

He was sitting in a city park with a book on a pleasantly cool afternoon during the first week of October when a snub-nosed urchin approached him.

"Hi," the kid—who looked to be about ten—said.

Resting the paperback on his knee, Riley studied the boy a moment before coming to the conclusion that he'd never seen him before. "Hi."

"Whatcha doing?"

Riley sat on a concrete picnic bench, his back to the table, facing the small, pretty lake that was the center of the park. A can of soda and the remains of a burger and fries were scattered on the table behind him. He figured it was pretty obvious that he was taking advantage of a nice, warm day to picnic, read and commune with nature for a while, but apparently the boy was simply trying to start a conversation.

"I'm just taking a break from work," he said. "What are you doing?"

"I'm going to feed the ducks." The boy held up a clear plastic bag filled with bread cubes.

Riley looked toward the lake, where several hungry-looking ducks were starting to congregate nearby, apparently deciding the boy looked like a promising food source. "I'm sure they'll like that. How come you aren't in school?"

"No school today," the kid announced with pleasure. "It's a teacher workday."

Glancing around at the few other people in the park, none of whom seemed to be monitoring the boy's actions, Riley asked, "You aren't here by yourself, are you?"

"No, my sitter's with me. Well, she's in the rest room with my little sister. I'm supposed to wait for them before I start feeding the ducks, because Maggie gets mad if I start without her."

"Maggie's your sister?"

"Yep. My name's Mark."

Because it seemed like the right thing to do, Riley extended his hand. "Nice to meet you, Mark. I'm Riley."

The boy pumped Riley's hand gravely. "It's nice to meet you, too. Now you're not a stranger, right? It's okay for us to talk, right?"

Riley couldn't help chuckling. "Weren't we strangers a few minutes ago—when you first spoke to me?"

The boy gave the question only a moment's consideration before replying airily, "I was just being polite then."

Although amused by the kid's logic, Riley thought it was probably time for him to offer some wise-adult advice. "Maybe you'd better not be quite so polite to strangers when your sitter isn't around."

"I don't talk to *bad* strangers," Mark replied confidently. "Only nice ones like you."

"But..." Riley paused and drew a deep breath, feeling himself hovering on the verge of stammering. This kid had an answer for everything. Must keep his parents on their toes all the time.

"Uh-oh! Mark's talking to a stranger again. I'm going to tell Mom."

The shrill announcement from behind them brought Mark's chin up defensively. "He's not a stranger. His name's Riley and he's my friend."

The teenager trailing after Mark's blond, blue-eyed little sister was someone Riley recognized. "Hi, Jenny."

Her heavily mascaraed eyes lit up. "Hey, Riley. What are you doing here?"

"You know each other?" Mark seemed pleased.

"Oh, sure, I've known Jenny since she was younger than you."

"Riley used to date my older sister," Jenny confided to Mark with a giggle. "But she stopped going out with him because he wasn't the marrying kind and she wanted someone who was."

Riley cleared his throat and quickly changed the subject. "So your school is out today, too, Jenny?"

"Yes. They all are. So I'm making a little extra money watching my neighbor's kids until their mom gets off work."

Mark and Maggie had already headed for the hopeful-looking ducks that had gathered on the grass at the edge of the lake. The moment Mark reached a hand into the bag and tossed a handful of bread cubes onto the ground, the ducks went wild, quacking and jostling for the food, making the children laugh at their eager antics.

"This is just a suggestion," Riley murmured to Jenny, "and of course I don't know much about kids or baby-sitting, but you might want to keep a closer eye on Mark. He's pretty chatty with strangers."

Jenny bit her lip. "I know. The kid's a real talker, and he's curious about everyone and everything. His mom says he's probably going to be a politician or something because he wants to talk to everyone he sees. I told him to stay close to the rest rooms while I was inside with his sister, but I guess he saw you and just couldn't resist striking up a conversation. I'll talk to him about it on the way home."

"Good idea. He needs to know he can't just start talking to any strange guy sitting in a park."

Jenny giggled again. "You're not a strange guy."

"Your sister might disagree with that comment," Riley murmured, his smile wry.

"Hey, Riley," Mark shouted. "You want to feed a duck?"

Riley reached for the portion of bun left over from his hamburger. "Feeding ducks just happens to be one of my favorite pastimes."

It was another generally held misconception that Riley didn't like children. It was true he didn't go to great lengths to seek them out, so he hadn't spent a great deal of time with them on the whole, but he didn't actively dislike them.

He enjoyed the time he spent feeding the ducks with Mark, Maggie and Jenny. Mark chattered almost endlessly, pelting Riley with a barrage of questions and humorous comments. A bit more shy at first, Maggie soon joined in the fun, treating Riley like a longtime friend, much the same way Jenny behaved toward him.

Knowing there were several people who'd be surprised to see him in this situation, Riley still had a good time. Cute tots, he thought. If more kids were as entertaining and well-behaved as these two—or three, if one counted a teenager as a kid—Riley wouldn't feel compelled to avoid them quite so often.

Still, it wasn't long before he glanced at his watch and said, "I'd better be going. I have a lot to do this afternoon."

Jenny checked the time on her own watch. "Oh, gosh, we'd better go, too. The kids' mom will be home soon."

It was only two-thirty in the afternoon. Apparently, Mark and Maggie's mom worked the early shift. A parttime job, perhaps.

"It was great seeing you, Riley," Jenny said as she herded her charges toward the parking area.

"You, too. Give my best to your family."

"I will. Bye, Riley."

"Bye, Riley," Maggie parroted, waving.

"See ya around, Riley," Mark called over his shoulder.

"Yeah. See you around." Who knew…it was a small town. Maybe they *would* see each other around sometime.

It occurred to him only then that he'd never gotten the kids' last name. It was entirely possible that he knew their parents, though he couldn't place them with anyone at the moment.

Cute kids, he thought again as he drove his car out of the parking lot. Their parents were obviously doing something right raising them. Not a job he wanted himself—*way* too much responsibility and pressure for Riley—but some folks seemed to have a talent for it.

He just didn't happen to be one of them.

Chapter Three

For some reason, Riley's thoughts were turned to past events as he entered the Edstown High School football stadium that weekend, along with a crowd of local football fans.

It had been several months since young Eddie Stamps had been arrested for arson, bringing an end to a troubling series of local fires. Most of the buildings that had burned had been vacant, the fires more of a nuisance than a dangerous threat to the community. Two of the fires had had more serious repercussions.

The Hightower Insurance office had burned to the ground, destroying valuable personal records and expensive office equipment. Five employees had lost their jobs, since R. L. Hightower had decided to retire rather than rebuild. The most devastating incident had occurred two months before the insurance company fire, in mid-January. A small hunting cabin in the woods just outside of town had burned, killing Truman Kellogg, who'd died in bed of smoke inhalation.

Unlike the other fires, that had been the only one in which there'd been no clear-cut evidence of arson. The cause was still listed as undetermined. It had been a fluke that Kellogg had even been at his hunting cabin that night. He had visited it only infrequently during the past few years and almost never at that time of the year.

Eddie Stamps had finally confessed to most of the arsons, yet denied responsibility for the insurance company and the hunting cabin. Most locals believed he was willing to confess only to the fires with the least serious consequences, hoping for a lesser sentence. Dan had pointed out to Riley that there were some differences in those two fires, but he, too, suspected that Eddie might have been involved with them. The timing seemed too coincidental to believe otherwise.

Dan tended to believe that Truman's death had been accidental. Since Truman so rarely stayed at the cabin, it was conceivable that the arsonist—if there was one in that case—could have believed the cabin was vacant. Because prosecutors had reluctantly decided to accept a plea bargain from Eddie's attorney and charge him only with the fires he'd confessed to, it was possible no one would ever know whether Truman's death had been the result of arson or merely a tragic accident.

Since Eddie's arrest, news had been slow for the two reporters for the *Evening Star.* Lindsey stayed busy covering school programs and civic meetings and doing features on interesting locals. She shared hard news coverage with Riley, informally taking turns showing up when real news occurred. Riley's regular responsibilities included attending and reporting on weekly city council meetings and sporting events and a twice-weekly column of biting political and social commentary.

The column was new, an idea of managing editor Cameron North. At first Riley had been reluctant to commit to the demands of a regular column. Cameron had talked him into it, assuring Riley that he could do most of his work at home, giving him plenty of freedom to work his own hours at his own pace, on the condition that he would produce two columns a week.

Riley enjoyed writing the columns more than he'd expected. It gave him a chance to get in a few digs at the mayor, the city council, local society leaders, the school board—he liked to think of himself as an equal opportunity needler. Even his friends weren't entirely safe from his barbs. Dan and his police department had taken their share of hits from Riley's keyboard.

"Hey, Riley." The city attorney approached him at the Friday night high school football game, an aggrieved look on his broad, mocha-toned face. "That wasn't an entirely fair column you ran today. Just because the state Supreme Court overturned one of our city ordinances doesn't mean I don't know my job. I honestly thought it would hold up in court."

"C'mon, Dwayne, every business owner in town has been insisting that ordinance was unconstitutional since the council drafted it almost two years ago. Just because you and the mayor persuaded one lower court judge—a golfing buddy of the mayor's, no less—to uphold it didn't make it legal. As the state Supreme Court justices told you quite succinctly, by the way."

Dwayne's scowl deepened. "Now that's just what I was talking about. You can't accuse a judge of being influenced by a longtime acquaintance with the mayor."

"Sure I can. Especially when it's true."

"Damn it, Riley—"

"Careful, Dwayne." Riley skillfully sidestepped a mob of kids dashing recklessly toward the concession stand behind them. "There are innocent ears listening."

He moved on before the mayor's most devoted minion could get further wound up. Dwayne would get over this offense—until the next time Riley took aim at the local political scene.

"Riley!" A towheaded kid in fashionably oversize clothes skidded to a stop in front of him. A slightly smaller, more feminine figure tagged at the boy's heels. "Hi. Remember us?"

"Mark," Riley said, identifying the boy he'd met in the park a few days earlier. "And Maggie," he added with a smile for the little girl. "Nice to see you again."

"We're going to get drinks and popcorn." Almost shouting to be heard over the noise surrounding them, Mark waved a five-dollar bill in one hand as he pointed toward the nearby concession stand with the other. "Mom's saving our seats. She said we have to stay close together, hurry back and don't talk to anyone."

"You're talking to me." Riley couldn't help pointing it out.

"Well, yeah, but that's different," Mark replied with his usual airy disregard for details. "We know you."

"Still, you'd better buy your snacks and get back to your mom before she starts to worry. I'll catch you later, okay?"

"Okay. See you, Riley."

"See you, Riley," Maggie echoed, staying close to her brother as they joined the shortest line at the crowded booth.

Nodding toward the uniformed officer stationed by the concession stand, one of several on duty in the generally problem-free high school stadium, Riley moved toward the bleachers. It was almost time for kickoff. He wasn't officially covering the game tonight—a high school senior with dreams of becoming a sportswriter had requested that privilege this evening—but Riley liked football and was a loyal supporter of the Edstown Eagles. He rarely missed a home game, even when he wasn't being paid to attend.

The crowd was already pumped up and ready for the action to begin. The band played—loudly if not flawlessly—and maroon-and-gold clad cheerleaders and pom-pom girls bounced and chanted. An announcer's voice boomed from scratchy speakers. The smells of fresh popcorn, hot dogs, nachos, coffee and hot chocolate wafted through the cool air. Young kids who couldn't care less about football played tag on the grassy hill beside the bleachers, and groups of teenagers strutted and giggled while trying to impress the opposite gender.

Some things, he thought, never changed.

Nodding greetings to people he knew, he spotted an empty stretch of bench with a good view of the field. Climbing over a few outstretched legs, he claimed a spot, settling carefully onto the chilly aluminum seat. He glanced idly left, froze for a moment, then slowly smiled.

The woman sitting only a few feet away hadn't noticed him yet. Her attention was focused on the cheerleaders, who were doing an intricately choreographed dance routine on the sidelines while the band members played enthusiastic accompaniment.

She seemed to be alone in the noisy crowd. Riley had every intention of changing that. He moved closer to her, waiting for her to recognize him.

Pulling her attention away from the field, Teresa

glanced at her watch, then craned her head to look toward the concession stand as if looking for someone. Maybe she *wasn't* alone. Maybe her date was getting drinks or something. Riley frowned.

And then she spotted him. Her eyebrows lifted in surprise at finding him sitting only a few feet away. He quickly turned his frown into a smile. "Hi."

"Hello." She could have been greeting a total stranger even though he knew that she'd recognized him.

She looked very pretty this evening, he mused. The thin red jacket, snug white pullover and faded jeans she wore were flattering to her—but then, most things would be. "So you're a football fan?"

She shrugged. "I like football, though I prefer watching basketball."

"Really? I like them both. But then, I like most sports."

She glanced over her shoulder again and murmured something he didn't quite catch because of the noise level around them.

He raised his voice a little, making sure she heard him. "Are you waiting for someone to join you?"

Still looking toward the concession stand, she replied, "Yes, as a matter of fact, I am."

So that was why she hadn't accepted any of his invitations. She was seeing someone else. He could deal with that, he supposed. But it didn't mean he had to like it. He'd rather fancied the prospect of getting to know Teresa Scott much better. They could have had a great time—for a while. But they could still be casual friends. He had quite a few of those. "Anyone I know?" he asked, following her glance.

"No. Actually, I—"

"Hey, Riley. Want some popcorn?" Young Mark

seemed to appear out of nowhere, stopping in front of Riley and holding out a fragrant, overfilled box of popcorn.

"I didn't want popcorn. I got candy." Maggie leaned companionably against Riley's knee, gazing at him with a slightly flirtatious smile. "You want an M & M, Riley? You can have a blue one—they're the prettiest."

"Thanks, Maggie. You, too, Mark. But I'm not really hungry right now. Um—hadn't you two better get to your seats? The game will start any minute." He assumed they'd seen him sitting there and had impulsively come over to share their treats with him. Apparently, these two had decided he was their pal—which was all very well, but he doubted their folks would approve of them joining him without permission.

Rather than moving on, Mark settled onto the bench between Riley and Teresa. "I'm going to sit here."

"But *I* want to sit by Riley," Maggie protested.

Wondering where their parents were, Riley glanced at Teresa. She looked thoroughly startled, he thought. He couldn't blame her, of course. She probably hadn't expected him to be descended on by a couple of chatty kids.

"How on earth?" she began, only to be interrupted by Mark, who informed his sister that he had already claimed the spot by Riley.

"But *I* want to sit there!" Maggie glared at her brother, then at Teresa. "Mommy, make him move over."

While Riley tried to decide if he'd heard Maggie correctly, Mark scooted defiantly closer, leaving no room for his sister. "You sit by Mom," he insisted. "The guys can sit together, can't we, Riley?"

"That's not fair. Mommy!"

Her eyes still locked on Riley's face, Teresa murmured absently, "Mark. Maggie. That's enough."

"You mean *you're*—" Riley began.

"How did you—" Teresa started to say at the same time. Each fell silent to allow the other to speak.

Maggie settled the argument with her brother by climbing onto Riley's knee and snuggling against his chest. "Will you open my candy for me?" she asked, holding the package up to him.

Either Riley had recently developed an irresistible magnetism for children, or these were the friendliest two kids he'd ever encountered. He was pretty sure that the last time he'd had an eight-year-old girl in his lap he'd been the same age. Debbie Glover had plopped herself down on his knee and tried to kiss him.

This scene was almost as disturbing.

Teresa tried again to speak over the pandemonium. "Riley, when did you meet my—"

"Please rise for the national anthem," the announcer's voice boomed from overhead.

"Stand up, Mom," Mark urged, leaping to his feet.

Riley set Maggie on the bench beside him when he stood, keeping a hand on her shoulder to steady her. Teresa leaned closer to Riley as the band launched into the anthem and the crowd surrounding them began to sing. "Where did you meet my kids?"

"At the park the other day. But I didn't know they were yours. I didn't even know you *had* kids."

"Shh," Maggie whispered loudly. "You're not s'posed to talk during the anthem. My teacher says it's disrespectful."

Properly chastised, Riley and Teresa fell silent, though they continued to give each other searching looks. Riley was trying to figure out how he could have known Teresa for almost a month without finding out she had two children.

With gossip such a popular pastime in this typical small town, he generally heard everything about everyone eventually. But then, Teresa was new in town and didn't seem to have gotten involved in the community yet. With the exception of finding her on the side of a road with a flat tire, he'd never seen her anywhere other than the Rainbow Café.

So why hadn't Marjorie told him about the children? All she had told Riley was that Teresa had met her younger daughter, Serena, in college and had come to her recently looking for a job. Marjorie had teased Riley about his obvious attraction to Teresa—without once mentioning that he'd been flirting with the mother of two. He couldn't help wondering if that omission had been intentional. Marjorie knew him well enough to be aware of his policy against dating anyone with kids.

He'd been aware, of course, that Marjorie had been not so subtly nudging him toward asking Teresa out. Marjorie was a compulsive matchmaker, and he knew she'd never completely given up on fixing him up with someone despite his repeated admonitions to her that he wasn't the marrying kind. But he'd never realized that dear, softhearted, well-intentioned lady could be downright devious.

The crowd remained on their feet as the two teams charged onto the field and held the kickoff. The Eagles were the receivers, taking the ball on their own twenty-five-yard line. Only then did Riley sit down. Maggie plopped onto his knee almost before he was fully settled. ''I can see better here,'' she announced, then popped a handful of candies in her mouth.

"Maggie, Mr. O'Neal wants to watch the game," Teresa said, looking flustered. "Come sit on my lap."

"I can see better here." It seemed inconceivable to the little girl that her presence would not be desired anywhere.

"But—"

"She's okay, Teresa." Riley cut in. "I'll send her to you if my leg goes to sleep."

Her expression was a mixture of apology and bemusement. Apparently she was still having trouble understanding how Riley and her children had become so chummy.

He was having a little trouble figuring that out himself.

Mark wasn't content to be ignored for long. He tapped Riley's arm and pointed toward the field. "Why did the judges throw down those yellow flags? Who did something wrong?"

"They're called referees," Riley answered. "And the other team just got a fifteen-yard penalty because one of their players grabbed our receiver's face mask to pull him down. It's a stupid mistake—especially this early in the game—and a major violation because it could cause serious injuries. Our team is fifteen yards closer to a touchdown."

"Now what are they doing?"

Riley patiently answered Mark's questions and Maggie's ramblings throughout the first quarter. It was very difficult, he discovered, to concentrate on the game with two kids competing for his attention. There was little chance to talk with Teresa, and he would certainly have felt awkward flirting with her in front of her children, anyway.

He was aware that he was drawing quite a bit of attention from the spectators around them. He had no doubt the word would soon be all over town that he'd attended a football game with Teresa Scott and her two kids. Wouldn't *that* cause avid speculation?

He lasted until halftime. Maggie had fallen asleep by then—and so had Riley's left arm. Growing bored with football, Mark had pulled a Gameboy out of his mother's purse and was industriously pursuing Pokémon.

"I think I'd better head for the press box now," Riley said, standing to deposit Maggie into her mother's arms. "I promised to check in with our high school sports reporter to see if he needs any help."

Which was at least partially true. Riley had told the young man he would read over the copy—but not necessarily during the game.

"Are you coming back? Can I come with you?" Mark asked eagerly.

Teresa interceded before Riley had to come up with a reply. "No," she said firmly. "I think it's time for us to go."

"Go? But the game isn't over," the boy protested.

"Your sister is tired. Our team is ahead by three touchdowns. And you haven't been watching the game, anyway."

"Yes, I was." Mark hastily hid the Gameboy behind his back.

"We're leaving, Mark. End of discussion," she added as he opened his mouth to continue the argument.

Riley noticed that the boy subsided immediately. There was no doubt who had the final say in that household.

After taking his leave of them, Riley headed for the press box in a pensive mood. He was stopped a couple of times by acquaintances who teased him about trying to get closer to the pretty waitress by being nice to her kids. Someone else asked him if he fancied himself in the role of step-daddy.

A sweet-faced matron, who was almost as avid a matchmaker as Marjorie and twice the gossip, patted his arm and told him how natural he'd looked holding a sleeping child. "I always thought you'd be a good father," she added.

Riley made a hasty escape, then changed his course from the press box to the parking lot. The Eagles could carry on without him to cheer them, he decided.

He needed some time alone.

Long after the kids were sleeping in their beds, Teresa sat staring blindly at the flickering television in the living room of the small house she'd been renting since she'd moved to Edstown. She kept remembering the expression on Riley's face when he'd left her at halftime—bolted, actually. It was a look she'd seen on the faces of other men during the past four and a half years—nearly every time they learned that she was the single mom of two preadolescents.

Something about her appearance obviously gave men the wrong impression about her. She usually kept her hair pulled off her face, wore a minimum of makeup and selected her clothes for comfort and practicality rather than sex appeal—but still men looked at her and saw a slender, blue-eyed blonde rather than a busy mother of two. Once they found out—well, they saw her differently then.

Riley O'Neal, of course, was no exception. Nor had she expected him to be.

She was still reeling from the shock of having her children greet Riley by name and then proceed to climb all over him as if they were longtime friends. Granted, her kids were gregarious—too much so at times. And she knew they were aware of the absence of a man in their lives—especially Mark. But couldn't they tell when someone wasn't entirely comfortable with children?

She'd asked Mark on the way home why he'd never mentioned meeting Riley at the park. Looking rather guilty, he'd replied that he hadn't wanted to get in trouble for talking to strangers again—even though, he had added with a touch of defiance, Riley was a very nice stranger and not a bad one. She hadn't had the energy to get into another circular discussion with him just then; she would start again on her precautionary lessons tomorrow.

Poor Riley had looked as though he hadn't a clue what to do when Maggie had crawled into his lap. Teresa had tried to rescue him, but he'd politely allowed Maggie to stay—even though he'd acted as if he were afraid she might grow a second head or something equally bizarre.

He couldn't seem to get away from them fast enough at halftime. Teresa supposed she couldn't blame him for that.

It had only been chance that she'd been at the football game with her kids. Mark had heard about the game from some of his friends at school, and he'd asked to go. Because she thought it might be a way to get more involved in the community—a little at a time—and because it was a fairly inexpensive form of family entertainment, she had agreed. She'd certainly never expected to end up sitting next to Riley.

At least one thing had been accomplished tonight, she mused. The man who had told his friend that he wanted nothing to do with children had discovered that Teresa came with two of them. That would probably put an end to him asking her out. Maybe he would even find a new place to have breakfast for a while.

It wasn't as if she'd expected anything to develop between them—or even wanted it to—but she would miss his flirting. A little. It had been amusing and maybe a little flattering. But she had other things to concentrate on, she thought, glancing at the apologetically worded eviction notice lying on her coffee table. This little rent house had been sold, and the new owners wanted to move in as soon as possible.

Teresa's first order of business was to find a new place for her and her children to live. She would talk to Marjorie at work in the morning. If there was anyone who knew everything about this town, it was Marjorie Schaffer.

"It's so nice of you to come with me to look at your friend's place," Teresa said to Marjorie Saturday afternoon. They had left the diner, which was open for breakfast and lunch six days a week, and were headed for a nearby neighborhood in which a friend of Marjorie's had a duplex apartment for rent.

Teresa didn't work Saturdays, and she had been able to hire Jenny to baby-sit for a few hours that afternoon to give her a chance to do some apartment hunting. At Marjorie's suggestion, they'd met at the diner at closing time, leaving Marjorie's car there.

Teresa couldn't believe this had all happened so quickly. She'd merely mentioned to Marjorie on the phone that morning that she needed to find a place to rent. Within a few minutes, Marjorie called Teresa back with the news that she'd made arrangements for Teresa to look at her friend's place.

Looking rather smug that she'd set things into motion

so quickly, Marjorie replied, "You're welcome, dear. I hope you like the duplex my friend owns."

Teresa braked for a red light. "I'm sure I will, if you recommend it. You've never guided me wrong before."

Marjorie cleared her throat. Teresa might have sworn the older woman looked vaguely guilty—but the light changed before she could ask if anything was wrong.

"Take the next left," Marjorie advised. "It's the last house on the right in the cul-de-sac."

"This *is* a good location," Teresa mused, admiring the neat lawns of the small houses and duplexes on the street. "Close to the diner and the school, not too much traffic, and the rent you quoted is certainly reasonable. There must be something wrong with the apartment."

"Nothing at all," Marjorie answered a little too quickly. "It's very nice. Small, of course, but big enough to suit your needs for now."

Following Marjorie's instructions, Teresa turned into the second driveway in front of the red brick duplex. She took a moment to study the place, approving of what she saw. Two stories. White shutters at the windows. Matching front doors with small covered stoops. Fenced yards with tidy if minimal landscaping. Marjorie explained that a fence divided the backyards, and that each unit featured a small patio.

It looked ideal. Ever the skeptic, Teresa couldn't help worrying that there would be some major drawback. Maybe it was all facade and the inside was a dump. Or maybe, she thought when the landlord opened the door in response to their knock, the problem wasn't with the house—but with its owner.

It appeared that this duplex belonged to Riley O'Neal.

Chapter Four

Riley was obviously as surprised to see Teresa as she was to see him. He recovered quickly, giving Marjorie a vaguely chiding look and saying, "So this is your friend who's looking for a place to rent."

"Yes. Didn't I mention that it's Teresa?" Marjorie asked with an innocent tone she couldn't quite pull off.

"No, you didn't. Your exact words, I think, were that you had a dear widowed friend who's looking for a quiet, safe place to live."

"Marjorie!" Teresa turned to her friend in exasperation, stunned that Marjorie had been so deceptive.

"What?" The older woman's still-sharp eyes widened even further behind her glasses. "It's all true."

"And did you mention that your dear friend has two children?"

"No, she didn't mention that fact." Riley seemed

more indulgently resigned than annoyed by the minor deception.

Teresa shook her head. "And I'm sure you have a policy against renting to anyone with children. So thank you for your time, but—"

She had already taken a step backward when Riley stopped her. "Wait a minute. Who said I wouldn't rent to anyone with children?"

"*Do* you?" she challenged.

He cleared his throat. "Why don't you come in and see the place before you turn it down?" he asked, side-stepping the question as he motioned them inside.

Teresa hesitated, but Marjorie took her arm in a surprisingly strong grip and urged her forward. "Yes, Terry, come inside. It's really very nice."

Reluctantly, Teresa allowed herself to be escorted in.

They entered a small foyer with a straight staircase that led to the second floor. A tiny half bath was tucked beneath the stairs. The foyer led into a cozy unfurnished living room with a built-in bookcase and a nice hardwood floor. At the back of the first floor was an airy, eat-in kitchen equipped with a range, a refrigerator, a dishwasher and a washer and dryer behind bi-fold doors in one corner.

Teresa looked longingly at the washer and dryer. The little house she'd been renting for the past couple of months hadn't come equipped with them. She had to take all her laundry to a nearby laundromat—an expensive and time-consuming process.

"Let's look upstairs." Marjorie nudged Teresa along with the ease of an experienced realtor. "Three bedrooms. Right, Riley?"

"Uh, yeah." He followed them, letting Marjorie take the lead—as if he had any real choice about that, Teresa thought with a slight smile. "Each one's the size of the average walk-in closet and they all share a bath, but there's a fair amount of storage tucked into various nooks and crannies."

He'd exaggerated only a bit about the size of the bedrooms, Teresa discovered. They were small but nice. Hardwood floors again, and good-size closets behind bifold doors. Multipaned windows let in plenty of natural light, preventing the rooms from feeling claustrophobic. The single bathroom was easily accessible to all three rooms. It held a shower-bathtub combination, a sink, a toilet and a roomy linen closet.

"My side of the duplex is a mirror opposite of this one except that I've taken out an upstairs wall to make one large bedroom. I use the smaller one as an office," Riley explained, obviously making conversation to fill an awkward pause when the tour ended.

It was nice, Teresa had to admit. Roomier than it looked from the outside. The kids would each have a bedroom, and the fenced backyard would give them a safe place to play. It was on the school bus route, so the bus would drop them off practically at the front door every afternoon.

Too bad she couldn't take it.

"Thank you for the tour," she told Riley a bit primly. "It's a lovely place. I'm sure you'll find a tenant very quickly."

"Actually, I'm pretty particular about who I rent to," he replied, leaning against a wall and studying her. "That's why I bought the duplex when the original owner put it up for sale three years ago. I'd been living here for a couple of years and I'd gotten used to it, but I didn't want just anyone living next door. So I became the landlord."

It had been a wise move, Teresa concluded. The rent he charged probably paid most of the mortgage, and he had equity building as an investment. All in all, it showed rather surprising foresight, considering her early impressions of Riley. "How long has this side been vacant?"

He shrugged. "A few weeks. The young couple who lived here decided to move to Memphis in search of higher-paying jobs."

"I've lived in Memphis," Teresa murmured, glancing out a window at the quiet-looking neighborhood. "There's something to be said for the slower pace of small-town life, even when it means a cut in pay."

"I'm sure that's especially true for a single mother," Marjorie commented. "Edstown is such a pleasant place to raise children."

Riley seemed to come to a decision. "If you're interested, you can move in as soon as you want."

Teresa's eyebrows rose. "You would let me rent this apartment?"

"Yeah. If you want."

"My children, too?"

He rolled his eyes. "No, you have to leave them on the street. Of *course* the kids, too."

For only a heartbeat she considered it—and then she shook her head. The thought of living here with Riley O'Neal on the other side of her bedroom wall was just too much to comprehend. "I don't think so."

Marjorie looked disappointed. "You don't like it, Terry?"

An image of that lovely washer and dryer flashed through her mind. "I like it just fine. But I don't think it's right for us."

"You've got something against the landlord?" Riley inquired.

"The landlord isn't used to children," she returned evenly. "Mark and Maggie are well-behaved, for the most part, but they're normal kids. Sometimes they get rowdy. Make noise. And they like you—they'd probably pester you half to death."

He straightened away from the wall, his expression suddenly serious. "I know what to expect from kids. They'd have their own yard to play in, and these walls are very well insulated for soundproofing. As for the other part, I'm quite capable of letting them know when I need to be left alone to work."

Teresa was shaking her head even before he finished speaking. "I just don't think it would work out."

"Your choice," he said cordially. "Of course there aren't many rentals available in Edstown, especially in this area. And as far as us being neighbors goes, whole days sometimes went by without me even seeing the couple who lived here before. You'd have plenty of privacy, just as I tend to protect my own."

"What makes you think I would be a good tenant?"

He lifted one shoulder in a shrug. "I think you'd be a responsible renter who'd pay your bills, take care of the place and not give me much hassle. That's pretty much all I look for. As for your kids—I've seen you keep them in line. I'm not worried about them being much trouble. I'm ready to get the place rented so I don't have to worry about it anymore, and Marjorie has vouched for you, which is good enough for me."

Teresa chewed her lower lip while she considered his words. As he'd said, there weren't a lot of other options. This neighborhood was ideal, the apartment—while a bit cramped—was adequate for her needs, and the rent was affordable. "Would I have to sign a lease?"

"Why don't we take it a month at a time until we find out if the arrangement works for both of us?"

She considered the suggestion for another moment. While there were certain disadvantages to not having a lease, there was also the advantage that she could move at any time if the arrangement didn't work out. Of course, that would mean uprooting the children again, something she would prefer to keep to a minimum. But they would enjoy that nice backyard—and they'd like being so close to the school and their friends....

"I think you should try it, Terry," Marjorie advised. "It's the most suitable place I know of in this school district."

"And Marjorie knows them all," Riley murmured.

Teresa had little doubt about that. She didn't think there was much that happened in this town that escaped Marjorie's notice. "All right," she said after drawing a deep breath. "I'll take it."

Marjorie looked rather smugly satisfied that her plan had worked out. Teresa couldn't read Riley's expression.

She wasn't sure what emotions her face might reveal, since she wasn't at all sure what she was feeling about the prospect of living next door to Riley O'Neal.

Hearing noises in the driveway next door, Riley stepped out his front door to investigate and discovered Teresa and the kids moving in.

It looked as if she had plenty of assistance. Teresa drove a bright orange rental van. Marjorie, her daughter, Serena, and Serena's husband, Cameron North, followed in another vehicle. All were dressed in jeans and casual shirts and looked ready to get to work. Fortunately it was a nice day, sunny and not as stiflingly hot as September had been.

Teresa looked very nice in her jeans and cherry red pullover, he couldn't help noticing, his gaze drawn inexorably to her. With her hair in a ponytail and her feet clad in trendy sneakers, she certainly didn't look old enough to have two school-age children.

When he'd discovered at the football game last weekend that she had children, he'd decided she must be divorced. He had come home from the game with a promise to himself that he had asked her out for the last time. He'd always been resolute in his determination not to date women with children. He'd seen too many kids hurt by adults moving in and out of their lives.

His best friend in high school had come from a broken home and had suffered through a series of his parents' girlfriends and boyfriends and the occasional stepparent and step siblings. Nick had once confided in Riley that it hurt every time he got attached to someone new only to have them leave him without a backward glance when the adult relationships ended. Riley didn't ever want to put himself in the position of hurting a child.

Learning that Teresa was widowed rather than divorced had been almost as big a shock as discovering that she had children. It had never occurred to him that she might be a widow until Marjorie had described her as a ''dear, widowed friend.'' Teresa was so young, so close to Riley's age. Her children were so small to have already lost their father. He suspected it was that surprise revelation that had made him change his mind about renting to someone with kids. His sympathy, for once, had overridden his selfishness.

He'd have to be careful or he'd ruin his reputation in this town, he mused wryly.

"Hey, Riley. You just going to stand there and stare or are you going to get over here and help me carry some of this stuff?" Cameron called when he spotted Riley standing on his stoop.

Pulling his hands from the pockets of his jeans, Riley resigned himself to a couple of hours of manual labor—something else he usually avoided whenever possible. "Just remember you're only my boss at the newspaper," he reminded his editor as he approached the rental van.

Cameron grinned, his golden hair gleaming in the early afternoon sun. "No problem. I have a feeling *neither* of us is going to be the boss on this job."

"Cameron, you should probably unload the bedroom furniture first," Marjorie called from the open doorway of the apartment. "I think it will be better to carry things upstairs before we start downstairs."

"Yes, ma'am," Cameron replied to his mother-in-law.

"Oh, Riley, how nice. You've come to help." Marjorie gave him a smile of approval before adding, "You boys make sure you don't bump the stairway walls with the furniture, you hear? You don't want to scuff those nice freshly painted walls."

"Yes, ma'am," Riley said.

Cameron chuckled and murmured, "See what I mean?"

Mark and Maggie dashed out the open front door, followed closely by Teresa and Serena. "Hi, Riley! We're going to live in your house," Maggie announced as if he hadn't already known.

"Not exactly in the same house," Mark corrected her impatiently. "Only in half of it."

Unconcerned with details, she shrugged. "I picked my room," she confided to Riley. "It's the one with the white fan. I like that one best. Mommy gets the biggest room and Mark gets the other.''

"That sounds like a good arrangement.''

"My room's closest to the stairs," Mark said, claiming his own bragging rights. "It's the best.''

"No, mine's best," Maggie insisted.

Teresa settled the brewing argument swiftly. "You each have the room that's best for you.'' She gave Riley a slightly distracted smile. "The paint job looks great. You didn't have to do that, but thank you.''

He shrugged. "It was something I'd already planned to do. The old paint looked dingy. I've been on the painter's schedule for a couple of weeks. I'm glad he was able to get the job done before you moved in.''

"Can we unpack my stuff first?" Maggie requested. "I want to fix up my room.''

"We'll unpack everything when we get to it," Teresa assured her. "Why don't you and Mark go check out the backyard while we carry some things inside?''

"But I want to help the guys," Mark insisted, moving closer to Riley.

"Me, too," Maggie added.

"We'll find things for them to carry," Cameron assured Teresa in a low voice that Riley overheard. "They want to feel useful.''

"Just don't let them get under your feet.''

"They'll be fine." Cameron turned to the van. "Okay, let's get some of these boxes out of the way so we can get to the furniture.''

"You don't have to do this, you know," Teresa said to Riley. "I have plenty of help if you have other things you need to do today.''

"I don't mind," he said carelessly, and was almost

surprised to realize it was the truth. "It'll earn me a few brownie points with my employers."

She smiled a little at the joke, then turned to take a box from Cameron. "Thank you," she said over her shoulder to Riley.

"Thank him after he's actually done something," Cameron suggested. "Riley, let's get this dresser first. It has to go upstairs."

Riley winced, pushed up the sleeves of his long-sleeved T-shirt and prepared to sweat. "Okay. Let me at it."

He soon noticed that Teresa had brought just enough belongings to furnish the few rooms of the duplex apartment. She didn't have an overabundance of possessions, but what she had looked very nice. Riley would almost bet another day of hard labor that some of the items he and Cameron carried to her bedroom were rather nice antiques. She had good taste.

Every tidbit he learned about Teresa Scott only increased his curiosity about her. Which might not be a good thing, he reflected, considering that he was always too easily intrigued by a puzzle.

Just before six, when almost everything had been brought inside, Marjorie laid out sandwiches for an early light dinner. It provided everyone a welcome break from hauling and arranging furniture and toting and unpacking boxes. Even the kids were starting to wear down, their excitement over the novelty of the move fading. Gathered around the kitchen table while the children picnicked on a tablecloth spread on the floor, the adults chatted for a while, something they'd been too busy to do so far.

"So you and Serena were college roommates?" Riley

glanced from Teresa to Serena as he asked the question, finally clearing up the connections between this group.

"Yes." Teresa sent Serena a quick smile. "I finished high school a year early and I was a bit younger than the average college freshman. I was scared spitless. It helped to discover that I'd been assigned a very nice and friendly roommate."

"And I was relieved that my roomy was neat and studious," Serena admitted. "I'd been so worried I'd get a slob who would spend more time partying than preparing for classes."

Riley chuckled, not at all surprised. A successful attorney, Serena was a notorious workaholic who took her responsibilities to her job, her family and her community very seriously. Riley had often accused her of being *too* serious.

She and Cameron made a good match, he reflected. While equally dedicated to his career, Cameron was more laid-back about it than Serena. He brought out her dry sense of humor and encouraged her to have fun. They'd been married a year and still looked at each other like they were on their honeymoon.

Riley had nothing against the institution of marriage. It certainly seemed to work well for some people—Serena and Cameron, Dan and Lindsey, his own parents, for that matter, who'd been contentedly wed for thirty-five years. He just couldn't really picture himself taking that drastic step—at least not with anyone he'd met to this point.

He wondered if Teresa had been as happy with her late husband as his newly married friends were with their respective spouses. How long had it been since she lost him? Was she still grieving for him?

He realized abruptly that Teresa was talking again,

filling in the gaps about how she came to be his tenant. "I visited Edstown with Serena a couple of times during college and I always thought it must be a wonderful place to grow up. When the neighborhood the kids and I were living in before started having more problems with crime and delinquency, I decided to move here for their sakes. Marjorie very kindly offered me a job. Since the diner is only open for breakfast and lunch, I drop Mark and Maggie off at a before-school program at the church next door to their school, and then I'm there to greet them when they come home in the afternoons. It's working out very well."

"You're doing me the favor," Marjorie insisted. "I've had so much turnover in staff at the diner during the past year or so that it's nice to have someone I can depend on to stay for a while."

Cameron cleared his throat and shifted in his chair. "Technically, I *am* still working for you," he reminded his mother-in-law.

Marjorie laughed. "I wasn't referring to you, dear."

Teresa lifted an eyebrow.

"You remember me telling you that Cameron worked in the diner when he first showed up in Edstown?" Serena prompted.

Teresa nodded, looking at her friend's husband. "You were working as a reporter for a newspaper in Dallas and you got involved in a dangerous story that almost got you killed. Something about a politician who was embezzling public funds, wasn't it?"

"Among other things," he agreed. "I followed a lead to Little Rock and I was snooping around outside his mistress's house when someone hit me from behind. The crook had hired a couple of guys to send me a message—if not to kill me. He still denies giving anyone instructions to harm me even though their paychecks were traced to him. His story is that he had simply hired a couple of guys as bodyguards for his platonic friend, who'd received some mysterious threats against her life."

"His platonic friend who just happened to be pregnant with his child," Riley added.

Teresa rolled her eyes. "Of course she was. How do these men keep believing they'll get away with this stuff?"

"Anyway," Serena said, picking up the conversational threads, "I—well, my dog, actually—found Cameron lying in a ditch beside the dirt road that runs behind our house late one evening. He'd been beaten unconscious and left facedown in high grass. It was practically a miracle that I found him then."

"I'd have probably been dead by morning." Cameron's matter-of-fact tone made Teresa's eyes widen.

Serena continued, "He woke in the hospital with no memory of who he was or how he'd gotten there. But instead of telling anyone about his amnesia," she added with a chiding glance toward her husband, "he concealed it, making up a tall tale about being a drifter who'd been robbed by a couple of strangers."

"Needless to say, Dan was not happy to find out a few weeks later that he'd wasted too many man-hours trying to track down those nonexistent muggers when he could have been finding out who Cameron was, instead." Riley shook his head ruefully as he remembered Dan's very vocal reaction to that news.

"I've heard most of this story before, of course," Teresa said to Cameron. "But I've never really understood why you didn't tell anyone you had amnesia. Was it because you were afraid?"

"In a way." Cameron looked uncomfortable. "I wasn't sure anyone would believe me, since true amnesia is such a rare phenomenon. I kept telling myself my memory would come back if I'd relax and not force it. But mostly I dreaded the attention I would receive if I told anyone the truth. I worried about being scanned and probed and prodded and questioned—treated like a medical oddity, written up in medical papers. I just couldn't deal with that attention at the time."

"So he prevaricated," Marjorie said, phrasing his actions generously. "He took a job working for me at the diner to support himself while he attempted to regain his memories. He was a very good waiter," she added a bit wistfully.

"He's a better newspaper editor," Serena responded firmly.

"Of course." But Marjorie still seemed to regret losing her popular server.

Teresa's gaze met Riley's across the table, and he saw his amusement reflected for a moment in her expression. She looked away abruptly, leaving him missing that brief moment of unison.

"How long, exactly, did it take you to regain your memories?" Teresa asked Cameron, her cheeks a bit pinker than usual. Had she, too, been caught off guard by that momentary connection with Riley?

"Snatches of memories started coming back almost immediately," he replied. "It took me three weeks to get up the nerve to admit the truth to Serena and Dan—"

"And by that time he and Serena had already fallen in love," Marjorie interrupted with a sentimental sigh.

Again, Riley and Teresa glanced at each other in shared amusement. Again, it was Teresa who looked away first.

"After I confessed, everything fell into place rather quickly," Cameron finished. "After seeing the photo of me that Dan circulated, my friend Shane came from Dallas with information about the story I'd been pursuing, and I went back with him for treatment. Within a month, I'd retrieved most of my memories. There are still gaps, and there probably always will be. But for the most part, I've completely recovered."

Riley had heard the tale numerous times, of course. He would have been much more interested in hearing Teresa's story. Did she have family? What, if any, careers had she pursued prior to waiting tables for Marjorie? How had she met her husband? Had he been a high school sweetheart? Teresa couldn't have been more than twenty-one when she'd had her first child. Did she have family to turn to? Why did she seem so alone?

Why did his curiosity about her seem different from his usual detached, journalistic interest in other people?

"I can't eat all my carrot sticks," Maggie announced from her cross-legged position on the red-and-white checked tablecloth. "I'm full. Can I go unpack some more of my stuff?"

"Me, too," Mark said. "I want to put my books in order."

Riley had noted with approval that both siblings had bookcases for their rooms, along with several boxes of books, drawing pads and art supplies. He had always believed literacy was the key to academic achievement, and Teresa seemed to agree with that philosophy.

Given permission to go to their rooms, the children dashed upstairs, fully refueled by the break.

"I wish my batteries recharged that quickly," Cameron murmured ruefully.

Serena chuckled. "Let's just hope we have enough

energy to keep up with *our* child. We're starting quite a bit later in life than Terry did."

There was a short, startled pause, and then Teresa asked tentatively, "Does this mean...?"

Serena smiled and nodded.

Riley glanced at Marjorie. "I *thought* you'd been in an exceptionally good mood today."

Her face beaming, Marjorie patted her daughter's arm. "It was all I could do not to let the news slip, but I knew Serena wanted to make the announcement in her own time."

"Oh, my gosh! You've been carrying boxes and furniture and stuff all day." Teresa looked reproachfully at her friend. "If I'd had any idea that you—"

Serena's expression turned a bit rueful. "Obviously you haven't noticed that Cameron's been watching me like a hawk all morning. The stuff he's been handing me to carry has been ridiculously lightweight."

Riley hadn't noticed, either. Since he usually prided himself on his observational skills, it bothered him that he'd allowed himself to be so distracted by Teresa. Considering that he was her landlord now, and that she was a single mother, he knew it was definitely best if their relationship remained casually friendly. He'd toned down the flirting and given up any ideas of a brief, passionate fling. But there were certain parts of him that hadn't yet gotten the message that she was unavailable.

Even now, as he watched her tuck back a strand of golden hair that had escaped her low ponytail, he felt his fingers twitch with the urge to feel her hair for himself. When she reached for her cola, he couldn't help noticing how nicely her red knit shirt moved with her, delineating her feminine curves.

A princess in denim and sneakers, he thought fancifully. And once again he'd let his absorption with her distract him from everything else going on around him. While he'd been watching Teresa, the others had been discussing Serena and Cameron's news.

Realizing that he needed to make some contribution to the conversation, he lifted his soda can in a mock toast. "To Serena and Cameron," he said when the others fell silent. "May they be blessed with the wisdom, the patience and the courage they'll need for the next eighteen years or so."

Marjorie laughed softly. "As if all the problems of parenthood end when they turn eighteen."

Setting his can on the table, Riley asked, "How is your older daughter?"

Shaking her head in bemusement, Marjorie replied, "She says she's having the time of her life. They're in a different city nearly every night on this whirlwind tour. She told me she still cries every time she hears Pierce's voice on the radio."

Marjorie's older daughter, Kara, was on the road with her fiancé, Pierce Vanness, an up-and-coming young singer. He'd just recorded his first CD, and his first single was making a respectable showing on the country music charts. He was on tour as the opening act for a well-known country group.

Kara had believed in Pierce since she'd first heard him singing in a local bar. She'd dropped everything in Edstown to follow him—including the management of the *Evening Star,* a job she had spent years preparing for. Some people thought she was crazy to take a risk like that, but nearly everyone believed it was because of her support and encouragement that Pierce's career was taking off so quickly.

Riley could identify with Pierce's dream. He had a

few of his own. The difference was, he didn't need any-one to cheer him or push him. When he was ready, he would pursue his goals on his own.

Cameron sighed and pushed away from the table. "There are a few more boxes waiting for us," he re-minded Riley.

Draining the rest of his cola, Riley stood. "Let's go," he said. "The sooner we get her moved in, the sooner she can start paying rent."

The others all laughed—even Teresa.

Riley wondered if he'd made a big mistake renting half his home to a woman he already found entirely too intriguing.

Chapter Five

Teresa's helpers were determined to finish their job before they departed. By the time they left just after dark, she was completely moved into her new apartment. Every stick of furniture was in place. Kitchen supplies, linens and personal possessions had been put away. Even her clothes were hanging neatly in her closet. There was very little left for her to do.

"I don't know how to thank everyone," she said, not for the first time, as Serena, Cameron and Marjorie prepared to leave. "Especially since it's the second time you've all helped me move in."

Cameron shrugged, his gentle smile illuminated by the security lighting overhead as they stood in the front yard, huddled into their coats against the chilly night air. "You can repay *me* with another one of those cakes you made me last time. Man, was that good."

"I'll make you two of them," she promised.

Serena laughed and patted her husband's flat tummy. "You do that and he'll be as fat as I expect to be in a few months."

Riley cleared his throat loudly. "I've only helped you move once, but I like cake, too."

Teresa couldn't help smiling at his hopeful expression. "I'll make you a cake, too," she promised.

He grinned. "I'll hold you to that."

She looked quickly away. There was something about his lazy smiles that made a funny little quiver run all the way through her. And she had no business at all quivering over Riley O'Neal.

She and Riley remained outside to see the others off. Their car had just pulled away and Teresa was preparing to thank Riley again for his assistance when a battered pickup truck turned into Riley's driveway. An older man in a camouflage cap and coat, jeans and battered boots climbed out of the cab. "Hey, Riley."

"Hey, Bud. Come meet my new tenant."

The visitor ambled toward them, his thumbs hooked in the pockets of his jeans. "Well, well," he said to Riley, studying Teresa in the artificial light of the security poles. "Ain't you the lucky landlord?"

Riley sighed. "Teresa Scott, this is my uncle, Bud O'Neal."

"Pleased to meet you, ma'am."

She extended a hand. "It's nice to meet you, too, Mr. O'Neal."

His hand was rough with calluses, testifying to a lifetime of hard work. "Call me Bud. Everyone does. So you just moved in?"

"Yes, just today."

"Well, you let me know if Riley gives you any problems, you hear? I'm the only one who could ever keep him in line."

Teresa couldn't help but return his contagious smile. "Thank you. I'll keep that in mind."

"Mom! We're hungry again. Can we have a snack?" Mark and Maggie tumbled out the front door as they made the familiar request.

"First say hello to Riley's uncle, Mr. O'Neal. These are my children, Mark and Maggie."

"Children?" Bud's bushy gray eyebrows nearly disappeared beneath the low-riding camo cap. He recovered quickly from his obvious surprise after only one searching glance toward his nephew. He gave his full attention to Mark and Maggie, and it was immediately apparent to Teresa that he enjoyed children.

"How do you like the new place?" he asked them.

"It's cool," Mark replied. "We didn't have stairs in our other house."

"My room's best," Maggie asserted. "It has a white fan and a big window and—"

"Let's not start that discussion again," Teresa interceded, seeing that Mark was prepared to start defending his own quarters.

"You like to fish, Mark?" Bud asked.

"I don't know. I've never been."

"Never been fishing?" Bud looked almost scandalized. "How old are you?"

"I'm ten."

"High time for you to try it out, then."

Riley moved a step closer to Teresa. "Bud thinks fishing and hunting are almost a religion. He's been taking me since I was big enough to walk."

Always keenly aware of the lack of a father or grandfather in her son's life, Teresa envied for Mark's sake the close relationship Riley seemed to have with his uncle. "My father took me fishing a few times when I was very young," she murmured. "I barely remember it, but I know I enjoyed being on the water."

Watching Bud easily charming Teresa's kids, Riley asked casually, "Is your father still living?"

"He and my mother died in a car accident when I was ten. It was their anniversary, and they had been out to celebrate."

Even though Teresa had kept her voice deliberately uninflected, Riley turned to her with sympathy in his eyes. "I'm sorry."

She nodded, watching Mark chattering to Bud about the move, his room, his school. Mark had never met a stranger—just like his father, she thought with a hard swallow. Her son's eager gregariousness worried her— he was so trusting, so curious about everyone he met. How could she keep him safe without dampening his extroverted spirit?

Sometimes it terrified her to think of how much responsibility rested on her shoulders. She loved her children so much it hurt sometimes. The feeling that she alone was accountable for their safety, their happiness, their futures, was almost overwhelming.

A night breeze ruffled her hair and wafted down the neckline of her knit top. It reminded her that it was getting late. "We'd better go inside," she said to her children, placing a hand on Maggie's shoulder. "You can each have an ice cream bar for dessert, and then it's time for your baths. It was very nice to meet you, Mr. O'Neal—"

"Bud," he reminded her.

The children bade good-night to Riley and his uncle,

then dashed inside to help themselves to ice cream bars from the freezer.

"Your door unlocked?" Bud asked Riley.

"Yeah. Go on in. There are sodas in the fridge."

"I know where to find everything. Take your time."

Riley turned to Teresa when they were alone. "So…if you need anything…"

"Thank you, but I'm sure we'll be fine."

"I wasn't offering my services," he corrected her. "I was just going to tell you there's a phone book in your kitchen."

She couldn't help but laugh. "Oh, gee. Thanks."

His smile was almost smug, and she knew he was pleased that he'd made her laugh.

Her smile faded. "Thank you again for all your help today. I'm sure you had better things to do."

"No problem. But I'm holding you to that cake you promised."

"You'll have it."

He couldn't seem to think of a reason to linger any longer—and neither could she. But still neither of them moved.

Riley cleared his throat. "Well…"

She tucked her fingertips into the pockets of her jeans. "Good night, Riley."

He startled her by reaching out to tuck a stray strand of hair behind her ear. His fingers grazed her cheek as he did so—and there was that annoying and decidedly inconvenient quivering inside her again. "Good night, Teresa. Sleep well."

He was standing entirely too close to her. Smiling at her entirely too warmly. She moistened her lips, deciding she'd better make something clear right from the start—just in case there were any misunderstandings. "Riley,

I want this rental arrangement to work out. And there's no reason it shouldn't if we set a few ground rules from the beginning.''

Even in the shadowy evening light she could see his left eyebrow shoot up in response to her wording. "Ground rules?"

She nodded firmly. "I intend to make it clear to my children that we're friendly neighbors, nothing more. They won't be allowed to pester you or pop in on you without permission, and I'll try to keep them from making too much noise when they're playing outside.''

"They're kids. Let them have fun.''

"I didn't say they couldn't have fun. I just won't let them get carried away with it.''

"Any other rules you want to spell out while we're at it?''

He was making fun of her, but she didn't let him get to her. She kept her chin high as she replied, "One or two.''

"Such as?''

"I know you were teasing me at the diner—you know, when you flirted with me and asked me out—but...''

"What makes you think I was teasing?''

She wouldn't let him see how his question—and the tone in which he asked it—flustered her. "I'm quite sure you were. But even if you weren't, you must see now that it would be entirely inappropriate. You are, after all, my landlord.''

He crossed his arms over his chest and leaned against one of the posts that supported the awning over her little stoop. "Going to charge me with harassment if I wink at you?''

There was the slightest edge beneath his lazy drawl—

just enough to warn her that he didn't find this as amusing as he pretended. "Look, I'm not trying to be difficult," she said. "I just—"

"You just want to warn me to keep my hands to myself, is that it? Making it quite clear that my nefarious plan to get you under my roof where I have you at my mercy won't work?"

She felt her cheeks flame in the cool night air. "There's no need to mock me," she said stiffly.

"Did anyone ever tell you that you have a tendency to sound a bit melodramatic at times?"

Now the edge was in *her* voice. "All I'm trying to say—"

He straightened away from the post as he spoke. "I know what you were trying to say. And now I think we'd better say good-night."

Great. She'd ended her first day in her new apartment by offending her landlord—and after he'd been so nice about helping her move in. "Listen, Riley, all I was trying to say is—"

"Don't worry about it. I'm sure we'll have a very pleasant landlord-tenant relationship. Let me know if you have any problems."

He was inside his apartment with the door closed between them before she could come up with a reply.

Shaking her head in self-disgust, she entered her apartment, locking the door behind her. She really was terrible at that sort of thing. All she'd wanted to do was let Riley know, as politely as possible, that she wasn't available for any sort of personal relationship.

After that awkward scene, she doubted it would be an issue in the future. She didn't expect Riley would ever ask her out again, even teasingly.

That was good, of course. Exactly the way she wanted

it. Which didn't at all explain why she was just a teensy bit depressed as she joined her children in the kitchen for ice cream.

Riley wasn't annoyed. He was royally teed off.

He'd been on his best behavior all day. He'd acted no differently toward Teresa than Cameron had—friendly, teasing, platonic. Almost brotherly.

Sure, he'd noticed things about her. Like the way her blue eyes sparkled when she laughed. The way she wrinkled her nose when she concentrated on something. The sway of her hips when she walked. The glimpses of creamy abdomen revealed when she'd raised her arms to place items on high shelves.

But had he acted on any of those observations? No. Had he said anything to make her uncomfortable? Absolutely not, even though he'd had to bite the words back occasionally. The only time he'd given in to impulse had been when he'd reached out to brush that strand of hair from her face as they'd said good-night.

And what had his hours of restraint gotten him? A lecture about landlord-tenant relationships. Ground rules.

He was the one who usually set the rules. He didn't date women with kids. He wasn't interested in long-term commitments. He carefully guarded his time, his space, his privacy. And if that made him selfish, well, that was just the way he was.

In other words, he should be relieved rather than irritated by Teresa's little speech. But for some reason, he wasn't. Maybe it was because he preferred to be the one to draw the lines.

Sitting on Riley's couch with a canned ginger ale in his hand and the TV playing in front of him, Bud looked up when Riley entered the room. "That's a glum look for a guy who just left a pretty girl."

"I was just saying a friendly and neighborly good-night to my tenant," Riley corrected with a scowl.

Bud's grin was wicked. "Shot you down again, did she?"

"She didn't shoot me down. I didn't even try anything."

Motioning toward the ginger ale he'd brought in for Riley, Bud was still smiling when he took another sip from his own. "Obviously not your choice."

Riley plopped down on the couch and opened the soda can, letting its hiss symbolize his frustration. "C'mon, Bud, be reasonable. Do you really think I would make a play for Teresa?"

"Well, let's see. She's pretty, nice, intelligent. Why *wouldn't* you want to go out with her?"

"Two reasons. Their names are Mark and Maggie."

"Oh. You don't like her kids?"

"Sure, I like them. They're okay—for kids. But I don't get involved with single mothers."

"It's a lot smarter than getting involved with married mothers."

Ignoring Bud's lame quip, Riley took a gulp of his beverage, swallowed without tasting it, then set the can aside. "I don't date women with kids. I have no interest in being anyone's stepfather."

Bud's gaze was on the football game playing on the television, but his attention was obviously focused on their conversation. "How about being someone's father? You aren't getting any younger, you know. Thirty-one may seem young to you now, but trust me, you'll be staring at sixty-five before you know it."

"It has nothing to do with age. I'm just not cut out

for marriage and parenthood and long-range planning. I'm the first to admit I'm much too self-centered.''

''You don't want to end up like me, do you? Washed up, worn out? Living in a trailer with not much to look forward to except getting older?''

Taken aback, Riley turned to study his uncle's profile. He'd never heard Bud talk that way. He'd always thought Bud enjoyed his life. Recently retired from a long career as an electrician, Bud had always seemed to have the time and money to hunt, fish, hang out with his friends—whatever he wanted to do. Bud had been divorced twice, confirming his assertion that he simply wasn't marriage material. Riley had gotten the impression that Bud had been fond of both his wives, but not deeply in love with either of them. It was a bit disturbing to learn that Bud lived with regrets and unfulfilled dreams. ''Uh…''

His uncle seemed to shake off the rare moment of melancholy. ''Hey, I was the lucky one. When I wanted a kid around, I just borrowed you. When I got tired of you, I gave you back to your folks. Being an uncle's the best way to have kids. But since you're an only child, you're going to miss out on that particular pleasure.''

''So I'll find other pleasures.''

''Yeah, well, just remember—you ain't going to be young and pretty forever. You'd better start thinking now about what you want when you're my age.''

Bud looked at his soda can as he spoke. For the first time, Riley thought his uncle looked old. He sensed that something was haunting Bud, and again he wondered if it was connected to Truman Kellogg's death. But before he could think of any way to ask, Bud hauled himself to his feet. ''I'm going to head home. I just stopped by to say hello and mooch a free soda.''

"You're sure you don't want to stay awhile? We can watch the rest of the game."

"Nah. I'm planning on cleaning out my tackle box tonight. Hey, what do you say you and I take that boy fishing sometime? A boy his age should know how to bait a hook and cast a line."

Riley wasn't surprised by the suggestion. He'd known from the moment Mark had admitted he'd never been fishing that Bud would feel the need to remedy the situation. As for himself, he didn't want to become involved in Mark's daily life, but he wouldn't mind taking the boy fishing. Especially if it put a gleam of interest in Bud's eyes again.

Would Teresa consider it breaking her rules if Riley and Bud took her son fishing? He'd better let Bud do the inviting when the time came.

A few minutes later, Bud was gone. Riley was left alone in his apartment, still disturbed by his uncle's odd mood, still smarting from Teresa's prim little speech. He found himself listening for noises from his new neighbors. There was the occasional thump or thud, but no more noise than there had been the last time the apartment had been occupied. As he'd boasted, the walls were well soundproofed.

He glanced at his watch. It was still relatively early in the evening. There was nothing of particular interest on TV, so he might as well get some work done. He could write another column for the paper, or a few more pages of his novel. Back to his usual routine—one he enjoyed, he assured himself with a touch of defiance. Total freedom to do what he wanted, when he wanted.

Sure it was a selfish existence—and he made no bones about it. Nor did he have any interest in changing it.

Because he suddenly found himself imagining what

that same routine might be like forty years from now, he pushed thoughts of the future forcefully out of his mind and sat down at his computer, determined to enjoy what was left of his solitary evening.

Nearly two weeks later, on a Friday evening, Teresa and her children were guests in Serena and Cameron's home for dinner. Marjorie joined them from the guest house she had moved into when Serena and Cameron married. Conversation was lively during the meal. Mark and Maggie, encouraged to participate, chatted about school and their friends. After dinner, Cameron took them into the den to play video games, leaving the women to gossip over coffee around the kitchen table.

"Cameron loves having someone to play video games with him," Serena commented with an indulgent smile. "Sometimes Dan and Riley come over to play, and they all act like kids with a cool new toy."

"He'll be such a wonderful father," Marjorie said, her expression misty.

"Or a terrific big brother," Serena murmured before taking a sip of her decaffeinated coffee.

Teresa gazed into her cup to hide the regret that was probably reflected in her eyes. She had thought her late husband would be a good father—and he had tried. He just hadn't been able to follow through on all his good intentions. He had died before he could keep the latest promises he'd made to her and their children.

From what Serena had told her, Teresa knew Cameron had spent years avoiding commitment, telling himself he wasn't the marrying kind. Coming from an unhappy, occasionally abusive home, he'd had few examples of loving, lifelong relationships. Falling in love with Serena had changed him. Taught him to believe in happily-ever-after endings. And he was willing to work very hard to ensure that blissful outcome.

That was the key, she thought wistfully. Realistically anticipating difficulties. Being committed to deal with them when they occurred. Being willing to put the welfare of the family above everything else.

Maybe Darren would have gotten to that point—eventually. But she doubted it. Believing he would change had been a mistake both of them had made.

"Terry? Are you all right?"

Teresa forced a smile in response to Marjorie's inquiry. "I'm fine. Just a little tired."

"You're working so hard at the diner," her employer fretted. "You really should take more breaks, you know. Shameka and Justine and I can handle things during slow spells, just as you fill in for us when we take breaks."

"I'm hardly overworked. I only put in seven hours a day, five days a week."

"At the diner," Marjorie agreed. "Then you leave to do the shopping and laundry and housekeeping and cooking for yourself and two young children. You don't have one full-time job, you have half a dozen. No wonder you're tired."

Teresa waved a hand dismissively. "Taking care of the kids isn't a chore—it's my greatest pleasure. Actually, the main reason I'm tired this evening is that I foolishly sat up half the night reading. I started a new romantic suspense novel when the kids went to bed and I just couldn't put it down."

Both Marjorie and Serena nodded sympathetically, looking as though they had experience with losing sleep because of a good book.

"At least you can sleep in tomorrow morning," Serena said.

Teresa laughed. "You don't know my kids. I have to practically drag them out of bed on school days, but Saturdays they're up at the crack of dawn to sit on the floor and eat cereal and watch cartoons. It's the only time I allow them to eat in front of the television."

"The children seem to have adapted well to their new home," Marjorie commented.

"They love it there. There are several children their ages in the neighborhood and that nice playground only a couple of blocks away. We've already spent two af- ternoons there, since the weather's been so nice lately."

"It's hard to believe it's the middle of October again already." Marjorie glanced toward the window as she spoke, as if to confirm that the seasons were, indeed, passing. "Things have changed so much in the past year or so. Serena and Cameron just celebrated their first wedding anniversary, and now they're expecting a baby. Kara and Pierce are making wedding plans, and Pierce seems well on his way to success in the music business. Dan and Lindsey are married—something few people would have predicted this time last year. And now you and Mark and Maggie are a part of our community."

"The past year seems to have brought changes for everyone," Serena agreed. "Except Riley, of course. Ri- ley never changes. He's still working on that novel no one's ever seen, still putting in just enough hours at the paper to keep his job, still keeping the local powers-that- be from getting too carried away with their self- importance."

Teresa couldn't imagine why hearing Riley's name made her cheeks warm. It was exasperating that the men- tion of him rattled her so much—a particularly incon- venient condition considering she lived right next door to him and mingled with his friends. Not that she had

seen him much since she'd moved in. If she hadn't
known better, she might have suspected he was avoiding
her.

He hadn't been to the diner for breakfast since she'd
become his tenant.

She'd seen his uncle as much as she had Riley. Bud
made a point to greet her and the children each time he
stopped by to see his nephew—three or four times since
she'd moved in. Trying to speak as offhandedly as Serena had, she said, "Riley and his uncle are taking Mark
fishing tomorrow. Mark's so excited he can hardly
wait."

Marjorie nodded. "I heard Mark talking to Cameron
about the fishing trip. I wasn't surprised. Bud loves fishing and children. He's been an honorary uncle to a lot
of boys in this town. I always thought it was a shame
he never had children of his own."

"He and Riley seem close."

"They've always been close, especially since Riley's
parents retired to Florida. Riley stays in contact with his
parents and visits them in Florida a couple of times a
year, but he seems to enjoy having his uncle Bud close
at hand." Marjorie sipped her coffee, then added, "You
needn't worry about your son when he's with Bud and
Riley. They'll take good care of him."

Teresa wondered if Marjorie had read her mind. It
hadn't been easy for her to give permission for Mark to
go on this fishing trip—for several reasons. One being
that she didn't want to infringe any more than necessary
on Riley's personal time. But he and Bud *had* been the
ones to make the offer, she reminded herself.

"I do tend to be overprotective of my kids," she admitted. "But I know Mark misses having a man in his

life, and he'll enjoy spending an afternoon with Riley and Bud.''

"I was always overcautious with mine, too," Marjorie confessed. "It's hard not to be when you read the newspapers. But you can trust me when I say that your son will be completely safe with Riley and Bud O'Neal. I would tell you if I had any reason to believe otherwise."

"Thank you. I'd already decided it would be all right or I never would have told him he could go. But it's nice to have you confirm my decision. There's no one whose judgment I trust more than yours."

A burst of laughter came from the den, Cameron's deep chuckle blending with the children's high giggles. The women all smiled. "The kids are getting kind of loud," Teresa commented.

"They aren't half as loud as Riley gets when he plays the game with Cameron and Dan," Marjorie said, then immediately asked, "so, how are you and Riley getting along?"

Uh-oh. That was a well-intentioned matchmaker's smile if Teresa had ever seen one. Surely Marjorie didn't think Riley O'Neal was a good match for a single mother. She kept her tone casual when she replied. "We get along very well. We always nod and smile when we cross paths."

That didn't seem to satisfy the older woman at all. "I would think you'd see quite a bit of each other, living right next door the way you do."

"We've both been busy," Teresa answered vaguely. "Riley has his work, and I have mine. I make sure the children don't encroach on his time or property, though he often wanders out to talk to them when they play in the backyard."

"And does he ever wander over to talk to *you?*"

"Mother," Serena murmured warningly.

Marjorie widened her eyes the way she always did when she was trying to look innocent. "I'm just asking."

"I know what you're doing. And so does Terry. Leave her alone."

Marjorie sighed wistfully. "But they make such an attractive couple. And Riley seemed so taken—"

Serena shook her head, then looked wryly at Teresa. "She's shameless."

"In this case, she's also misguided." Teresa softened the comment with a smile, but she meant every word of it.

Marjorie seemed about to say something in her own defense but was interrupted when Mark burst into the room. "Mom, you have got to see this game. It's so cool. And Cam's the best player I've ever seen."

Relieved at the distraction, Teresa allowed herself to be towed into the den to watch the play.

She only hoped Marjorie had gotten the message. But she had a foreboding that it wouldn't be the last time Marjorie tried to nudge her in Riley's direction.

Chapter Six

Mark was sitting on the front stoop of his side of the duplex when Riley stepped outside his door early the next afternoon. "Hi, Riley! Is it time yet?"

Riley couldn't help but grin in response to the boy's eagerness. "Almost. As soon as Bud gets here. How long have you been sitting there?"

"Just a little while. Mom was getting tired of me asking her if it was time yet, so she said I could sit here and wait for you to come out."

Riley noted the boy was dressed appropriately for the outing in jeans, sneakers, a pullover and a thin jacket. A Tennessee Titans cap rode low on his forehead, shading his face from the sun.

"What are your mom and your sister going to do while we're fishing?"

"They're going to a movie. A *kid* movie. I didn't want to see it."

Riley nodded gravely, hiding his amusement at the gruff tone Mark had adopted in an attempt to sound older. He and Bud had debated taking both the children on the outing, but they'd decided one was all they could handle on this first excursion. Teresa had assured them she would keep Maggie entertained, so they needn't feel guilty. It was nice for her to have a chance to spend some one-on-one time with her daughter, she'd added.

The front door opened and Teresa peeked out. "Mark? Are you— Oh. Hello, Riley."

"Hi." Why was it, he wondered, that the sight of her made him automatically stand straighter? And why did the sight of *him* so often seem to make her stop smiling? "I hear you and Maggie are going to take in a movie."

Teresa wrinkled her nose, probably an unconscious reaction to the mention of the film. He didn't envy her the next couple of hours; he'd rather scrub toilets than sit through one of the animated merchandise commercials that passed for children's films these days. Just another example of how lousy he was with kids, he reminded himself.

"We're really looking forward to it," Teresa said, and he couldn't help grinning again.

"Yeah, I can tell. Don't worry about Mark. We're going to have a great time."

"Is there anything else he needs?"

"No, he's dressed fine. Bud and I will provide everything else."

"You have a life jacket for him?"

He wondered if she knew she was twisting her fingers in front of her. He spoke as reassuringly as he could. "We have a life jacket. Kid size. Bud borrowed one from a neighbor. I won't let Mark take it off even for a minute. Cross my heart."

That solemn vow made her smile a little. "Thank you."

Bud's truck turned into Riley's driveway, and Mark started bouncing in excitement. "He's here! We can go now."

Riley rested a calming hand on the boy's shoulder. "Careful, buddy. You're going to float right off the porch."

Mark grinned. "I'm excited."

"Really? I hadn't noticed." He couldn't help being pleased by the boy's enthusiasm. It felt pretty good to be partially responsible for making a kid this happy.

Bud sauntered toward them with a smile for Teresa and a thumbs-up sign for Mark. "You ready to catch some fish, boy?"

"Yes, sir!"

"Well, go get in the truck."

Almost before the words were out, Mark was making a dash for Riley's driveway.

Bud gave his nephew a wry look. "I think he's ready. I'll go make sure he's belted in."

Riley noticed that Teresa was chewing her lower lip. "We'll take good care of him."

"I know," she said, obviously trying to sound nonchalant about it.

He could still see very faint impressions from her teeth in her soft lower lip. Because he could so clearly picture himself soothing those marks with the tip of his tongue, then erasing all evidence of them with a long, hard kiss, he took a quick step back from her. "I'll, uh, see you later. You and Maggie have fun at your movie."

The slightly quizzical look she gave him let him know she must have read something odd in his expression. He bolted before he could make her more nervous than she already was.

Teresa stood by her son's bed that night, watching him sleep. The soft glow of a night-light gave just enough illumination for her to see that he was smiling in his sleep. Was he reliving his fishing trip in his dreams?

He'd had a wonderful time on his all-guy outing. He hadn't stopped talking about it from the moment he'd returned home until she finally tucked him into bed, where he'd fallen asleep almost immediately.

Lying there sleeping in his Pokémon pajamas on his Star Wars sheets, his worn stuffed monkey beside him, he looked very young and small. She couldn't resist reaching out to brush a lock of sandy hair from his forehead. He didn't even stir.

She knew he wouldn't appreciate her thinking of him as her baby boy, especially tonight after his adventure.

He was growing so quickly. It seemed like only yesterday that she'd nursed him, rocked him, snuggled him in her arms in the wee hours of the morning. Now she looked at the soft skin of his sleep-flushed cheek and imagined it covered with a wiry five o'clock shadow. She pictured his slender little body filled out with a man's muscles, covered with a man's hair. And she wished—as she had many times before—that there was a way to slow down the passage of time.

She knew it was selfish on her part, but she wanted to keep her children little for a while longer. Keep them to herself. Delay for as long as possible that inevitable time when they went off to lives of their own.

What would she have then? Who would she be when

she was no longer a full-time mother to Mark and Maggie?

Impatient with the melancholy that she could feel settling in, she shook her head and stepped away from Mark's bed. He was only ten years old, Maggie only eight. They had many years of mothering left. Just because Mark had spent a day away from her, enjoying an activity that held little interest for her, casually bonding with a couple of nice men who'd offered him much-needed masculine attention didn't mean he no longer needed his mom. He was still a few years away from shaving and borrowing the car. She needed to savor every moment of his childhood and not waste it worrying about the future.

Leaving him to his dreams, she wandered down the hallway, stopping to check on Maggie, who'd kicked off the bedclothes again. Teresa covered her daughter's tiny form, then picked up Maggie's favorite doll from the floor where it had fallen and tucked it into the bed with her. She brushed a kiss across Maggie's warm, soft cheek, then tiptoed out of the room.

A glance at her watch told her it wasn't quite ten o'clock. A bit early for her to turn in, since she wasn't at all sleepy. There was nothing interesting on television, and she'd finished the book she'd been reading last night.

The apartment was clean, the laundry folded and put away. For once, there was nothing that needed to be done. She wished there were some chores pending as she paced through her neat rooms with an uncharacteristic restlessness. She ended up in the kitchen, where she plucked a couple of Oreos from the cookie jar. Boredom eating, she thought with a sigh. She might as well rub them directly on her thighs.

She ate them anyway, standing at the sink and gazing through the small window at the moon-washed backyard. Though Indian summer was still dragging its heels, making the days warm, it would be winter soon. Halloween, Thanksgiving, Christmas and then another new year.

Darn it, she was dwelling on the passage of time again. What was with her tonight, anyway?

On an impulse, she opened the back door and stepped onto the flagstone patio. The air was still warm enough that she was comfortable in the denim shirt she wore with a pair of khaki slacks and leather loafers. Someone a couple of houses down had thrown a backyard barbecue party earlier that evening. Closing her eyes, she could still smell faint hints of charcoal, beer and citronella—like an aromatic echo of summer, she thought with a touch of whimsy.

"Having trouble sleeping?"

Though he'd spoken softly, the sound of Riley's voice made her jump. She turned toward his yard, eyes open and one hand covering her heart. "I didn't see you there."

He stepped out of the shadows so his face was illuminated by the overhead security lighting. He'd changed out of the clothes he'd worn earlier, she noted automatically. He wore a white T-shirt and baggy plaid pajama pants with sandals. His longish hair looked damp, as if he'd just stepped out of the shower. "I didn't mean to startle you."

Even though a chain link fence separated them, she still found herself resisting a cowardly impulse to move backward as he stepped toward her. "I stepped out for a moment to enjoy the nice evening," she said, feeling the need to fill the silence between them.

"It is nice, isn't it? Hard to believe it will be winter soon."

"I was just thinking the same thing."

He crossed his arms on the top rail of the fence and leaned against it, one foot propped against the bottom. "Kids asleep?"

"Soundly. They're both tired after their busy day. Mark had a wonderful time on the fishing trip. He hasn't stopped talking about it since you brought him home."

"I'm glad he had fun. Bud and I enjoyed having him with us."

"I doubt that either of you got to do much fishing with Mark along, but he was thrilled that he managed to land a couple."

"He learned quickly. Bud had him fishing like a pro within the first twenty minutes."

"I, um, hope he didn't talk your ears off."

Riley chuckled. "That boy does like to talk."

"I know." She winced at the thought of what might have spilled from her son's lips during the outing. She'd tried to warn him not to talk too much—specifically, not to talk too much about his family. Even as she'd stumbled through that little speech, she'd been afraid she was wasting her time.

"So you worked as a stripper in a men's club before you moved here, hmm? I understand your stage name was Diamonds LeFlash."

Teresa stared at Riley through the shadows. "What on earth are you talking about?"

"Oh, just repeating what Mark told us during the fishing trip. I found it very interesting."

She sighed and shook her head. "He did not say those things."

"Are you sure?"

"He doesn't even know what a stripper is—I hope."

Riley laughed softly. "Yeah, well, I wouldn't be so sure about that. Kids grow up a lot faster these days than they used to."

Great. A few minutes earlier, she'd been fretting about whiskers and driving. Now she had to add strippers to the worry equation. "Just tell me you didn't really talk about strippers with my ten-year-old son."

"I was just teasing you. We talked about fish, not flesh."

"Thank you."

"You're welcome."

Joking aside, maybe Mark had been fairly discreet during the outing, she reassured herself. Not that there were any big secrets to reveal about their little family, but it made her uncomfortable to think of her son discussing her with other people. Okay, specifically, it was the thought of being discussed with Riley that felt particularly awkward.

He seemed to be studying her face, as if searching for something in her expression. "What?" she asked involuntarily.

His eyebrows lifted. "Was I staring at you?"

"Yes."

"Sorry. It's just…"

She found herself taking a step toward him, curious about what he was going to say. "What?"

His smile was crooked. Almost sheepish. "You look very pretty in the moonlight."

She felt her cheeks warm in response to the unexpected compliment. "Oh."

He didn't seem to notice the inanity of her response. "Of course, you look pretty in daylight, too," he continued. "But the moonlight really makes your eyes sparkle."

She frowned at him. "I thought you'd stopped doing that."

He was almost as bad as Marjorie at feigning innocence. "Doing what?"

"Flirting with me."

"I was merely stating facts. Can I help it if I'm just naturally charming?"

She rolled her eyes. "And possessed with such natural modesty."

"Another one of my assets."

"Don't you ever stop joking?"

"There are some things I take *very* seriously." The look he gave her came perilously close to a leer. "Would you like me to demonstrate for you sometime?"

"You're incorrigible. And, besides, we agreed that we would maintain a friendly, professional relationship."

"I can be *very* friendly."

"Stop it." For some ridiculous reason, she felt herself smiling—probably because his tone was more silly than suggestive. She straightened her expression immediately. "That isn't what I meant."

He sighed with exaggerated regret. "I know. But that doesn't stop me from daydreaming."

Shaking her head, she took a step toward her door. "It's getting late. I'm going inside."

"Afraid to spend any more time alone in the moonlight with me?"

"Yes, that's it." She kept her voice dry as she shot back her answer. "I'm afraid I'll be too tempted to climb over this fence and throw all caution to the wind."

He gave her a quick, ridiculously hopeful grin. "Don't let me stop you."

"Good night, Riley."

"Good night, Teresa. Sweet dreams."

Riley could make even that well-worn and generally meaningless phrase sound too perceptive. As if he suspected he might play a role in her dreams. It bothered her that she couldn't absolutely swear he wouldn't make an appearance there—or that he never had before.

She let herself in her house quickly, locking the kitchen door behind her. Now she really was wide awake. She opened the pantry and started pulling out the ingredients for muffins. She supposed it wouldn't hurt to have breakfast prepared a few hours early.

She wasn't quite ready to face her dreams tonight.

Riley's telephone rang at two-thirty Tuesday morning, jarring him out of a sound sleep. "What?" he barked into the phone, groggy and disoriented.

"It's Lindsey. Someone just tried to kill R. L. Hightower."

The succinct statement brought him upright in a hurry. "Where are you?"

"Outside R.L.'s house. You might want to come. Bud's here, and he's understandably upset."

"I'm on my way." He was already reaching for his jeans when he tossed the phone into its cradle.

The scene outside R.L.'s house was chaotic. It was a normally quiet, middle-class neighborhood with big yards putting some distance between the early seventies ranch-style houses. Accessed by a circular concrete driveway, R.L.'s house was set back several yards from the road. That driveway was filled with vehicles, including a fire truck, an ambulance and two marked police cars. Groups of people stood around the vehicles, among them several faces Riley immediately identified.

The scene took him back several months to the fires that had distressed the community, including the one that had killed R.L's friend Truman. But the arsonist had been caught and was now in jail. What on earth had happened?

Even as he hurried toward one of the groups, Riley automatically noted the damage to the house. Several windows were shattered, all on the right front side of the house. Because he'd visited his uncle's friend several times, Riley knew the windows were in R.L.'s bedroom. He watched as the ambulance was maneuvered carefully out of the crowded driveway, lights flashing as it turned onto the street and disappeared.

"Riley," Lindsey called. "Your uncle is over here."

Moving toward his co-worker, he saw that she was standing beside her husband, Chief Dan Meadows. Dan was talking to Bud, who was gazing toward the house with a look of shock on his slack face.

"Bud?" Riley put a hand on his uncle's shoulder. "Are you okay?"

Bud's response was slow in coming. "R.L. was hurt, not me."

"Is he all right?"

"He will be." It was Dan who answered. "He's lucky. Had he been sleeping in his bed, he would very likely have been killed. But his back was hurting tonight, so he slept on the floor, instead. He was hit by some debris, got a few cuts and bruises, but he'll recover. He called Bud even before he called nine-one-one. We got here close to the same time, about twenty minutes ago. R.L.'s been taken to the hospital for observation."

"What happened?" Riley addressed the question to Dan, since Bud still seemed too shaken to answer.

"Someone shot into R.L.'s bedroom through the windows. The bedding looks like Swiss cheese. Lamps and mirrors and damn near everything else in the room are all busted up. Like I said, if he'd been in bed…'' Dan let Riley mentally complete the grim alternative.

"Have you caught the shooter?"

"No. I've got officers combing the neighborhood for witnesses now."

Riley's attention was torn between wanting to know more details about the attack and worrying about Bud, who was uncharacteristically quiet and unresponsive. "R.L.'s going to be okay, Bud. Dan said he wasn't badly injured."

Bud merely nodded.

"Maybe you should take him home," Lindsey murmured, touching Riley's arm.

"Yeah. You're covering the story?"

"I've got it. Take care of your uncle."

"C'mon, Bud, let me take you home." Riley tugged lightly at the older man's shoulder. "Just leave your truck here. We'll get it tomorrow."

"I, uh…" Bud fell silent, looking old and confused.

Riley was getting seriously concerned by his uncle's behavior. "Maybe we should stop by the hospital and let Dr. Frank take a look at you."

Bud shook his head. "I'm okay. I want to go home."

"He needs some rest," Dan suggested. "It's only natural that something like this would shake him up."

"I want to go home," Bud repeated.

Though he still wasn't convinced that a visit with Dr. Frank was out of order, Riley conceded to his uncle's wishes. Tuning out the noise and confusion around them, he led his uncle away from the disturbing scene.

Teresa hesitated outside Riley's door the next afternoon. She'd just gotten home from work, and the children's bus wouldn't bring them home for another hour. She'd never knocked on Riley's door before—hadn't had a reason to—but she felt compelled to do so now.

She was beginning to think he wasn't going to answer when the door abruptly opened. Wearing jeans and a logo T-shirt, his feet bare, Riley looked as though he'd just crawled out of bed. His hair was tousled, his eyelids heavy, and he hadn't shaved. He certainly wasn't looking his best. Yet she still had to moisten her suddenly dry lips before she spoke. "I'm sorry. You were sleeping. I didn't mean to disturb you."

He ran his fingers through his hair, restoring some semblance of his usual casual style. "No, that's okay. I fell asleep on the couch."

"I heard about what happened to your uncle's friend. It was all anyone talked about at the diner today. Some people mentioned that your uncle seemed very shaken. Is he okay? Is there anything either of you need?"

She'd never seen Riley look quite so serious when he answered. "I stayed with him most of the night and part of the day. He couldn't go back to sleep. He just paced or sat staring at nothing. He wouldn't eat and he barely responded when I spoke to him. I finally called Dr. Frank and had him prescribe something to help Bud relax a little. I wanted to bring him home with me, but he absolutely refused. He said he wanted to stay in his own home."

"So you haven't had much sleep yourself. You should get some rest." She started to back away.

Riley stopped her. "Wait. Why don't you come in for a minute? The kids won't be home for a while, will they?"

"No, but—"

"I'll make some coffee. I'd like to hear what everyone was saying at the diner today. I've been sort of out of the loop."

"Don't you want to rest?"

"If I go back to sleep now, I'll be up all night. So, how about that coffee?"

Maybe it was because he looked so tired and somber that she couldn't refuse his offer. She stepped inside his apartment, allowing him to close the door behind her.

Chapter Seven

Teresa had never been inside Riley's half of the duplex, and his decor rather surprised her. She had expected Early Bachelor Pad; instead, she discovered that he leaned toward rustic country with Shaker and primitive accents. She recognized several characteristically heavy Bob Timberlake pieces and a couple of nice antique reproductions. Hunting prints and duck prints hung on the walls. Colorful throws and thick pillows were invitingly arranged on upholstered chairs and sofas. "This is very nice."

He gave her a weary facsimile of his usual lopsided grin. "You were expecting cinder blocks and two-by-fours?"

"I'm not sure what I expected. But I like what you've done."

"Thanks. Come into the kitchen. I'll put on the coffee."

The first word that came to Teresa's mind when she entered Riley's kitchen was "efficient." The appliances were stainless steel, and several timesaving devices were grouped on the spotless countertops. He walked straight to the impressive-looking coffeemaker. "This is quite a change, isn't it?"

"What is?" she asked, drawing her attention away from his kitchen accessories.

"Me serving you coffee. Have a seat, it'll be ready in a minute."

She pulled out a bow-backed chair from the round oak table. The cushions on the chairs matched the curtains at the single window above the sink—a bold plaid that looked neither too masculine nor too feminine. "Did you hire a decorator?"

He answered without pausing in his coffee preparations. "No. I had help from friends when I needed it."

Girlfriends, she clarified mentally. It was easy enough to imagine any number of single young women who'd have been more than happy to assist Riley with his decorating. Because gossip flowed as freely as the coffee at the Rainbow Café, she knew he'd dated quite a few of the women in town. None of the relationships had led even close to the altar, according to the local tattle mongers, not that a few of those women hadn't tried their best.

He set a steaming mug of coffee in front of her. "Cream or sugar?"

"No, just black, thank you."

Placing his cup on the table, he started to sit, then paused. "I have some homemade cookies in the jar— oatmeal-raisin, I think. Would you like some?"

"No, thanks. Um, you baked cookies?"

"A friend made them for me." He settled in the chair opposite her at the small table.

Another friend. Riley O'Neal was one popular guy, she thought, lifting her mug to her lips. "Good coffee," she said after taking a sip.

"You're sure you wouldn't like something to go with it?"

"This is fine. How is your uncle's friend?"

"I called the hospital just before I left Bud's house a couple of hours ago. He was doing very well then—shaken up, of course, and sore from quite a few cuts and bruises, but he'll recover. He's being kept in for observation—and possibly for his own safety while Dan tries to figure out who tried to fill him full of holes."

"So it's true that no one knows who did this or why?"

"That's what I've been told. R.L. denies any knowledge of who it could have been. There were no witnesses to the shooting. Everyone in the houses nearby was asleep."

"People are scared," Teresa murmured, remembering the somber conversations in the diner that day. "They say there's never been anything like this in Edstown."

"With the exception of the fires Eddie Stamps set, there have been very few serious crimes here," Riley agreed. "Break-ins, fights, drunk drivers, domestic abuse—we've had our share of all those. But drive-by shootings? That's a new, unwelcome development."

Teresa gazed into her coffee cup. "I moved here to get my children away from urban violence. I would hate to think it had found us here."

"I'm not sure there's any place that's completely free of crime and violence anymore," Riley mused. "Edstown's been slower than some places to come into the twenty-first century, but we're getting there. Still, I doubt there's a reason for the locals to start digging trenches or wearing flak jackets. This wasn't a random shooting or a psycho attacking the first house he passed. This was someone with a grudge against R.L. Someone who knew where he sleeps and targeted his bed.''

"How could someone have an enemy like that without knowing who it is?" Teresa asked in bewilderment. "If someone hates him badly enough to want to kill him, wouldn't Mr. Hightower know about it?"

"If he knows, he isn't saying. He told Dan he didn't have a clue."

"What about Bud? Do you think he has an idea who shot at his friend?"

"He told me he doesn't know who it could have been."

"And did you believe him?"

Riley hesitated for a telling moment before answering. "I don't know. All I know for sure is that Bud's having a very hard time dealing with this. He lost one friend this year. He isn't ready to lose another."

"One of his friends died?"

Riley nodded. "He died in a fire in January. No one has ever decided for sure if the fire started accidentally or if it was deliberately set. It was a fishing cabin in an isolated location, and it burned completely to the ground before anyone reported seeing smoke. The fire marshal said the exact cause hasn't been determined."

Teresa remembered now. "I heard about that one. There was a lot of speculation that the teenager who set all those fires in town might have set that one, too, though he denied it."

"Yeah. I watched Eddie answer questions about the fires. He confessed to all of them except Truman's fishing cabin and the insurance office R.L. had owned for more than thirty years.''

"Could you tell whether he was lying?"

Again, a hesitation before Riley's reply. "I don't know. But there wasn't enough evidence to charge him with those two. The prosecutor agreed to drop those charges in return for his confession to the others."

"You don't think he set those two," Teresa reported, studying the look in his eyes.

Riley pushed his hand through his hair again, leaving it tumbled around his face. "I had my doubts," he admitted. "It seemed too coincidental that the only fires Eddie denied involved two of three longtime buddies. Truman, R.L. and Bud met in junior high school and they've been practically inseparable ever since. Through marriages and divorces, diverse careers and the usual temporary falling-outs, they stayed friends. Now Truman's dead. R.L. watched his business burn and was almost shot in his own bed."

"And you're wondering if something's going to happen to your uncle next," Teresa finished for him when his voice trailed off.

He sighed. "It's probably a groundless concern. Truman could have died from smoking in bed, for all I know. R.L.'s troubles are probably due to a disgruntled insurance customer, someone whose claim was denied for one reason or another, so he blamed the agent who sold him the policy. None of that would have anything to do with Bud."

"You're probably right. Why would anyone suddenly be after three old buddies?"

"Exactly. Makes no sense at all. They've all lived here in Edstown their entire lives. They never caused any trouble, never made any enemies that I know of.

They were all hard workers—R.L. had the insurance company, Truman owned a car sales lot, and Bud operated his own electrical contracting company until he retired a few years ago. They were all successful, in their own ways. They had enough money to hunt and fish and travel a little, but they all lived fairly modestly for the most part. Bud jokes that he spent most of his earnings on alimony for his two ex-wives, but he lives comfortably in his double-wide, and he's actually stayed on pretty good terms with his exes.''

Teresa nodded, sensing that Riley needed to talk for a while.

''What I'm saying is that I can't imagine why anyone would have a grudge against my uncle or his friends. They're not the type to make enemies like that. So Truman's death must have been an accident—or one of Eddie's arsons—and R.L.'s shooter had to be an angry insurance customer. It's the only explanation that makes sense.''

''It does sound reasonable.''

''So why do I have this gut feeling that there's something more I need to know?''

The worry and frustration in his voice made her instinctively want to reach out to him. To pat his hand and reassure him, the way she would her son. And yet there was nothing even remotely maternal about her reactions to Riley. ''I'm sure your police chief friend will be investigating the shooting extensively,'' she said. ''If there's anything for you to be concerned about, Chief Meadows will probably uncover it. I've heard he's good.''

''He's *very* good. If anyone can find answers, it's Dan.''

''There you go, then,'' she said bracingly. ''You can

relax and let the police handle everything. I'm sure once your uncle has rested and seen his friend again, he'll feel much better—and so will you."

"I'm sure you're right."

She could tell he'd made an effort to speak confidently, but there was still concern reflected in his silvery-gray eyes. He forced a smile. "Thanks for letting me unload on you."

"I know you're very close to your uncle. I can understand why you're so concerned about him."

"Actually, it felt pretty weird taking care of him today. Bud's always been the one who thought he had to look out for me."

"Families look out for each other." Or so she'd heard.

Propping his elbow on the table, Riley rested his chin on his fist as he studied her face. "Do you have family, Teresa? I know you lost your husband and your parents, but is there anyone else? Grandparents? Cousins? A favorite uncle of your own?"

"A few cousins, none close. I was raised by my grandmother after my parents died, but she passed away a few years ago. I've lost touch with my aunts and uncles." She didn't add that Darren had alienated most of her family. He hadn't cared for any of them, and he'd convinced Teresa that they weren't particularly fond of her, either.

It had only been when their marriage was falling apart that Teresa had finally seen through Darren's charm and promises, that she had finally realized he had deliberately separated her from her family and the friends she'd had before their marriage. His insecurities had made him want to keep her to himself, totally dependent on him.

"What about your husband's family?"

Teresa wasn't comfortable discussing Darren with Riley—she didn't usually talk about her late husband with anyone—but she answered his question. "He has a sister. She lives in California. I haven't seen her since before Maggie was born. His mother still lives in Tennessee, just outside of Memphis."

"Do the children see their grandmother often?"

She hesitated, tempted to brush off the question with a monosyllabic answer. But Riley had been so candid with her she felt compelled to answer honestly. "My mother-in-law is one of the reasons I moved here. She's a bitter, neurotic woman who divides her time between feigning illness, fighting with her neighbors and threatening to take my children away from me. They don't enjoy being around her, and neither do I. I couldn't take it anymore."

She bit her lip before she could babble any further. Riley had only asked a simple question, and she'd answered in more detail than she'd intended. Apparently, he wasn't the only one whose tongue had been loosened by this impromptu chat session.

He wasn't smiling. "She threatened to take your children away from you?"

"Periodically." She tried to speak matter-of-factly, intending to change the subject very quickly. "Every time I refused to cater to her whims. She's never had a case, of course, and she wouldn't really want to be bothered with the full-time care of two young children, anyway, but she made it a hobby to call me every so often and threaten to file a custody suit."

"On what grounds?"

"Why, that I'm an unfit mother, of course."

She'd never heard Riley utter an expletive, but he did then, making her blink in response. "Have you talked to Serena about this?"

"Of course. She has assured me she'll represent me in the unlikely event that Edna actually files suit. She promises there's no way Edna could ever take my children. But it did become...bothersome," she said, settling for an understatement.

"Can't you file suit against her? Charge her with harassment or something?"

"I suppose I could—but I'd rather not, unless she makes it necessary. She might be bitter and difficult, but she's just an aging woman who alienated a husband and a daughter and lost her son. I'm not going to inflict her on my children, but I have no desire to be vindictive against her. And besides, since I've moved here, I haven't heard from her. I suppose she's realized that the children and I are out of her reach, and she's turned her attentions to harassing someone else. Her neighbors, probably. She loves to file lawsuits against them."

"You're more generous than I would be under the circumstances," Riley muttered.

"I just prefer to avoid confrontations whenever possible." She drained her coffee.

"Do you mind if I ask how you lost your husband? Was he ill?"

Growing more uncomfortable with the increasingly personal nature of the conversation, Teresa answered briefly this time. "No. He died in an accident." She glanced at her watch. "The kids will be home soon. I'd better go get ready for them."

Riley stood when she did. "Thanks for stopping in to check on my uncle and me."

"Just being neighborly," she said lightly, moving toward the doorway. "Let me know if you need anything."

He tagged at her heels to the front door. "I'm sure

you must be greatly disappointed," he said as she reached for the knob.

"What do you mean?"

"Well, I had you alone in my house and I was too tired to even make a pass at you. I'll try to do better next time."

She was torn between exasperation and a touch of relief that the smile was back in his eyes. His appealingly crooked grin looked almost natural again.

It was nice to think she'd made him feel better by providing a sympathetic ear, but she had no intention of letting him get carried away. He certainly had no shortage of female friends, she reminded herself, thinking of those homemade cookies in the kitchen. "Try anything next time and you'll be drinking coffee through a straw."

He laughed, and she was ridiculously pleased that she'd caused him to do so. "I'll keep that in mind."

She found herself wearing a faintly bemused smile as she entered her place a few moments later. Riley O'Neal was definitely one of a kind.

R. L. Hightower left town as soon as he was released from the hospital. He didn't leave word of where he went, though Riley suspected his uncle was in contact with his friend.

"Your uncle knows something he isn't telling," Dan said bluntly on Saturday evening, his deep voice rough with frustration. "He won't admit it, but I think he has a pretty good idea who shot at R.L."

"If Bud knows who tried to kill his best friend, why wouldn't he say anything?" Lindsey demanded, looking skeptical. "He would surely want the guy caught so R.L. would feel safe to come home."

Dan and Lindsey were sitting at a dining table with Riley and their hosts, Serena and Cameron. Usually there was a great deal of laughter and teasing when this group got together, but tonight the conversation was more serious. Dan had been preoccupied since he arrived, and his friends all knew him well enough to understand why. A serious crime had been committed in his town. Dan wouldn't relax completely until the culprit had been caught.

In response to his wife's question, Dan shook his head. "I don't know why Bud's not talking. Maybe he's not sure about his suspicions and he doesn't want to cast doubt on someone who could be innocent. Or maybe he knows too much," he said with a quick glance at Riley.

"You think he's afraid to speak?" Serena asked, sounding concerned.

"It's a possibility," Dan agreed. "I need your help here, Riley. Bud clams up every time I try to talk to him. Hasn't he said anything to you?"

Riley took a sip of iced tea, then set the glass down. "He puts me off, too. It's something he's never done before. I don't know how to get him to talk to me if he doesn't want to."

"Have you asked him if he has suspicions about the shooter?" Cameron inquired from the other end of the table.

"Several times. He shrugs or shakes his head. When I pushed a little harder, he tuned me out. Stared into space like he couldn't even hear me."

"That's pretty much what he did with me," Dan muttered.

"I hated it," Riley admitted. "To be honest, it scared me a little. It was so unlike him. So I stopped asking. As long as I don't mention R.L. or the shooting, he talks to me. He's still quieter than usual, definitely distracted, but at least he responds.''

"This must be upsetting for you." Softhearted Lindsey reached out to cover Riley's hand with her own.

"I'll just be glad when we find out what the hell's going on so things can get back to normal.''

Dan scowled. "I wish I could assure you that will be soon. But with R.L. out of town and Bud not talking, we're not making any progress."

"It is possible that Bud doesn't know any more than we do," Cameron suggested.

"Yeah. It's possible." Dan didn't sound overly confident.

"When's R.L. planning to come back home?" Serena asked.

Dan answered with a grumble. "Beats the hell out of me. He didn't even tell me he was leaving town.''

Riley shrugged. He didn't know where R.L. was nor when he would return.

For the next few minutes, they all concentrated on the excellent food Serena and Cameron had prepared for them. Marjorie was off on her regular Saturday night outing with a group of friends, and this dinner party had been planned for a couple of weeks. As she always did, Serena had encouraged Riley to bring a guest and, as always, Riley had declined. Dining with these two blissfully married couples was likely to give a date ideas, he figured. The wrong ideas, when it came to him.

"How's your new tenant working out?" Dan asked Riley, apparently deciding he needed to stop talking shop and lead the conversation into a lighter direction.

"No problems so far. Half the time I don't even know they're there." Which was, of course, a lie. Riley was always too well aware that Teresa lived in the other half of his house.

Lindsey smiled. "The kids are cute, aren't they? I've met them at church a couple of times."

"They're great kids," Serena said with a smile. "I've known them since they were born, of course, so I'm not exactly objective, but I do think they're exceptionally well behaved."

"You must have known Teresa's husband."

"Of course," Serena answered Lindsey. "I attended their wedding."

Riley wondered if the others had noticed a sudden change in Serena's voice.

If Lindsey had noticed, it didn't stop her from asking, "What was he like?"

Serena glanced at her husband before admitting, "I didn't know him very well, really. Teresa and I didn't get to see each other very often while she was married. I was in law school while she was having her babies—we were just busy with different things."

Blunt as always, Lindsey concluded, "You hated him."

"Lindsey," Dan murmured, shaking his head in resignation.

"I didn't hate him," Serena insisted. "I just didn't particularly like him."

"Was he a jerk?"

"Lindsey," Dan said again.

"What? I'm just asking. Teresa's part of our community now. It's only natural that I'm curious about her."

"Gossip," Cameron stated.

"A fine old Edstown tradition," Lindsey retorted. "So why'd you hate Teresa's husband, Serena?"

Serena shook her head. "I'm not going to sit here and gossip about my friend's late husband. I've already admitted that I didn't care for Darren, but that was just my opinion. I don't see any need to go into the reasons."

The young reporter had never been easily dissuaded from a line of questioning, as everyone at the table had good reason to know. "How did he die?"

"He was trimming some tree limbs and he accidentally hit a live wire with the tool he was using. He was electrocuted. Lindsey found him when she returned home after doing some shopping with the kids."

Riley felt the stark force of Serena's words hit him solidly in the chest. Hearing the details of Teresa's husband's death made him even more aware of all she had been through—losing her parents so young, finding her husband dead, raising two children alone, battling an embittered mother-in-law. It was a wonder she was as positive and upbeat as he'd usually found her to be. And no wonder at all that she was so independent and wary of getting involved with new people.

After a moment of silence, Lindsey asked, "How long ago did it happen?"

"It's been four and a half years. Mark was in kindergarten and Maggie was just a toddler."

"And she's been raising them on her own ever since."

Serena nodded. "She's such a good mother. I expect I'll be calling on her quite a bit for advice."

"I'm surprised Marjorie hasn't started trying to fix her up with someone." Lindsey grinned. "Your mother does love matchmaking."

Cameron groaned, as did Dan and Riley—all of them had been recipients of Marjorie's less-than-subtle matchmaking attentions at one time or another. Of course, with

Cameron and Dan, her efforts had led to matrimony. Riley intended to be another story.

Serena's smile was rueful. "Actually, Mom has started making lists of local eligible bachelors. She's leaning toward Neal McClain and Bill Jungkind. I've been trying to discourage her from fixing Teresa up with anyone, but as you said, my mother loves being a matchmaker."

Riley scowled at his plate. As fond as he was of Marjorie Schaffer, this matchmaking was getting out of hand. She'd stopped trying with him, of course, which he appreciated, but he didn't see any reason for her to turn her attentions to Teresa.

Lindsey frowned thoughtfully. "Neal McClain's a nice guy—but he's a little old for Teresa, isn't he? I'm guessing he's close to fifty."

"Mother said he would be good for her because he's so steady and settled and financially secure. And he likes kids."

"He's a grandfather," Riley muttered. "His oldest daughter just had her first kid. Why would Teresa want to get involved with a grandfather?"

"Bill Jungkind's closer to the right age," Lindsey mused. "Mid-thirties. Of course, he has joint custody of his own three kids, so that would be a lot of children involved."

Abruptly losing his appetite, Riley set his fork on his plate. "You know, I really don't think Teresa would appreciate knowing we'd been talking about her this way."

"You're right," Serena agreed, her expression a bit sheepish. "I wish she could have joined us this evening, but she'd promised to take Mark and Maggie to a school party at the skating rink."

Cameron changed the subject by bring up the local reaction to Riley's latest column in the *Evening Star*. Serena deftly picked up the new conversational thread, and Dan and Lindsey went along. Riley was grateful to his hosts for the change of subject.

Now if only he could figure out a way to stop thinking about Marjorie pushing Teresa into the willing arms of one of the bachelors Serena had mentioned.

Chapter Eight

Teresa wasn't exactly sure how she and her children ended up in Riley's apartment the first Sunday afternoon in November watching a NASCAR race with Riley and Bud. She suspected that Mark had finagled an invitation for himself. Maggie hadn't wanted to be excluded for a second time, so she'd been invited, too. Bud had insisted that Teresa be included since everyone else was. He seemed so disappointed when she initially declined that she allowed herself to be persuaded.

She'd only seen Bud a few times in the ten days since the still-unsolved shooting, but even those brief encounters had been enough to let her see the changes in his behavior. He seemed quieter, more withdrawn. And he looked older.

She could understand why Riley had been worried.

But watching Bud now, as he sat on the couch between Mark and Maggie, slugging ginger ale and ex-

plaining the fine points of stock car racing, she thought
he seemed more like the man she had first met. He
chuckled as he patiently answered Mark's many questions and made a place on his knee for Maggie's head
when she tired of watching the colorful cars passing by
on the screen.

Teresa sat in a chair next to Riley's recliner. They'd
made casual conversation during the past hour and a
half, but Mark had claimed most of the attention for the
afternoon. The boy was obviously wearing down a bit;
he'd stopped talking quite so much and leaned companionably against Bud's side as he watched the race with
a fascinated concentration that rather surprised Teresa.
Though this was the first time he'd ever watched a car
race, he'd already chosen a driver to cheer for. His attention was focused on the flame-decorated car that was
currently battling for second place with another equally
determined driver.

Mark cheered when his driver took the spot, then
gasped when two other cars slammed into each other,
setting off a chain reaction of noisy crashes. Because of
the efficiency of the high-tech safety equipment, no one
was hurt in the incident, but debris on the track brought
out a caution flag. The lead cars took advantage of the
opportunity to head into their pits, where pit crews
jumped the wall and started changing tires, pouring gas
and washing grills and windshields with amazing speed
and well-coordinated efficiency.

Teresa glanced from the frantic activity on the television screen to Riley, who sprawled in his chair beside
her. "That's what you once pictured yourself doing?"

He chuckled. "Hard to imagine, isn't it?"

She watched as a crew member changed a tire in less

than ten seconds. "It took you a bit longer than that to change my tire."

He grinned. "Yeah. But I looked better doing it."

She fought an answering smile. "If you say so."

He reached for his soda can, shook it, then sighed. "Empty. Now I have to walk all the way into the kitchen."

"I think it's a good thing you didn't join a pit crew."

He chuckled. "I think you're right."

He started to rise.

"I'd be happy to bring you another soda if you want to watch the race," Teresa offered.

"Thanks, but I'd rather have coffee, anyway. You can come keep me company while I brew a pot."

Taking the hint that he wanted to speak to her, she stood. "Sure."

"Anybody need anything from the kitchen?" Riley asked.

Bud smiled as he looked at the little girl dozing blissfully on his knee. "I think Maggie's okay. How about you, Mark?"

"Got any ice cream?" the boy asked hopefully.

"Mark—"

"But, Mom, he asked."

Riley chuckled. "I imagine I have some ice cream in the freezer."

"You and Bud are coming perilously close to spoiling my children," Teresa said as soon as she and Riley were alone in his kitchen.

"Hey, I'm about ready to go buy them a toy store. Have you watched Bud's face this afternoon?"

Teresa glanced in the direction of the living room. "Yes, I've watched him. He seems to be enjoying himself."

"It's the first time I've seen him really smile since R.L. left town. Bud's grown very fond of your kids, Teresa."

"They're very fond of him, too. Bud is what they imagine a grandfather would be like."

While the coffee brewed, Riley opened the freezer and pulled out a half gallon of ice cream. "Today has been good for him. I don't believe he's given a thought to R.L. or the shooting since the race started."

"There's been no further progress on finding out who was responsible?"

"No. Not a clue."

"When do you think Mr. Hightower will come home?"

"Not until he feels safe, I'd imagine. But I don't know how he can feel safe until the shooter is caught. And I don't know how anyone can be caught until someone tells Dan who has a grudge against R.L."

"Do you still think your uncle has suspicions about that?"

"Yes, I do. But I've given up on him sharing those suspicions with anyone—including me. I've stopped asking because it just upsets him when I bring it up."

"Then you probably should let it rest," Teresa agreed. "He'll tell you when he's ready—if he ever is."

"Yeah. You think Maggie will want ice cream?"

"I'm sure she will. She and Mark both love ice cream."

He pulled another dish from a cabinet. "How about you?"

"No, thanks."

"Are you sure? It's chocolate chip. The premium kind," he added enticingly.

She paused, then said, "Well, maybe just a scoop."

Her kids weren't the only ones in the family who liked ice cream.

"We might as well all have some." He lined up five dishes on the counter, then opened the carton and picked up the scoop. "There's a tray in the cabinet to the left of the oven if you'd like to get it out."

She found the tray and carried it to him. Standing beside him, she set the ice cream dishes on the tray as he filled them. The aromatic scent of fresh-brewed coffee filled the room, and she could hear Mark and Bud talking over the television in the other room. Mark laughed at something the older man said, and Bud's deep chuckle followed.

A very domestic scene, she thought with a faint pang. It was going to be difficult to keep her children—Mark especially—from getting too close to these men. As tempting as it might be for them to think of Bud as a surrogate grandfather, they needed to understand there was really no connection between them, no obligation for Bud or Riley to keep spending time with them.

It was something she needed to remind herself occasionally, she thought as Riley's hand brushed hers when he passed her an ice cream dish. The contact made a pleasant shiver run through her, as did the warm, almost intimate smile he gave her.

The O'Neal men were entirely too appealing. Especially this one. It would be all too easy for a woman who wasn't very careful to allow liking to turn into more. Especially a woman with a historical weakness for charmingly irresponsible men.

Maggie woke up sick early Monday morning. Her temperature was above normal, and she complained of headache and nausea.

Because Teresa had been warned that a highly contagious virus was making its way through the school, it wasn't hard to diagnose the illness. A quick telephone conversation with the doctor on call for the medical clinic she'd been using since she moved to Edstown confirmed her suspicion. She was told to make sure Maggie rested and drank plenty of fluids and was given instructions about the use of over-the-counter medications. The virus generally caused several days of discomfort, the doctor added, but rarely led to serious complications.

Reassured about Maggie's health, Teresa began to worry about what to do with her for the day. Already she would be late for work. Normally she knew Marjorie wouldn't mind her taking a day off to take care of her sick child, but this was the date for the monthly luncheon meeting of a large local civic club. Even then it wouldn't have been quite such a problem had Shameka not been out of town for a family event, leaving Marjorie already one worker short.

Surely Marjorie would know someone who could either baby-sit, at least through the meeting, or take Teresa's place at the diner. Marjorie knew nearly everyone in Edstown. She would surely come through.

"If you feel comfortable leaving Maggie with someone else while she's sick, I'd really like to have you here," Marjorie said when Teresa phoned her. "I know a couple of great baby-sitters, but no competent servers. Still, if you think you should stay with Maggie, we'll get by here. Your child is definitely more important."

Teresa hesitated a moment, then said, "I think she'll be fine for a few hours. Do you really know a good sitter who would be available on such short notice?"

"I think so. I'll make a call and get right back to you with the details. But, really, Terry, stay home if you need to. The Rotarians can wait a little longer between coffee refills this morning.''

It was the classic tug-of-war for any working mother, whether waitress or office worker or doctor—the need to be available to nurture her sick child and the obligation she felt to her job. Teresa knew Maggie wasn't seriously ill, and she hated to leave Marjorie—who'd been so good to her—in the lurch.

"I can come in for a while," she said again. "At least for the meeting, if you can suggest someone to sit with Maggie."

"I'll get back to you," Marjorie repeated, and disconnected.

After making a quick call to the church where Mark and Maggie attended a before-school program to inform them that her children wouldn't be attending that day, Teresa spent the next fifteen minutes getting Mark ready for school and herself dressed for work. Maggie had gone back to sleep, so she hadn't had a chance yet to prepare her for a baby-sitter. She decided to let Maggie sleep until she knew for certain who the sitter would be.

Teresa couldn't help being a bit nervous about leaving Maggie with someone new, especially when the child was sick, but she trusted Marjorie's judgment completely.

"Why can't I stay home, too?" Mark asked, dawdling over his cereal and fruit.

"Because you aren't sick. And, besides, you've been looking forward to finishing your painting in your art class today, remember?"

"Oh, yeah. You're really going to hang it on a wall?"

"Absolutely. I can't wait to see it."

"It looks pretty good. I'm the best artist in my class," the boy said matter-of-factly.

Distracted by a knock on her front door, Teresa decided to talk to her son later about displaying a bit more modesty. "Go brush your teeth and put on your shoes. I'll find out who's at the door."

She certainly hadn't expected to find Riley on her doorstep. Looking a bit sleep-rumpled, he gave her a lazy smile. "I hear you're in need of a baby-sitter."

"Marjorie called *you?*" And to think Teresa had been thinking about how much she trusted Marjorie's judgment!

"Yeah. She knew I wouldn't mind keeping an eye on Maggie for a couple of hours."

"But don't you have to work?"

"I'm working at home today, writing a column. I don't have to be anywhere until three this afternoon."

"But—"

"It's no big deal, Teresa. Marjorie said she really needs you at the diner this morning, and I owe her a few favors, so she called me. I'm happy to help out."

"Have you ever actually taken care of a sick child?"

"No," he admitted. "But Marjorie said Maggie's not badly ill. She said it was just a bug. She's right, isn't she? There's no reason to be seriously concerned?"

"No. It is just a virus that's going around the school. But feeling bad makes her whiny and cranky. And very demanding. I'm not sure how much work you'll get done when she wakes up."

"I can handle this, Teresa. Go to work."

She hesitated, not at all sure this was a good idea. She still found it hard to believe Marjorie had called Riley to baby-sit—even though he certainly was close and apparently available. It wasn't that she didn't trust him to take care of Maggie. It was mostly that she hated to be obligated to him.

Torn between obligations, she wavered only another moment before saying, "I'll only be gone three or four hours. I'll come home as soon as the meeting is over. Um, don't you usually cover that meeting for your paper?"

"Lindsey's taking it today. Maggie's sleeping now?"

"Yes."

"Okay. I'll go get my notes and my laptop and I'll be right back."

The phone rang almost as soon as Teresa closed the door behind him. She picked it up, knowing who would be on the other end. She was right.

"I found you a baby-sitter," Marjorie announced.

"Yes, he just told me. I can't believe you called Riley."

All innocence, the older woman asked, "Why? Do you have a concern about Riley watching Maggie for a few hours?"

"Of course not. It's just not something I ever would have asked him to do."

"You didn't ask him, dear. I did. And as a favor to me, he agreed."

"I really hate to impose on him, Marjorie. When I moved in as his tenant, I promised myself I wouldn't cause him any problems."

"What problem? He said he was working at home today, anyway. Keeping an eye on Maggie is certainly no great imposition."

"Still—"

"He really doesn't mind, Terry. I thought of him immediately when you said you needed someone today. After all, he lives right next door and he often works at home. He was the logical first choice to call."

Teresa still didn't see it quite that way, but there was

no need to argue with Marjorie about it now. After all, Marjorie had only been trying to help. Promising to be at work as soon as she dropped Mark off at school, she hung up and headed upstairs to her daughter's room.

Maggie lay sprawled in her bed, her face still flushed, her fair hair tumbled on the pillow. Teresa placed a hand on her daughter's shoulder, leaning close to say, "Maggie? I need you to wake up for a minute."

Blinking, Maggie peered blearily at her mother. "Mommy?"

"I have to leave for a little while, okay? But Riley's going to sit with you until I get back."

Maggie's first reaction had been to shake her head to protest Teresa leaving. Riley's name changed her attitude. "Riley's going to stay with me?"

"Yes. For a little while. Is that okay with you?"

"I like Riley."

"I know you do. He'll take good care of you, and I'll be home early. He knows the number at the diner, so he can call if you need me and I'll come straight home, okay?"

"When will he be here?"

"In just a couple of minutes. I have to go very soon."

"Okay." Maggie snuggled more comfortably beneath her covers, her eyelids already getting heavy. "'Bye, Mommy."

Teresa found herself frowning as she stepped back from the bed. She was glad, of course, that Maggie felt comfortable with the arrangements and wasn't putting up a fuss. But Maggie could have shown a *little* more reluctance to see her go.

Mark was not so happy with the developments. "Maggie gets to stay with Riley? No fair!"

Her purse in her hand, Teresa had let Riley into the

apartment. Riley tousled Mark's hair in response to the boy's outcry. "I'm only staying with your sister for a little while because she's sick. It's not as if we're going to do anything fun without you."

"I could stay home and help you take care of Maggie."

Keeping his expression straight, Riley replied, "Thanks, buddy, but I can handle it. I'd hate for you to miss seeing your friends at school just to sit here and watch me work and Maggie sleep."

Teresa could see that Mark still wasn't convinced, but she didn't have time to argue. It was almost seven forty-five and Mark was supposed to be at school by eight. The luncheon meeting was scheduled from eleven-thirty to one, which meant she could be home by one-thirty at the latest.

"Get in the car, Mark," she said in her don't-push-me voice. "Riley, Maggie needs plenty of fluids. You'll find juice and Sprite in the refrigerator. There are also some flavored ice pops in the freezer if she doesn't feel like eating anything solid. She can have some children's acetaminophen if her fever goes back up, but not until ten-thirty. The number at the diner is—"

"I can find the number," Riley cut in. "You'd better go or Mark will be late for school. Maggie and I will be fine."

"You'll call if she wants me?"

"I'll call. Go."

She hesitated, searching Riley's face, and then she moved toward the door. She was coming home the moment she saw that Marjorie could get along without her, she promised herself. And she would make sure she didn't have to ask Riley for any more favors.

* * *

As far as Riley could tell, taking care of a sick child was a snap. Teresa had left more than half an hour ago, and he hadn't encountered a problem yet. He'd set up his laptop on the coffee table in her living room, his notes scattered around him, the canned soda he'd brought with him at his side. He'd checked on Maggie several times, rousing her once or twice to take a few sips of juice, but she'd gone straight back to sleep each time.

And to think he'd been worried that he couldn't handle this.

When Marjorie had awakened him at a ridiculously early hour with her phone call, he'd thought she'd lost her mind. "You're asking *me* to baby-sit a sick child?"

"Just for a little while," she'd replied airily. "I really need Teresa at the diner today. I hate to take her away from poor little Maggie even for a short time, but I honestly don't know how I'll get through that meeting without her. It's an election meeting, and you know how crowded those can be. They expect their coffee cups and water glasses to stay filled."

"So why couldn't I just come schlep coffee for you?"

"Sorry, dear, I couldn't afford the lawsuits after you dump hot coffee down a few notable backs. All I'm asking you to do is sit with little Maggie for a couple of hours. Just this once."

"Does Teresa know you're calling me?"

"She knows I'm calling *someone*," Marjorie prevaricated.

"But not me. She's not going to like this."

"I'm sure she'll agree that it's a wonderful idea. Maggie knows you and trusts you, and so does Teresa. And you live right next door, so it's convenient for everyone."

As stubborn as he could be, Riley had always had a hard time saying no to Marjorie—just like everyone else who knew her. He'd held firm about not letting her play matchmaker for him, but there had been plenty of occasions when he'd found himself going along with some of her schemes. Like today when, somehow, he found himself baby-sitting Teresa's sick daughter.

It hadn't been bad so far. No one could have been more surprised than he was, but he'd turned out to have a knack for baby-sitting. Not that he intended to make it a regular practice, of course. But it felt good to know he had another talent.

His somewhat smug reverie was interrupted by a call from upstairs. "Riley."

"On my way, Mags," he said, pushing the computer aside. Probably she wanted another drink. Maybe something to eat.

He could handle that. This really was a snap.

The smell hit him the moment he stepped through Maggie's doorway. Maggie sat in the middle of her bed, her face beet-red, her fuzzy pajamas and bedclothes soiled. "I threw up," she said, and then burst into noisy tears.

Riley's stomach gave a lurch, but he forced himself to move forward.

So maybe this wasn't going to be as easy as he'd thought.

Chapter Nine

It was exactly one-fifteen when Teresa walked into her home that afternoon. She'd gotten away from the diner as soon as she could. She'd called home twice during the day to check on Maggie. Both times Riley had assured her that everything was fine.

Something in his voice during the second call had been different. It had been that difference that had made her rush home as soon as she could get away.

Riley was sitting in a big chair in her living room with Maggie curled in his lap, wrapped in an afghan. Looking a bit frantic, he quickly lifted one finger to his lips. ''Don't wake her,'' he said in a stage whisper. ''She just went back to sleep.''

Quietly crossing the room, Teresa stopped beside the chair. She noted that Maggie was pale except for the splotches of red on her damp-looking cheeks. Her hair was damp, too, probably from fever. She had on different pajamas than she'd been wearing when Teresa left.

As sick as Maggie looked, Teresa wasn't sure Riley looked much better. His hair was sticking straight up in places, and there were shadows beneath his eyes. Lines of strain had carved themselves around his mouth, which was, for once, not curved into his usual lazy smile.

"It has been worse than you told me, hasn't it?"

His mouth twisted. "Let's just say we've had a few interesting moments. She can't hold down juice, by the way. Sprite and Popsicles are okay, but you'd better hold off on the juice. Oh, and you're out of air freshener. I used the last of the can I found upstairs."

"Oh, Riley, I'm sorry. She wasn't so nauseous when I left this morning. I didn't realize it would get worse."

"I called my doctor the second time she got sick. I was a bit concerned about her. Dr. Frank said nausea is definitely part of this bug that's going around. He said to keep her hydrated with clear fluids and make her comfortable and she should be better in a few hours. He said if she takes a turn for the worse you should take her to the emergency room, but he doesn't expect that to happen."

Teresa knelt beside the chair to brush a limp lock of hair from Maggie's face. Guilt gnawed at her. "She really didn't seem this sick when I left this morning. I never would have left her if—"

"Don't beat yourself up about it," Riley murmured. "We got by just fine. However, there is kind of a mess upstairs. I tried to clean up some, but Maggie kept me pretty busy until she went back to sleep."

"I'll clean up. Thank you so much for all you've done today, Riley. I owe you."

Before he could answer, Maggie stirred and opened her eyes. "Mommy?"

"I'm here, sweetie."

"I threw up."

"I know. I'm so sorry I wasn't here to take care of you."

"Riley took care of me." Maggie spoke around a big yawn. "He's pretty good, but he gets kind of nervous sometimes."

Under other circumstances, Teresa might have smiled at that. Riley did smile. "You got that straight, kid," he said and dropped a light kiss on the top of the child's head.

"Here, I'll take her now." Teresa reached for her daughter. "I know you have things to do and I don't want to take up any more of your time."

Riley didn't argue with her. He transferred Maggie carefully, then stood with a stiffness that indicated his legs had gone to sleep while he'd sat there. "Let me know if you need anything, okay?"

Sitting in the chair with Maggie in her lap, Teresa smiled. "We'll be fine. You've done enough."

"It's definitely been...interesting," Riley said as he collected his things. He let himself out, closing the door behind him. Teresa thought he'd moved with a bit more speed than his usual unhurried amble.

Poor Riley. She'd never thought those words would enter her mind, but she couldn't help thinking them as she remembered the way he'd looked when she came home. Whipped, she thought. Very close to exhaustion.

She could only imagine how stressful the morning must have been for a bachelor who wasn't used to children. Especially sick children. If Riley had been concerned enough to call a doctor, he must have been genuinely unnerved. So why hadn't he told her what was going on when he'd called?

Male ego, she decided. He hadn't wanted to admit that he couldn't handle the favor he'd been doing for Marjorie and her.

Every time he started flirting with her again, as he had in his kitchen yesterday afternoon, something like this happened. She couldn't imagine him wanting to get more involved with her knowing all the baggage she would carry with her into any sort of relationship. Especially after today.

Mark came down with the virus during the night, waking Teresa with a miserable call. Fortunately, Shameka was back on the job, and there were no more events scheduled in the diner, so Marjorie assured Teresa they could get along without her for a few days. "Take care of your children," she added warmly.

Tuesday was a busy day with both children demanding her time and attention, but Teresa was glad she was able to stay home to take care of them. They needed their mother—and she needed to nurture them while they were ill.

Riley called to check on the kids that afternoon, and she assured him she was managing well enough. She stayed inside all day, so she didn't see him.

Maggie felt considerably better Wednesday, though Mark was still achy and droopy. Teresa stayed home again with Marjorie's blessing. She didn't hear from Riley, though she knew he was home because his car hadn't left the driveway all day—something she just happened to notice, of course.

The children were able to hold down light food, so she made a big pot of chicken soup that afternoon. She vaguely remembered her mother serving her homemade chicken soup when she was ill. The old memory brought a familiar wistful pang to her heart.

On an impulse, she filled a bowl with soup and covered it with a plastic lid. She carried it carefully into the living room where her children were lying on blankets and pillows on the floor, watching a video. "I'm going to take some soup next door to Riley for his dinner," she told them. "You stay put until I get back, okay?"

"'Kay, Mom," Mark answered without taking his gaze from the television screen.

"Okay, Mommy," Maggie said, as engrossed in the animated feature as her brother was.

Confident that they would be fine for a few minutes, Teresa stepped outside her front door. It was finally starting to feel like autumn, she thought. There was a light nip in the breeze against her cheeks, just enough to be felt through the thin fabric of the long-sleeve T-shirt she wore with a lightweight long denim jumper. The sun was setting, reminding her of how short the days were getting.

Time passing. The phrase echoed in her mind, as it had so often lately. And as she did each time, she pushed it aside.

It took Riley so long to answer her knock that she was beginning to think he wasn't home, after all. Maybe someone had picked him up?

But then the door opened and Teresa grimaced at the sight of him. "Oh, no. You're sick."

"However did you guess?" His face almost as pale as the white T-shirt he wore with baggy gray sweatpants, he propped himself against the doorjamb with one hand. He wore an expression she recognized well after the past two days.

"Have you seen a doctor?"

"No need. I know what to do." He swayed a bit as he spoke.

"You need to lie down, or at least sit down before you fall." She nudged him backward, and it was an indication of how badly he felt that he walked so compliantly to the couch. He dropped to the cushions, half-sitting, half-reclining against them.

"I brought you some soup," she said, nodding toward the container in her hand. When he suddenly looked a bit green, she added quickly, "I'll put it in the refrigerator. You can heat it when you feel like eating."

"That could be a while." He pressed one hand to his flat stomach as he spoke.

"I'll be right back."

His usually neat kitchen was cluttered with used glasses, crumpled paper towels and empty soda cans. A large plastic bottle of acetaminophen sat open on the counter, the lid lying beside it. She set the soup in the fridge, then took a moment to straighten the kitchen before carrying a glass of water into the living room with her.

Riley had slid a bit lower on the couch, his eyes half closed. She sat beside him, holding the glass toward him. "Here, drink some of this. You have to stay hydrated."

"I'm not thirsty right now."

"Drink a little, anyway. You have to take plenty of liquids until you're able to eat something."

He sighed, but took a couple sips of the water before setting the glass on a coaster on the table in front of them. "Who's with the kids?"

"They're watching a video. I have to get back to them. What can I do for you before I go?"

"Nothing. I'm fine, really."

Before she'd even known she was going to do so, she reached out to touch his face, feeling the excessive warmth of his skin. "You don't look so fine."

He caught her hand, held it to his cheek for a moment, then gave it a little squeeze before releasing her. The gesture was sweet, somewhat weary but completely natural, as if they'd touched each other often. It was enough to make Teresa's throat tighten.

This guy was dangerous even when he was ill, she couldn't help thinking as she rose quickly to her feet. "Do you want me to call someone for you? Your uncle, maybe?"

"No. This bug's too contagious. I wouldn't want Bud to get it."

"Then you'll call me if you need anything? Promise you will."

"I'll call if I need anything. Um, how come you aren't sick?"

She smiled faintly. "Don't you know that moms never get sick? We don't have time."

"That must explain it, then." He let his eyelids drift downward. "Go home to your kids, Teresa. They need you."

Maybe it was that compulsively maternal side of her, but she didn't like leaving Riley alone and ill. As she quietly let herself out, she found herself wondering if Riley O'Neal ever really needed anyone—and if he would ever admit it if he did.

With the amazing resiliency of childhood, Mark and Maggie rebounded quickly from their illness. By Thursday Maggie was back in school, and Mark returned Friday, letting Teresa get back to work. She knew Riley was feeling better, too, because she had checked on him several times during the past couple of days to make sure.

She was greatly relieved that she had managed to avoid becoming ill. Despite her bravado to Riley and her almost obsessive hand-washing while she was taking care of her sick children, she had been afraid the virus would get to her. Apparently her luck had held this time.

Business was brisk at the diner Friday. She was warmly welcomed back by the customers who had come to expect to see her there.

Though serving was a physically demanding job and often stressful during the main rush times, she enjoyed her work. She liked visiting with the customers, getting to know the regulars, hearing the local gossip flowing so freely from table to table. The flexibility Marjorie offered her was another definite perk. She was never going to get rich waiting tables, of course, but she was getting by well enough for now.

She offered to work Saturday to make up for the days she'd missed, but Marjorie told her that wasn't necessary. Because she'd spent several days at home that week, the housework she usually tackled on Saturday mornings was already done. So Teresa woke with two healthy, energetic children and a rare day of leisure ahead of her.

They lingered over a breakfast of blueberry pancakes and crisp bacon. "What are we going to do today, Mom?" Mark asked when their plates had been cleaned.

"This would be a good day to do some shopping," she replied, setting down her empty coffee cup. "Both of you need a few things."

"I need some new jeans," Mark agreed. "Mine are getting too short."

"Yes, I've noticed." Her son was growing up so fast.

"Can I get a red sweater, Mommy?" Maggie begged. "Vanessa has a red sweater with a zipper down the front. I want one like that."

"We'll see if we can find one you like." And that she could afford, Teresa added silently.

Fortunately, her children had never gotten into name brand competition. They didn't care whose advertising logos were splashed across their bodies, and Teresa intended to keep it that way. She never wanted them to feel that they had to measure their worth through material possessions.

"Can we have hamburgers for lunch?" Maggie asked, pushing her luck. "They're putting Barbie toys in the kids' boxes this week."

"I suppose we can arrange that," Teresa agreed with a smile. At least the kids were still young enough to be satisfied with inexpensive cuisine. "Go upstairs and get ready, and we'll leave as soon as you're dressed."

They raced eagerly upstairs. As Teresa straightened the kitchen, she reflected on how little it took to make her children happy. She really was very fortunate. She resisted an impulse to cross her fingers as she hoped their teen years proceeded as smoothly.

The telephone rang as she finished cleaning the kitchen. She tossed a damp paper towel into the trash and picked up the kitchen receiver. "Hello?"

"Hi. It's Riley. How's everyone feeling today?"

Just the sound of his voice made her fingers clench more tightly around the receiver. She made a deliberate effort to loosen them and speak lightly. "Everything's back to normal here. And you?"

She heard a smile in his voice when he answered, "There are some who would say I'm never normal. But I'm as close as I get."

"That's good. I guess."

"Yeah. Uh, the reason I called is…well, there's this thing tonight. A Chamber of Commerce dinner to honor Edstown's citizen of the year. The food will be bland, the program boring, and everyone will act stiff and uncomfortable. So—you want to go?"

She frowned, trying to decipher what he'd just said. "Are you selling tickets?"

His laugh was rueful. "No, I'm not selling tickets. I have tickets. Two of them. I thought maybe you'd like to use the second one."

Though he was speaking very casually, this was beginning to sound suspiciously as if he were asking her for a date. Surely she was mistaken. "Um…"

"It was Bud's idea, actually," Riley added offhandedly. "I mentioned to him that I was supposed to go to this thing and he said you might like to go, too, after being stuck in the house all week with two sick kids and all. He even offered to come to your place with a pizza and a couple of family-friendly videos and baby-sit for the evening."

Teresa didn't know what to say. "Riley, I—"

"It's not really a date, if that's what you're worried about," he interjected. "Just a couple of friends attending a community event together. And it's sort of a favor to Bud, too. He would really enjoy spending a couple hours with your kids rather than alone in his trailer."

Oh, now that was just shameless. "Well, I…"

"I know it's short notice. To be honest, I've felt so lousy this week I wasn't sure I'd be up to going. I'm sort of expected to be there, but if you already have other plans or just don't want to go, I'd certainly understand."

Maybe it was guilt because Riley had gotten sick taking care of her daughter. Or maybe it was sympathy for

Bud, who was so anxious to avoid another lonely evening that he looked forward to baby-sitting two kids. Or maybe it was just the fact that it had been so long since she'd had a real grown-up evening out without her children. Whatever the reason, she blurted, "Okay. I'll go."

"Okay. Great. It starts at seven. So—maybe we should leave around six-thirty?"

"I'll be ready."

"I'll call Bud."

"Okay. So I'll...see you later." She hung up the phone, then immediately hit herself in the head with the palm of one hand. What was she doing? After all the lectures she'd given herself about not getting involved with Riley, all the mental warnings about ruining a pleasant friendship—not to mention a satisfactory tenant-landlord relationship—she was going to attend a fancy dinner with him.

For all his assurances that it wasn't a real date, she knew people would talk about seeing them there together. That was exactly the kind of speculation she had wanted to avoid.

She was tempted to call him back and tell him she'd had a change of heart. But that would be terribly rude, and he'd probably already called Bud by now. When she picked up the phone again, it was Serena's number she dialed.

"It's Teresa," she said when she heard her friend's voice. "Are you going to the Chamber of Commerce thing tonight?"

"Yes. I go every year."

"Good. Then you can tell me what the heck I should wear."

"You're going?"

"It looks like it." She drew a deep breath. "I'm going

with Riley. It's not a date. He just thought I'd enjoy the event.''

"I see.''

Teresa eyed the receiver suspiciously. Was there a grin reflected in Serena's voice? "I'm going as sort of a favor to Riley so he won't have to go alone," she added. "After all, I owe him for taking care of Maggie for me. And then he came down with her virus and he didn't really have a chance to make arrangements with anyone else.''

"That's very nice of you.''

Teresa definitely heard the smile this time. Deciding that more explanation would be overkill, she asked, "What do I wear?''

"You'll see everything there from sequins to Sunday dresses. A lot of women who go to this thing see it as a rare opportunity to get all dressed up. I'm wearing a black velvet pantsuit. Cameron will wear a dark suit and a tie. Riley—well, it's anyone's guess what he'll wear. He claims that socks are formal wear for him.''

Teresa couldn't help smiling. She'd noticed that Riley didn't usually bother with socks, and she had rarely seen him dressed in anything more formal than jeans and pullovers. "Okay, that helps. I'll find something to wear.''

"Who's going to watch the kids?''

"Bud volunteered. I haven't told them yet, but they'll be delighted. They've grown very fond of Bud.''

"I hear it's mutual. Riley told me Bud's crazy about your kids.''

"I'm sure he'll take very good care of them.''

"Of course he will," Serena agreed reassuringly. "Bud's wonderful with children. He was like a second father to Riley. He'll be a great baby-sitter.''

Teresa supposed it demonstrated how much faith she

had in Marjorie and Serena that she was willing to so readily accept their recommendations for baby-sitters. In Memphis, she'd been extremely particular about who she entrusted with her children's care. She'd practically required fingerprints and blood tests. But here, she had left her children with young Jenny and then Riley and now Bud. She hadn't been guided wrong so far—she hoped.

Telling Serena she would see her that evening, she hung up. She turned to find her children standing side by side in the kitchen doorway. "We're ready to go, Mom," Mark announced.

"Good," she murmured, moving toward them. "It looks as if I'm going to have to do a little shopping for myself while we're at it."

Asking Teresa to the Chamber of Commerce dinner had been an impulse—and not, as Riley had told her, an idea conceived entirely by Bud. Riley had met his uncle at a favorite restaurant Friday night, and the subject of the Chamber dinner had come up in their conversation. Riley had mentioned he had a couple of tickets, and Bud had asked who he was taking. Riley had been considering inviting Teresa even before Bud suggested that he do so.

"I doubt that she'll accept," he'd said.

Bud shook his head. "Any why wouldn't she? She'd probably enjoy having a nice evening out without the kids. Heck, I'll even baby-sit. It'll be fine."

Riley had been half convinced that she would turn him down, using the short notice of the invitation as an excuse. He was a bit surprised that she had accepted.

It wasn't a date, he reminded himself as he opened his closet door late that afternoon. He'd been in possession of an extra ticket and he'd thought Teresa might enjoy accompanying him. She didn't seem to get out much without the children, and she would probably enjoy mingling with some of the local adults.

He'd really thought she would turn him down.

As he draped the clothes he'd selected on his bed, he mentally replayed the telephone conversation with her. Had he made it clear that he'd only asked her to accompany him as a friend? Had he made *anything* clear? For some strange reason, he'd found himself stammering and stumbling through that invitation like an adolescent asking for his first date. But he specifically remembered saying that this wasn't a date.

Neither of them wanted that kind of involvement.

Not that he wasn't attracted to Teresa. Just the opposite, in fact. Had things been different, he'd be doing his best to charm her, as he'd been trying to do before he'd seen her at that football game with her kids.

Things had changed that night. He'd stuck to his long-time rule of not getting involved with single mothers—or at least he'd tried. He couldn't have predicted that Teresa would move into his house. Or that his uncle would practically adopt her kids. Or that he would end up doing baby-sitting duty himself. And *that* had been such a stressful experience that he still hadn't completely recovered. Still, here he was, getting ready to spend another evening in Teresa's company.

It wasn't a date, he repeated as he shoved his arms into his shirt sleeves. Maybe Teresa was very clear about that—but he seemed to have to keep reminding himself for some reason.

Chapter Ten

Bud answered when Riley knocked on Teresa's door at the appointed time. He gave Riley a once-over, then waggled both bushy eyebrows. "Don't you look spiffy?"

"Don't start with me, Bud." Riley stepped into the living room, where he was greeted enthusiastically by Teresa's children.

Maggie wrapped both her arms around one of Riley's, hanging there like a little blond monkey. "Hi, Riley. You look very nice."

"Thanks, Mags. So do you. I like that red sweater you're wearing."

She preened. "It's new."

"Very becoming."

Mark wouldn't be left out for long. "Hey, Riley. Uncle Bud brought pizza and videos."

"Let me guess. Pepperoni and Jerry Lewis."

Bud nodded. "Kids today don't know real funny stuff when they see it. Only choices they get are those smutty sitcoms and syrupy cartoons. I brought real family movies. Funny ones, without any bad language or half-nekkid people in them."

"Bet I even know which ones you brought. *The Family Jewels* and *The Geisha Boy*." They were the two films that Riley could remember watching with his uncle every time they were replayed on television, before the era of videocassettes.

"Good guess. I thought I'd save the Lewis and Martin films for future showings."

Even as he fondly remembered those pleasant boyhood hours, Riley couldn't help thinking about how confident Bud seemed that there would be future evenings with Mark and Maggie. And he couldn't help worrying a little about the complications of getting this tangled up with the Scott family.

Teresa entered the room then, and Riley had to make a conscious effort to keep his jaw from dropping. Until now, he'd seen her dressed only in her work clothes and what he'd come to think of as her PTA mom clothes—khakis, sweaters, jumpers and long, loose skirts.

She didn't look like a PTA mom tonight. She looked more like the princess he'd often mentally compared her to.

Cut from a rich midnight blue fabric, a close-fitting long-sleeve jacket hugged her curves from the deep scoop neckline to the hip-length hem. A mid-calf-length skirt of the same deep color moved softly around her legs when she walked. Those legs looked even longer and shapelier than usual in sheer stockings and strappy black heels. She had twisted her blond hair into a smooth

updo, and wore a bit more makeup than usual for a so-
phisticated evening look.

"Wow," he said.

Maggie giggled. "He thinks you look pretty,
Mommy."

"So do you," Teresa murmured to Riley, eyeing him
with the same surprised interest Bud had shown when
he'd opened the door. "I had no idea you even owned
a tie."

"I own several, actually. I just don't wear them very
often."

"As in almost never," Bud informed her.

Riley tugged at the collar of the pale gray shirt he
wore with a deep maroon tie and dark charcoal suit. He
wasn't fundamentally opposed to dressing up occasionally—he just didn't like being told when to do so. "Now
that we've admired each other, shall we go?"

"Yes, I'm ready. Mark and Maggie, I want you to be
good for Bud, do you hear? No quarreling, no breaking
the rules. Okay?"

"Yes, Mommy."

"Okay, Mom."

"We're going to be just fine here," Bud assured her.
"Now you kids go on and have a good time—although
I can't imagine how you're going to manage that at one
of those boring Chamber things."

"You're right." Riley glanced wistfully at the pizzas
and videos. "Maybe we should skip the dinner and hang
out here."

"And waste those pretty clothes? Absolutely not."
Bud practically pushed them toward the door. "Go. Enjoy."

"I think he wanted us to leave," Teresa commented

dryly when they were outside, her door closed behind them.

Riley chuckled. "He wanted those pizzas and movies—and your kids—to himself."

"He's certainly enthusiastic about baby-sitting."

Riley's smile faded. "Sitting with your kids gave him something to look forward to this evening. That's something he hasn't had much since R.L. left town."

"I hope Mark and Maggie don't give him any trouble."

Riley smiled again as he opened the passenger door of his car for her. "Have him tell you someday about the time he was baby-sitting me while my parents went out for an evening and I got a marble stuck up my nose. He had to rush me to Dr. Frank to have it extracted."

Teresa slid gracefully into the low seat of his two-passenger sports car. "Dr. Frank has been practicing for a while, I take it?"

"He delivered me." Riley closed the passenger door and walked around the front of the car to the driver's side.

Belted into his seat a few moments later, he started the engine. A blast of heavy metal music filled the small confines of the vehicle, making Teresa wince, and Riley reach hastily for the power button. "Sorry," he said. "I'm usually alone in the car."

"Don't you worry about your hearing?"

"Enough that I make myself cut it down most of the time. Just every once in a while I have to blast it, you know?"

"I see."

Turning the steering wheel in the direction of the country club where the evening's event was being held,

Riley asked lightly, "Don't you ever have an urge to let it blast, Teresa?"

"I don't have a lot of opportunity for blasting."

"Too busy taking care of your kids, I guess."

"That's certainly a big part of my life."

Riley shook his head. "I had a houseplant once, but it died from neglect. Someone offered me a puppy not long after that—but I was afraid to take it."

Teresa laughed, as he'd hoped she would, but it was a very brief laugh. He doubted that she could identify with the way he chose to live his life, responsible for no one but himself. It wasn't as if she'd had any illusions about him, anyway. She'd known even before he had what a mismatch they were.

There was a brief silence, which Teresa broke by asking, "Who *is* Edstown's citizen of the year, anyway?"

"Didn't I tell you? It's Dr. Frank."

"The doctor who delivered you and has been taking care of you ever since? No wonder you want to be there tonight."

"Yeah. He's a great guy. Have you had a chance to meet him yet?"

"Not in his professional capacity. He's been to the diner a couple of times for breakfast and lunch. I started calling him Dr. Purtle, but he said everyone around here calls him Dr. Frank."

"That's because his older brother used to practice here, too. Two Dr. Purtles got confusing, so they became known as Dr. Fred and Dr. Frank."

"Dr. Fred retired?"

"He died a few years ago. He was ten or twelve years older than Dr. Frank. I think they had a couple of sisters between them."

The country club was in sight, and they joined a long

line of cars waiting to enter the parking lot. "It looks like a big crowd turned out," Teresa commented, sounding a bit nervous.

"Yeah. You've probably met most of them at the diner at some point. Almost everyone in Edstown eats breakfast or lunch at the Rainbow Café occasionally."

"Yes, but it's a little different serving them and dining with them."

"We'll have fun," Riley assured her. Then he felt compelled to add, "Well, as much as possible at one of these things, anyway."

"You don't think anyone will find it odd—that we're here together, I mean?"

"Teresa, people around here find nearly everything I do odd. Haven't you figured that out yet?"

She wrinkled her nose at him. "You know what I mean."

He parked the car, turned off the engine, then twisted in his seat to face her. " I think everyone will simply assume I brought my friend and neighbor, a relative newcomer to our town, to meet and mingle with some of the prominent members of our community."

He watched as she drew a deep breath, possibly for courage. He'd be willing to bet that she had no idea what the inhale did for the seemingly modest scoop neckline of her top.

Dragging his gaze away before she noticed that he was staring at the creamy, smooth skin of her upper breasts, he reached hastily for his door handle. Friends didn't sit around staring at their friends' busts, he reminded himself. This friend would probably tear off a nice-size strip of his hide if she caught him doing so.

He noticed signs of nervousness in her again as they approached the entrance. Looping her arm through his, he spoke bracingly. "Ready to turn this place upside down?"

"Do *not* do anything to embarrass me," she said through clenched teeth as she pasted on a smile for the people who were already starting to head their way.

"I could never resist a challenge."

"Riley..."

Laughing, he pulled her into the crowd, thinking maybe the evening wouldn't be quite so dull, after all.

Although she hadn't expected to, Teresa enjoyed the dinner. The other guests, a surprising number of whom she recognized from the diner and other places around town, were quite pleasant to her. The food wasn't bad—not nearly as bland as Riley had predicted. The entertainment wasn't completely boring. She enjoyed hearing speakers telling funny anecdotes about their beloved Dr. Frank. The high school audition choir sang during dinner, and they were very good.

All in all, it was the most grown-up evening she'd spent in a very long time.

Riley, of course, was thoroughly amusing. He kept everyone at their table, including Teresa, laughing at his droll observations concerning the festivities. Though his wit could often be described as biting, he was never cruel, merely blunt. She imagined he made more than his share of people angry, but it wouldn't surprise her to learn that those same people usually ended up forgiving him and then laughing with him at his next barb.

She detected no real surprise that she and Riley had attended the event together. Maybe he was right; maybe everyone assumed that they were attending as casual friends. Knowing Riley as well as they all did, they had to be aware that she wasn't the type of woman with whom he would get intimately involved. She came with way too many responsibilities, something Riley had made a lifelong hobby of evading.

He hadn't even wanted to take care of a puppy.

Funny how often she had to remind herself of things like that. Something about Riley's attractive face and seductive smile seemed to periodically erase her more rational thoughts.

The only person at the dinner who seemed to eye them with any speculation was Marjorie Schaffer. Marjorie, who had been less than subtly trying to fix Teresa up with nearly every single man in town, despite Teresa's repeated assertions that she wasn't interested. Surely Marjorie wouldn't turn her attention to trying to set her up with Riley. Even a confirmed, compulsive matchmaker like Marjorie wouldn't be foolish enough to try *that* match.

She and Riley were standing in the elegantly decorated lobby of the country club after the dinner, chatting with Marjorie, Serena and Cameron, when they were approached by an older couple Teresa had seen only one time before, when they'd lunched at the diner. The woman's steel-gray hair was lacquered into a helmet of curls, and several splashy pieces of jewelry adorned her heavy bosom, thick wrists and stubby but perfectly manicured, fingers. The man was potbellied, balding and nondescript in comparison to his wife. Teresa recognized them immediately.

Even had she not noticed the very faint chill in Marjorie's eyes, Teresa knew Marjorie didn't care for Beatrice Herter because she had told her so. Beatrice was one of the most difficult and demanding customers Teresa had encountered at the diner, but she'd managed to hold on to her poise until the couple left—leaving behind a meager tip.

Marjorie had complimented Teresa on her patience. "You wouldn't have been the first of my employees to tell her off," she'd added.

Marjorie had gone on to explain that Beatrice was a snobby, arrogant and occasionally even cruel woman who was tolerated around town only because her husband had a lot of money and didn't mind spending it on community projects. "Every town has people like Beatrice," Marjorie had added with a sigh. "And I try very hard to like her. But I just can't."

Beatrice greeted Cameron and Serena as if she were doing them a favor to notice them. Teresa imagined that the woman considered Cameron worth her attention because he came from a wealthy Dallas family and had quite a bit of money of his own. Serena, of course, was an attorney and the daughter of longtime members of Edstown society, so Beatrice treated her comparatively cordially, as well. She turned her attention to Riley only after she had taken her time with the Norths.

"Well, Riley. You've been stirring up trouble with that column of yours again," she said frostily. "I didn't much appreciate your tasteless jokes about my Eastern Star lodge."

"Sorry, Beatrice," he returned irreverently. "But how can I help it when y'all give me so much great material?"

"You said we reminded you of a fleet of sequined battleships surging through the dining room of the Ramada Inn," she quoted indignantly. And then she turned to Cameron. "And you let him print it. Don't you have any control over this man?"

Cameron wasn't doing a very good job of camouflaging a grin. "No one has much control over Riley."

Marjorie interceded quickly. "Beatrice, Charles—you've both met our friend Teresa Scott, haven't you?"

Beatrice studied Teresa through her oversize, glittery plastic-framed glasses. "I don't believe we have."

"Of course you have. She works for me at the diner."

Beatrice's chin rose a bit higher. "The new waitress? Of course. How generous of you to bring her with you tonight, Marjorie."

Though she didn't appreciate being made to sound like a charity case, Teresa wasn't particularly offended. It was the sort of comment she would have expected from this woman.

"Actually, Teresa's here with me," Riley said, moving a step closer to her. "And I was honored that she accepted my invitation."

"I see." Beatrice gave Teresa the same sort of smile she might have directed toward a small child. "Did you have a nice time?"

"Yes, very nice, thank you."

"It must have been very exciting for you to dine with the distinguished members of Edstown society this evening. Instead of serving them as you usually do, I mean."

Marjorie gave a little gasp in response to Beatrice's deliberately condescending tone.

Teresa felt Riley stiffen at her side, and she just *knew* he was going to say something outrageous. She put her hand quickly on his arm, letting her fingernails sink lightly into the fabric of his jacket.

"It was nice to see so many of the new friends I've made through the diner," she said before Riley could speak.

Beatrice's attention had already wandered off. "Oh, Charles, there's the mayor. I want to catch him before he leaves. I want to ask him just when that pothole in front of our house will be repaired."

Without even bidding good evening, she started to move away.

"Instead of sequined battleships, I believe my next column will be about sequined battle-*axes*," Riley said, clearly enough for Beatrice to hear him. Teresa saw her stiffen for a moment, but her husband urged her toward the mayor.

"That old witch." Marjorie turned to Teresa with uncharacteristic anger burning in her blue eyes. "Don't let her bother you, dear. She just seems compelled to treat everyone as a social inferior. As if I didn't know that she grew up poor as a church mouse and was Charles Herter's mistress for two years before she finally convinced him to divorce his first wife and marry her thirty years ago."

Serena rested a calming hand on her mother's shoulder. "Careful, Mother, before you say something you'll regret later."

"I can't *believe* she was so deliberately rude to Teresa!"

"I'm the one she's mad at, for what I wrote about her lodge," Riley muttered, looking as angry as Marjorie. "So she took a swipe at Teresa because she was with me. Wait until Beatrice reads what I write about her next."

"Riley, it's okay," Teresa said firmly, embarrassed by the attention. "Don't get so upset about it. After all, she merely pointed out that I'm usually waiting tables rather than being waited on, and that's true."

"It was the way she said it," Riley growled. "As if working in the diner makes you inferior to her."

"Well, since I enjoy my job and do it because I choose to, I won't let her attitude bother me. You shouldn't, either."

The glare he sent in Beatrice's direction made it clear that he wasn't appeased.

Because she wasn't going to allow one less-than-gracious woman to ruin her nice evening, Teresa put Beatrice out of her mind and changed the subject. "We'd better go. Heaven knows what condition we'll find your poor uncle in after an entire evening with my kids."

With one last glower across the room, Riley turned to Teresa. "Maybe you should be wondering what condition your kids will be in after an evening with my uncle and Jerry Lewis."

Cameron shook his head in feigned dismay. "A couple of hours of that, and they'll be saying, 'hey, lay-deeee' instead of 'hey, Mom.'"

Teresa covered her cheeks with her hands. "Oh, my goodness. We'd better hurry home."

"Could be worse," Riley said with a grin. "They could have spent an evening watching Bud's Three Stooges collection. Then they'd be poking each other's eyes and saying, 'whoop, whoop, whoop.'"

"You're right." Teresa pretended to shudder. "It *could* be worse."

She was relieved that Riley's flash of temper had cooled. She never would have suspected he even had a hot temper; lazy, rather detached amusement seemed to be his usual reaction to other people. That he'd lost his composure on her behalf was equally surprising. She would have assumed he knew she was perfectly capable of taking up for herself, if necessary.

"I had a very nice time tonight," she told him when they had taken their leave of the others and were belting themselves into his car. "Thank you for bringing me."

"I hope Beatrice didn't spoil the evening for you."

She sighed. "Will you forget about Beatrice? I have."

"Sorry. I can't tolerate a snob."

Teresa shrugged. "Some people just feel compelled to put other people down in a pathetic attempt to build themselves up. Work in my line long enough, and you learn to deal with them."

Keeping his eyes on the road ahead, Riley asked, "You really like what you do?"

"I wouldn't do it if I didn't enjoy it. I could work in an office or a sales job, if I wanted, but I wouldn't have the freedom that Marjorie gives me at the diner. I wouldn't be home in time to greet the kids when they get home from school. I start earlier at this job than I would at some, but that works out with the before-school program the kids are enrolled in. All in all, it's a very satisfactory arrangement."

After a brief pause, Riley spoke again. "You said you and Serena were roommates in college. I know she majored in political science and went on to law school. What was your major?"

"Elementary education. But I dropped out at the end of my junior year to get married. I planned to finish my education later, after my husband was established in a career, but Mark was born ten months after the wedding. Then Maggie came along two years after that and...well, you know how that goes."

"Do you ever regret not becoming a schoolteacher?"

"I would have enjoyed teaching, I think," she answered carefully. "But I've enjoyed my children more."

Whatever regrets she might have, whatever unfulfilled dreams, whatever disappointments her troubled marriage had caused her, the joy her children had brought her more than made up for all of it.

"What did your husband do?"

As she had once before, she felt awkward talking about Darren to Riley. "He had several jobs after we were married. His last job was working for an insurance company as an adjuster."

"How long were you married?"

"Six and a half years. Mark turned six just a few months after Darren died in an accident." Because she didn't want to go into the details of the accident, she abruptly changed the subject, spending the rest of the short ride home talking about the dinner they had attended and asking questions about some of the people who'd been there. Riley went along, making her laugh several times with anecdotes about some of the guests, most of whom he had known all his life.

"Will you write a column about tonight's festivities?" she asked as they neared the duplex. "With all the local notables there, I'm sure you were taking mental notes."

Braking in preparation to turn into his driveway, he shot her a quick sideways glance. "Actually, I was paying too much attention to my lovely companion to notice what everyone else was doing."

Teresa rolled her eyes in response to his outrageous comment. "Puh-leeze."

Riley chuckled. "You're a hard woman to impress, aren't you? That was one of my best lines."

"That was your best?" She clucked her tongue and shook her head. "I'm disappointed in you."

He lifted an eyebrow. "That sounds a lot like a challenge."

"I was just joking," she said quickly, holding up both hands in a conciliatory gesture. If there was one thing she didn't need to do, it was to challenge Riley to try to captivate her!

After parking his car, he turned off the engine. "I'll walk you to your door, of course. I'm curious to see how things went while we were gone."

"Yes, so am I."

She reached for her door handle, but Riley stopped her by placing a hand on her shoulder. "You're sure you're okay about what happened tonight? With Beatrice, I mean."

"I'm really okay," she answered firmly. "I haven't given it another thought."

"You won't let her attitude keep you from attending more local events like this in the future?"

"Riley—have I ever given you the impression that I'm either shy or lacking in self-esteem?"

He considered that for a moment before replying. "No, actually. I'd say you seem quite comfortable with who you are."

"Exactly. I'll attend any future event that interests me—and I'll tell anyone who asks that I'm a waitress at the popular Rainbow Café. If Beatrice would rather be served by me than dine with me—tough. That's her problem, not mine."

The smile he gave her expressed his approval. "Good for you."

She expected him to release her and move away. Instead, he remained where he was, his hand lying warmly on her shoulder, his face only inches from hers. The inside of the little sports car seemed suddenly smaller, the shadows surrounding them deeper. Funny how quiet it had suddenly become. She could almost hear her own heartbeat—and it wasn't a reassuringly steady sound.

She cleared her throat. "I suppose we should go inside."

"Yeah. We should." But he didn't move.

Swallowing hard, she tried again. "You were going to walk me to my door?"

"Yeah. In a minute."

"There's something else you want to say first?"

"In a way. I'm trying to talk myself out of it."

"Why? What is it you want to say?"

He took her completely by surprise when he slipped a hand around the back of her neck. "This," he murmured—and covered her mouth with his.

The kiss didn't last long—which didn't mean it wasn't powerful. Whether because it was so unexpected or simply because it was from Riley, that firm press of lips left Teresa's head spinning and her heart pounding.

She drew back with a faint gasp. "Why did you do that?"

"Call it an impulse. Or maybe a response to your challenge."

"I didn't challenge you," she retorted gruffly. "And we agreed we would keep our friendship strictly platonic."

"I know. But you really could tempt a saint, Teresa. And I think we both know I'm no saint."

He found her tempting? She had enough feminine ego to be secretly pleased by that admission, even though she immediately chided herself for her weakness.

"Just...don't do it again," she said, and maybe she was talking to herself as much as to Riley.

"I'm not sure I can promise that." He was wearing his mischievous grin again, the one that dared her to try to put him in his place. "But I will promise that I won't kiss you again unless you want me to."

That brought her chin up. "Don't hold your breath."

He ran a fingertip across her still-tingling lower lip. "I don't have to. You want me to kiss you again right now. But I'll wait."

The arrogance of this man flabbergasted her. Even if he considered himself teasing her—and with Riley it was hard to tell—that statement was outrageous. "I'm going in," she said, reaching for her door handle.

"Probably a good idea." He opened his door. "Who knows what would happen between us if we stay out here much longer. Considering your problem with will-power when it comes to me, of course."

Okay, so he was trying to provoke her for some reason. Needling people was one of Riley's special talents and favorite hobbies—something she should have remembered sooner. To show him she wasn't one of his easy targets, she answered coolly, "I'm not certain exactly what would happen, but I can assure you that only one of us would emerge uninjured. And it would be me."

He laughed and climbed out of the car. Without waiting for him to walk around, Teresa got out and closed the passenger door with a snap.

Maybe he'd been on his party manners for as long as he could stand it that evening. Maybe he was trying to downplay any serious intent behind that impulsive kiss. Or maybe he was just being Riley, and she would be wasting her time trying to analyze his behavior. Since she didn't expect many more evenings like this between them, she supposed there was no need to try to understand or predict him.

He met her at the front of his car and placed a hand at the small of her back as they moved toward the walkway that led to her door. Annoyed by the shivery sensations that radiated from that point of contact throughout the rest of her body, she moved a bit abruptly ahead of him, dislodging his hand.

She'd played with fire enough for one evening, she decided. Perhaps Riley had only been teasing her in his eccentric way, but it was time to put an end to it. Their date was over.

"The movie's almost over, Mom," Mark said the moment she walked in the door. "Let me finish watching it, okay?"

She took in the scene at a glance. Maggie had fallen asleep on the couch. Mark had piled a couple of throw pillows on the floor and used them to prop his head as he watched the video. Bud sprawled in a recliner, a cup of coffee on the end table beside him. The room was as tidy as she'd left it.

She looked toward the television screen, where Jerry Lewis was sadly boarding an airplane to leave Japan. Because she'd seen the movie, she knew it was, indeed, nearing the end. "Of course you can finish the movie. Riley, would you like some coffee?"

"Sounds good, if Bud's left us any."

"Just made a fresh pot," Bud replied. "I figured you two might want some coffee when you got in. And it's decaf, so it won't keep you awake later."

Teresa had encouraged Bud to make himself at home in her kitchen, and she kept both regular and decaffeinated coffee in her pantry. It had been thoughtful of him to have a pot waiting for them.

She brought a mug of coffee to Riley, who'd settled into the chair beside his uncle, and then she turned toward the couch. "I'll put Maggie to bed while you guys watch the end of the film."

The three males merely grunted in response, their eyes glued to the screen. Guys must be born knowing how to make that particular noise, Teresa mused as she bent to rouse her daughter. She didn't know how else Mark had learned to reproduce it so perfectly.

Yawning hugely, Maggie didn't protest going to bed. She never did when she was sleepy, though Mark was likely to resist bedtime until he nodded off on his feet.

Maggie stopped to give Bud a hug and a sweet kiss on his lined cheek—which, Teresa noted, made him blush like an embarrassed but delighted schoolboy. And then the child stopped beside Riley's chair, leaning toward him. "Good night, Riley."

He hesitated only a moment before giving her a quick peck on the forehead. "Good night, Mags. Sweet dreams."

The drowsy smile she gave him was angelic. And then she turned to take her mother's hand, saying over her shoulder, "G'night, Mark."

Teresa almost felt Riley watching her as she led her daughter out of the room and up the stairs to bed.

Chapter Eleven

Riley *was* watching Teresa and Maggie as they left the room. They made a pretty picture, mother and daughter. Both blond and willowy, both graceful in their movements. Had Teresa's late husband realized how lucky he'd been to have this nice family? Why had Serena disliked him so much? Surely he hadn't been unkind to his wife and children. Riley couldn't imagine Teresa staying with a man who mistreated her, and definitely not her kids.

He'd tried to get a sense of how Teresa felt about her husband when they'd talked of him earlier. The only conclusion he'd drawn was that Teresa didn't like to talk about him. Whether it was just with Riley or whether she never talked of her late husband, he didn't know. Maybe it was still too painful for her. Maybe the grief was still too raw. The memories too vivid.

She was a young, attractive woman. He wondered if

she would ever let another man into her life. And then he thought of the men Marjorie was lining up for her and he scowled, convinced that none of them were right for Teresa or her kids.

The film ended and Mark began to chatter, his concentration on the television screen broken. Riley tried to pay attention as the boy began to recount the movie to him scene by scene, even though Riley had told him he'd seen it several times.

"And then the rabbit was floating on this little raft wearing swim trunks and sunglasses, but he got sunburned and he turned all pink and Jerry Lewis said, 'Oh, Harry.'" Mark leaned on the arm of Riley's chair as he talked, a broad smile splitting his face. "Maggie liked the first movie better because it was about a girl, but I really liked the rabbit in the other one."

Teresa entered the room, glancing in her son's direction. "Don't get in Riley's face, Mark. Back up and give him some air."

She smiled at Bud as she took a seat on one end of the sofa. "It looks like you had everything under control here."

"No problems at all," Bud boasted. "You've got good kids. Smart, too. They laughed at all the right places in the movies."

"My uncle's own version of an IQ test," Riley murmured.

Ignoring him, Bud asked Teresa, "Did you have a good time tonight?"

"Yes, very nice. Thank you again for watching the children."

"I enjoyed it." Placing his work-worn hands on the arms of the recliner, he pushed himself to his feet. "I guess I'd better be going. It's getting pretty late."

Mark bounced to Bud's side. "We're going fishing again, aren't we, Uncle Bud? The next nice Saturday?"

"If it's okay with your mom," Bud amended with a glance at Teresa.

"Of course it's okay."

Riley wondered what she'd been thinking during that split-second hesitation. He knew she trusted Bud with her children's safety; she never would have left them with him tonight if she didn't. Was she worried about the boy becoming too attached to Bud? A bit jealous, perhaps, that someone else had become important to her son?

Considering those possibilities, he stood to accompany his uncle out. Sending Mark upstairs to get ready for bed, Teresa followed Riley and Bud to the door. Bud stepped out first, glancing over his shoulder to tell Teresa good-night. Moving over the threshold at his uncle's heels, Riley noticed a dark van parked at the curb across the street, a shadowy figure sitting behind the steering wheel. Odd. He knew every vehicle that belonged on this cul-de-sac, and that wasn't one of them.

"Bud? Does that van look familiar to you?"

Bud glanced across the street and froze. After a moment he said, "I don't think so. Why?"

"Teresa? Have you ever seen the van before?"

She stepped into the open doorway. "No, not that I recall."

Whoever was sitting behind the wheel must have realized the van had attracted attention. He took off with a slight squeal of tires, disappearing into the darkness in excess of the neighborhood speed limit. Riley noticed that there were no license plates on the vehicle, which only increased the bad feeling he had about it.

Bud seemed to have been affected much the same

way. The jovial mood of earlier was gone, replaced by the grim expression that had become too familiar to Riley during the past weeks. "You better go back in the house, Teresa," Bud said. "Lock your door and don't worry about anything. You've got Riley right next door if you need anything, so there's nothing for you to worry about."

Teresa looked from Bud to Riley. "What was he doing there? Why did he speed away when he saw us watching him?"

"Probably just some teenagers drinking beer and cruising around," Riley answered lightly. "They park on quiet side streets sometimes, hoping no one will notice them."

It was a possible explanation—but he didn't believe it. He could tell that Teresa didn't, either. He gave her his most reassuring smile. "Go tuck your son in. Everything's fine out here. If it makes you feel any better, I'll give Dan's office a call, maybe have a squad car drive through the neighborhood, just to be safe."

"The van is probably long gone by now," she said, seeming to relax a little in response to his calm tone. "I just don't like the thought of people who don't live here hanging around at this hour."

"Neither do I," he assured her. "I'll keep an eye out. And you know you can call on me if you need anything."

Teresa nodded and moved back in the doorway. "I'll see you both later. Good night."

"Good night, Teresa," Riley replied.

Obviously lost in his thoughts, Bud murmured something Riley didn't catch.

Waiting only until Teresa had closed her door and he'd heard the dead-bolt lock snap into place, he turned to his uncle. "Why don't you come in for a few minutes?" he suggested, waving a hand toward his door. "We need to talk."

Bud shook his head. "I'm getting kind of tired. I think I'll head on home."

"Damn it, Bud, there's something going on with you. I want to know what it is. I saw your face when we spotted that van. You looked scared. Why?"

His uncle wouldn't meet his eyes. "I'll admit it made me nervous to think someone could have been lurking out here for some reason."

"Bud, I know there's something you aren't telling me. Something that's been on your mind since someone shot at R.L., if not before."

Bud looked at him, his expression grim. "There's nothing I want to talk about right now. Just know that I won't do anything to put you or anyone else I care about in danger. And that includes those kids in there. I probably won't be spending much time with them for a while. You make an excuse for me if they suggest anything, make sure their feelings don't get hurt."

"Bud, I want you to come in my house now," Riley said, speaking more firmly than he ever had to his uncle. "There's obviously something I need to know."

"We'll talk later. I need to go home now. Got a few calls to make."

Riley could tell by the older man's mulish expression that he would be wasting his breath to argue any further. Once Bud set his mind on something, there was little chance of changing it. "At least let me follow you home."

His bushy brows drawing into a fierce scowl, Bud shook his head. "I've been taking care of myself since long before you were born. You just let me be, you hear?''

"But—"

"I'm all right, Riley. You keep an eye on your pretty tenant and her sweet kids. And by the way, if you're not making a real effort in that direction, you aren't near as smart as I always gave you credit for being.''

Riley was no more interested in talking about his relationship—or lack of one—with Teresa than Bud was in talking about whatever was bothering him. "You be careful," he said as his uncle moved toward his truck.

Bud waved without looking around again. Shortly afterward, he was gone, leaving Riley standing on his doorstep, worrying.

Making a sudden decision, he went inside and picked up the phone, dialing a number he knew as well as his own. "Lindsey, it's Riley," he said a moment later. "Is Dan there?"

"He's here. Is something wrong?" she asked, her notorious curiosity piqued by the late call.

"I just really need to talk to Dan.''

"Okay, hold on.''

A moment later, Dan's deep drawl came through the line. "Riley?"

"I know it's late, but can you come over? I'd offer to come there, but I don't want to leave Teresa and the kids in the duplex alone right now.''

Dan's voice sharpened. "What's going on?"

"Probably nothing more than a monumental overreaction on my part. But I'd still like to talk to you.''

"I'll be there in fifteen minutes. Have the coffee ready.''

"I'll do that.'' Even as he hung up the phone, Riley

wondered if he'd made a mistake calling Dan. Bud wasn't going to like it. But something had to be done.

Despite his concerns about his uncle, he found his thoughts turning to Teresa as he started a pot of decaf brewing. He wondered if she'd gotten over her irritation with him for kissing her and then teasing her about it.

Kissing her had been an impulse he hadn't been able to resist. Teasing her had been his instinctive reaction to the aftermath of that brief but memorable embrace. A way of diffusing the tension and awareness that had been building inside him all evening until he simply couldn't wait any longer to find out if her soft, beautifully shaped lips tasted as sweet as they looked.

He'd thought a sample would be enough. A quick kiss, and his curiosity would be satisfied, his attention free to move in other directions. He'd known almost the moment his lips had touched hers that it wasn't going to be that easy. One taste wouldn't be enough to satisfy him for long. Not unless he made a determined effort to remind himself of all the many reasons he didn't need to be kissing Teresa Scott.

The doorbell rang, and he put that imprudent kiss out of his mind—or at least he tried to. He knew the memory was still lurking in the shadows, ready to haunt him again later, as he lay alone in his bed, separated from Teresa by no more than a couple of walls.

His life was getting much more complicated than he liked.

Teresa heard the news at the diner Monday. Bud O'Neal had left town, as silently and unexpectedly as his friend R.L. had a couple weeks earlier. Gossip had it that Riley was very upset.

She rushed home as soon as her shift ended, arriving

a full hour before the children were due home. She headed straight to Riley's door when she saw that his car was in the driveway.

He jerked the door open almost before the sound of her first knock had faded. It wasn't exactly disappointment she saw on his face when he recognized her, but she could tell he'd been hoping to see someone else.

"You haven't heard from your uncle," she said.

He pushed a hand through his hair—which seemed to be even more in need of a trim than usual, probably because he'd tugged at it so much during the past hours. "You heard he left town, I guess."

"Yes." The look in Riley's eyes made her speak gently. "Are you all right?"

"I don't know." As if he'd suddenly realized that she was still standing on his doorstep, he stepped back and motioned her inside. "Come in. Can I get you anything?"

"No, thanks. Tell me about Bud."

Waiting until she was seated on his sofa, he sank to the cushions beside her, his hands lying limply on his knees. "He left me a note. He didn't tell me where he was going or how I could reach him."

"What *did* he say?"

"That he was all right, but that he needed to get away for a little while. He said he'd get in touch with me eventually, but for me not to worry about him in the meantime. As if that was even a possibility."

"He gave you no hint of where he might be?"

"None. I called my parents, but they haven't spoken to him since last week. My father didn't seem overly concerned. He said Bud can take care of himself and that he'll show up again when he's ready."

"Do you think your uncle is with his friend? Mr. Hightower?"

"I think that's a definite possibility."

Because he still seemed so unhappy, Teresa laid a hand tentatively over Riley's. "I'm sure he's fine. If there was any reason to be concerned, Bud would have told you."

He stared at their hands without expression. "There was a time when I would have said Bud told me everything. I didn't think there were any secrets between us. Now..."

She clutched his hand more firmly. "You're just upset right now. You and your uncle are as close as any father and son I've ever known. You know how much he loves you."

Riley cleared his throat. "I know. I just wish I knew what the hell is going on with Bud and R.L. And whether Truman's death had anything to do with it."

She hadn't considered that possibility. She was beginning to understand exactly why Riley was so concerned. "When did Bud leave?"

"Sometime last night. I talked to him at about six. When I went by to check on him this morning, he was gone. He left the note to me taped to his front door in an envelope with my name on it."

"Seeing that van parked on our street Saturday seemed to bother him. Do you think that had anything to do with him leaving this way?"

"I keep coming back to that," Riley agreed. "Before we saw the van, he seemed to be cheering some. He was even making plans to take Mark fishing again soon. After we saw the van, he seemed to withdraw again."

"He thought whoever was in the van was watching him?"

"Apparently. He wouldn't tell me why. He seemed to be worried about having your kids around him—as if he was afraid that there was some risk to them if they were with him."

She moistened her lips, an instinctive ripple of fear going through her at the very suggestion of any threat to her children. "Do you think there's any reason for me to be concerned?"

He gave her hand a reassuring squeeze. "No. Bud seems to think the people he cares about are safe as long as he's not around."

She thought of the connotations of that statement. "Your uncle is afraid that whoever shot at Mr. Hightower will come after him next."

"I think so."

"But you have no idea why."

"Not a clue," Riley answered grimly. "Dan's looking into it, trying to find some record of trouble in their past, but so far he has nothing. Bud and R.L. have lived here all their lives, never got into any trouble that I know of, other than the usual hell-raising when they were kids."

"What are you going to do now? Are you actively trying to find your uncle or are you going to wait until he decides to contact you?"

"There's not a whole lot I can do," he admitted, frustration in his voice and in his expression. "Without knowing where Bud and R.L. are staying, I certainly can't ask them any questions. I've already called everyone I know who might have had a suggestion of where to look, but if anyone knows where they are, no one's talking."

"Then you'll have to wait until Bud calls you. He will, you know—when he's ready."

"I'm not sure I can wait for that."

"I'm not sure you have any other choice."

"I'm a reporter. I can dig up information. Find out if there's anything in Bud or R.L.'s past that could come back to haunt them now."

"How would your uncle feel about you doing that?"

"I can't just do nothing while I wait for Bud to come home. Or sit here worrying about whether I'll ever see him again."

"Then do what you have to do. Bud loves you enough to understand."

"I hope so," Riley said after a pause. "Because I'm going to keep digging until I find out what's going on."

Suddenly aware that she was sitting there holding his hand, Teresa tried to release him. He tightened his fingers around hers, turning to face her. "Thanks, Teresa. For stopping by, I mean."

"I was concerned about you. When I heard Bud left town, I knew you would be upset. I just… Well, is there anything I can do?"

He glanced at their linked hands. "You're being a friend. I appreciate that."

She swallowed, feeling waves of warmth radiating from her hand throughout the rest of her body. The connection between them was beginning to feel a bit more than friendly—at least to her. Which made her feel the need to put some distance between them. "I suppose I'd better go. The kids will be home soon."

On an impulse, she added, "I'm making chicken and dumplings for dinner. Would you like to join us?"

After a momentary hesitation, he nodded. 'Yeah. I'd like that. Thanks."

She was rather surprised that he had accepted. Apparently, he didn't want to be alone with his worries tonight. She untangled her hand from his and stood, as-

suring herself again that she was only being neighborly.
"We usually eat early, at around six."

"I'll be there."

She found it more difficult to leave than she had expected. Riley always seemed so in-control and self-
sufficient. Even when he'd been sick and she'd reacted
with a somewhat maternal impulse to offer assistance,
he had quickly convinced her that he didn't need anyone
to take care of him. Other than bringing him a bowl of
her homemade chicken soup, she'd left him to recover
on his own, and he'd seemed to prefer it that way.

It was different this time. For the first time since she'd
met him, Riley seemed to be at a loss. Thoroughly
shaken. Maybe he hadn't realized quite how important
Bud was in his life, how much he'd depended on always
having his uncle there. His anchor. His family. Maybe
Riley wasn't quite the independent loner he liked to pretend to be.

"I'll see you at six," she said, and let herself out. She
would use the time until she saw him again to remind
herself that she had enough in her life to worry about
without adding Riley O'Neal's problems to the list.

Somehow Riley ended up spending the entire evening
with Teresa and the kids. He didn't intend to; he'd
planned only to eat some of her chicken and dumplings
and then return to his place. Keeping his cordless phone
by his side in case his uncle tried to call, he found himself lingering over the meal, listening to the children
chattering about their activities at school. They had both
asked about Bud, but he'd simply told them that his
uncle was away for a vacation, which seemed to satisfy
them for now.

"We're doing a program for Thanksgiving and I get

to be a pilgrim lady,'' Maggie informed him over dessert, which consisted of red Jell-O with sliced bananas suspended in it. ''And we're going to sing songs. And then everyone gets cookies and punch. You're supposed to make cookies, Mommy.''

Teresa raised her eyebrows. ''I am?''

Maggie nodded. ''Mrs. Cooper sent a note. It's in my backpack. And then we're going to…''

Letting the happy young voice flow around him, Riley watched Teresa, who was listening to her daughter with a faint smile playing on her unpainted lips. She was the PTA mom again tonight, he mused, studying her simple ponytail and the loose-fitting, thin-wale brown corduroy jumper she wore over a beige knit top. Yet he could still picture her in the midnight-blue dress she had worn to the Chamber of Commerce dinner. And the way he'd first seen her, in enticingly snug jeans and a waitress's apron.

She looked beautiful to him no matter what she wore.

As if she'd felt his gaze on her, she glanced his way. Their eyes locked for a moment, and he wondered if he was the only one who felt an arc of awareness between them. She moistened her lips in an apparently subconscious gesture that served only to move his attention to her mouth. He could still very clearly remember the way her lips had felt and tasted beneath his.

''Riley? Did you hear me?''

Dragging his attention away from Teresa, Riley looked at Maggie. ''Sorry, Mags—what did you say?''

''Are you coming to my program?'' she repeated patiently. ''At school next week.''

''Oh, I—''

''Riley's very busy, Maggie,'' Teresa interceded

quickly. "He can't make any commitments right now. So don't bug him tonight, okay?"

Having been relatively patient during Maggie's turn to speak, Mark was ready to reclaim some attention for himself. "I've got to do a science project after dinner tonight, Riley. I'm supposed to mix colored water with cooking oil in a bottle and see what happens. Do you want to help?"

"Mark, I just said Riley's busy," Teresa repeated with a slight frown.

"I'm not too busy to help Mark with his science project," Riley refuted gently. "It sounds like fun."

She studied his face for a moment, then nodded. "You're welcome to stay and help. We can always use an extra scientist."

"I want to help, too," Maggie insisted.

"I'm sure we'll find something for you to do," her mother replied. "Now finish your dessert so we can clear away the dishes."

Two hours later, Riley was still there. The kitchen had been cleaned and the science project completed. Afterward, they'd relaxed in front of an old sitcom on a cable oldies station for half an hour. Teresa sat on the couch with Maggie curled at her side. Riley and Mark were in the two chairs, legs stretched comfortably in front of them.

Something amusing happened on the television. Maggie and Mark responded with peals of giggles and Teresa with her soft, musical laughter. Riley looked from one to the other and smiled, thinking what a happy family they were. Mark and Maggie squabbled occasionally but seemed to get along quite well compared to many siblings he'd spent time around. Teresa enforced her rules firmly, but lovingly.

He'd read recently that the most effective parents set high expectations yet provided a high level of support and approval, as opposed to setting high expectations backed with little support or just generally setting low expectations. Teresa seemed to belong to that first category, and her success was evident in her children's self-confidence and good behavior.

Wryly amused at the direction his thoughts had taken, he wondered why he was suddenly philosophizing about parenting styles, Teresa's in particular. He must really be working hard to keep from worrying about Bud—not that he was succeeding.

"Okay, guys, time for bed," Teresa announced when the program ended. "Tell Riley good-night and head upstairs."

Maggie immediately climbed to her feet, but Mark protested. "Can't I stay up a little longer? I'm not sleepy yet."

"You will be as soon as you're in bed," Teresa answered firmly. "No more arguments tonight."

Mark sighed gustily, but he didn't press his luck any further. "G'night, Riley," he muttered. "Thanks for helping me with my science project."

"You're welcome. I hope you get an A."

Maggie climbed onto Riley's chair, threw her arms around his neck and planted a noisy kiss on his cheek. "Good night, Riley."

He swallowed before he answered. "Good night, Mags. Sweet dreams."

"You have sweet dreams, too," she replied with her angelic, gap-toothed smile.

"Thanks. I'll try."

"I'll be up in a bit to tuck you in," Teresa told her children. From her seat on the couch, she watched them dash up the stairs, then she turned to Riley with a smile. "Mark never goes to bed without a fuss. Tonight was relatively easy."

"I used to fight bedtime every night," Riley admitted. "My mom finally started deducting fifteen minutes from the next night's bedtime for every time I complained."

Teresa chuckled. "I bet you were a handful."

"Some people would say that's still true."

They were looking at each other again, and Riley thought he saw a wave of self-consciousness cross her face. He wondered if she, too, was suddenly remembering that brief, shadowy interlude in his car. Clearing her throat, she dragged her gaze away from him, looking toward the stairway as she asked, "Is there anything I can get for you? Something else to eat or drink?"

"No. You need to take care of your children." He stood. "Thanks for dinner. It was very good."

She walked him to the door. "Try not to worry too much about your uncle tonight. I know he'll call you soon. He'll miss you too much to stay away permanently."

Standing in front of the door, he traced the faint line of concern between her eyes with the tip of one finger. "You have enough people to worry about without adding me to your list. I'm all right."

Searching his face, she asked, "Are you really?"

"Mostly," he amended. "Tonight helped."

"I hope so."

On an impulse he didn't try to resist, he leaned down to place a firm kiss on her lips. "Sweet dreams, Teresa. Lock the door behind me."

He slipped out before she could answer—and before he could be tempted to stay longer. He closed the door firmly between them. There was a noticeable pause before he heard the dead bolt slide home. Only then did he enter his own apartment.

He turned on the television as soon as he walked into his living room—not because he particularly cared about watching anything, but because his rooms seemed too quiet without it. Hearing a faint mental echo of the Scott family's laughter, he went upstairs to his office and straight to his computer. He figured it was as good a time as any to start his search for answers.

It wasn't as if he had anything else to do.

Chapter Twelve

All the way home from work Tuesday afternoon, Teresa mentally debated whether she would knock on Riley's door when she arrived. She didn't want to pester him and she certainly didn't want to give him the wrong ideas about what she wanted from him, but she worried about him. And she was terribly curious about what, if anything, he'd learned about his uncle.

Her quandary was decided for her when she saw that his car was not parked in his driveway. Not certain whether she was more relieved or disappointed that he wasn't home, she unlocked her door. She might as well take advantage of the hour before the children arrived home to do some housework. She started a load of laundry, then opened the refrigerator. It was a cool, overcast day. A pot of chili and a pan of corn bread sounded good. She always made more than enough for herself and the children—so if Riley happened to show up at dinnertime, that wouldn't be a problem.

Not that she expected him to join them for dinner again tonight, of course. But just in case...

It was a little too early to start dinner. Reassured that she had all the ingredients for chili, she took out a canned diet soda and closed the refrigerator door. Her kitchen, with its green and white checked curtains and chair cushions and apple accessories, was perfectly tidy, so there was really little for her to do until time to start the next load of laundry.

A neatly folded newspaper lying on the white laminate countertop caught her eye. Yesterday's *Evening Star,* she realized. She'd never gotten around to reading it. She opened her soda, took a seat at the kitchen table and spread the thin paper in front of her.

The lead story bore Riley's byline and concerned an ongoing dispute between the mayor and some local business owners. Something about a tax that had recently been ruled unconstitutional by the state supreme court, and which the mayor was now scrambling to replace. The subject didn't interest her much, but she read it because Riley had written it. He really was good, she thought, not for the first time. Concise, clear, completely objective in his news coverage. A very different voice than the one he used for his column, which was filled with irony and opinion.

She'd like to read the novel she'd been told he was writing. She and Riley had never talked about that; she wondered how he really felt about being published. Was writing merely an entertaining hobby for him, or was it a cherished dream? Was he any good? She would be willing to bet that he was.

She had a feeling writing wasn't all Riley was good at.

Unbidden, the memory of his kisses crept into her mind, and her lips tingled as if with a memory of their own. He'd kissed her only twice, and both had been relatively brief embraces but powerful in their effect on her. As much as she'd tried to pretend they hadn't meant anything to her, as often as she'd told herself that they had done nothing more than satisfy her curiosity—and his—she knew there was more to them than that. The kisses had reminded her of what was missing in her life. Adult intimacy. Romance. Sex.

Despite all its problems, her marriage had been fine in that respect. The handsome, dashing, witty and romantic charmer who had convinced her to quit college only a year prior to her graduation and marry him had been a skilled lover. And if there had been times when she had suspected he was sharing those talents a bit too generously, she had kept her concerns to herself for the sake of the children. Having lost her own family so young, she'd been determined to raise Mark and Maggie in a typical two-parent household.

Fate had had other plans for them.

Someone knocked on her door, bringing her abruptly back to the present. She glanced at her watch. The children weren't due home for another half hour. Somehow she knew who she would find at her door.

Smoothing her palms down the front of her jeans, she peeked through the tiny security window in her front door, confirming her guess. Making every effort to keep her expression bland—she certainly wouldn't want Riley to guess that she'd just been thinking about him and his kisses—she opened the door. "Hi."

He gave her a faint, somewhat weary smile. "Hi."

"Have you heard from your uncle?"

His smile faded. "No."

"Want some coffee? A soda, maybe?"

"I'm sure you have things to do."

Reading between his words, she stepped out of the doorway. "Come in. You can watch me fold towels."

"That sounds more interesting than anything going on at my place." He moved past her. "Do you have any ginger ale?"

"Root beer, grape soda or diet cola."

He chuckled. "I'll have the root beer."

"That's Mark's favorite." She turned to walk toward the kitchen, and Riley followed closely behind her.

He motioned toward the newspaper spread on the table. "Read anything interesting?"

"Just catching up on local news," she replied as she opened the refrigerator door. "I'm a day behind—just getting around to reading yesterday's paper."

"Wait'll you see today's. The lead story is about the winner of last weekend's Little Miss Edstown pageant. There's a big photograph. A four-year-old kid with big hair, trowled-on makeup and a ruffly, beaded dress starched so stiff it could probably walk down the runway by itself."

"Don't tell me you covered the pageant."

He shuddered. "I'd quit first, and Cameron knows it. He sent Lindsey. She isn't much more fond of pageants than I am, but he bribed her with next weekend off. Please tell me you don't enter Maggie in spectacles like that, as pretty as she is."

"No way. I want my daughter to find success with her brains and her ambition, not her face or her body."

"Good for you."

Setting a glass of root beer in front of him, Teresa

took her seat again and reached for the soda she'd been drinking before he arrived. "It's nice for you to be able to choose your assignments."

"Why do you think I stay in this job? It's not for the big bucks. And I don't think I'll be winning any Pulitzer prizes for local news coverage. I like the freedom. The chance to work out of my house."

"And the extra time to work on your novel, I'm sure."

He shrugged. "That, too."

"What's it about?"

He sipped his drink, then set the glass on the table. "It's a fantasy novel. Good against evil in a world populated with wizards and spirits and mythical beasts."

"Really?"

"You sound surprised. What did you think I was writing?"

"Oh, I don't know. A mystery or a thriller, perhaps. A tough-talking, hard-living detective story, maybe."

"Too normal. I like weird."

She couldn't help laughing. "Imagine that."

"Surely you aren't calling *me* weird."

"I didn't say that."

"You didn't have to."

Smiling, she watched as he took another drink of his root beer. "I would like to read your book."

"I've never let anyone read it."

"Why? Isn't that why you write? So people can read and enjoy your stories?"

"When it's ready."

"When will it be ready?"

His smile was lopsided. "Good question."

"Wouldn't you like feedback?"

"Only good feedback. I don't take criticism well."

She didn't find that statement surprising. "So let me read it. If I don't like it, I'll lie and tell you I do."

Laughing softly, Riley shook his head. "Something tells me you would be the world's worst liar. Your eyes would give you away."

She batted her lashes. "You think I have honest eyes?"

"You have very expressive eyes. I can't always tell what you're thinking, but I can usually sense when you're holding something back."

Because that made her uncomfortable, she looked away from him—just in case he could read something in her eyes she didn't want him to see. Standing, she moved toward the apple-shaped ceramic cookie jar on the counter. "I have some peanut butter cookies that Marjorie sent home for the kids. Would you like one?"

"No, thanks."

She hadn't realized he'd risen from his chair until she heard his voice from directly behind her. She turned quickly, almost bumping noses with him. He chuckled and steadied her by placing his hands on her shoulders. "Careful."

She cleared her throat. "Is there something else you want?"

Tugging her a bit closer, he bent his head until his mouth was only inches from hers. "I think you already know the answer to that."

She tried to frown intimidatingly. "I don't want you to do this."

His too-perceptive gray eyes searched her face. "I was right. You're a terrible liar."

She swallowed. "I don't think this is a good idea."

"Now you're being honest. And very sensible." His

lips brushed across hers as lightly as a warm breeze. "I've never been known as the sensible type myself."

It was probably a good thing he was still supporting her, because her knees were going weak—along with her willpower. "Then I suppose it's up to me to be sensible for both of us," she whispered.

"Looks like it." He kissed her again, a little harder this time. She lifted her hands to his chest. She was quite sure she'd intended to push him away. Instead, she seemed to be resting against him.

She really was going to be sensible and put an end to this. In a minute, she promised herself as his lips settled onto hers again.

It had been very difficult for her to stop thinking about those two brief kisses they had shared before. But the memory of those kisses evaporated in the heat of this one. His mouth moved on hers with a hunger that hadn't been evident before, an eagerness he didn't even try to disguise.

The kitchen counter dug into her back as he pressed against her. The intensity of the kiss wasn't the only evidence that he wanted her. A quiver of instinctive response ran through her, and a hollow ache centered somewhere deep inside her. Once again she was reminded of the missing elements in her life—and she suspected that Riley could provide all of them. At least for a while. Until his attention moved on.

That sobering thought—or was it the sad voice of experience?—gave her the strength to pull her mouth from his. "We have to stop this."

He threaded the fingers of his right hand through her hair, and only then did she realize that he'd somehow released the clip that had been securing her hair at the back of her neck. The fact that he'd done so without her noticing was disturbing.

"I know. Your kids are going to be home soon."

She almost groaned. The kids. They *would* be arriving home at any minute—and she hadn't even thought of that until Riley pointed it out. "Yes, but—"

"You're thinking that I'm the last guy on earth you need to get involved with. I'm commitment-phobic, unpredictable, irresponsible…am I missing anything?"

"Yes." She reached up impulsively to rub a smudge of lipstick from his lower lip. "You're a bad influence on my son. This morning he tried to leave for school wearing shoes with no socks. When I told him to put on his socks, he said, 'But Riley doesn't wear them.'"

He appeared to give that a moment's thought before he asked, "If I start wearing socks, would you consider having a wild, passionate affair with me?"

She tried not to smile. She tried to look stern and disapproving. Instead, she shook her head with a reluctant laugh. "You're incorrigible."

"Another of my flaws."

"Riley—"

"Is this where you give me another lecture about maintaining a professional tenant-landlord relationship?"

"I think that would be a waste of time at this point," she said in resignation.

His mouth quirked into an appreciative half-smile. "I think you're right."

He started to lower his head again. She sidestepped quickly, evading the intended kiss. "But, as you just reminded me, my children will be home very soon, and I need to get ready for them."

He sighed regretfully and moved to give her some space.

Her hands weren't quite steady when she reached to gather her hair at her nape again, securing it with the clip he'd placed on the counter. She cleared her throat and tried to speak normally. "I'm making chili and corn bread for dinner, if you'd like to join us."

"Sounds good. But I have a few things to do first."

"I'll have dinner ready at six-thirty. If you can get away by then, you're welcome to join us."

"I'll be here." Probably just to be irritating, he reached up to remove the clip again, letting her shoulder-length hair swing free. The fact that he did it so quickly and so deftly attested to a wealth of experience that made her nervous all over again. "See you later, Terry."

It was the first time he had used the nickname that only her closest friends called her. As she watched him walk out, she thought of how intimate the familiar diminutive had sounded coming from him.

As she had acknowledged, it was too late to pretend there was nothing between them. Riley seemed to be drawn increasingly to spend time at her place, and she seemed to be taking for granted that he would be hanging around. And wasn't that exactly what she'd wanted to avoid? Getting too accustomed to his presence in her life?

It would be hard enough on her children if Bud decided not to return now that they had grown so close to him. She had to keep reminding herself that Riley was just as free to take off as Bud had been.

Her children announced their arrival with the crash of the front door opening and a clatter of footsteps. "Mommy! We're home," Maggie called unnecessarily.

"Mom! Come see the ribbon I got for my painting," Mark shouted. "First place!"

Pasting on a smile, she went to join them. Her life really was very full, she reminded herself. If there were a few holes—well, the blessings more than made up for them. She simply had to keep reminding herself of those facts when Riley O'Neal was around to tempt her to forget.

It hadn't been easy, but Riley convinced Teresa to hire a baby-sitter and go out with him Saturday evening. Although he'd spent nearly every evening that week with her and the kids, she had been hesitant to commit to what could only be considered a date.

He wasn't sure why she'd finally agreed, whether it was because she really wanted to get out or to shut him up or because she still felt sorry for him because he'd made no progress in locating his uncle. Whatever her reason, he promptly took her up on her acceptance, setting a time and making arrangements before she could change her mind.

As he dressed for their outing, he tried to analyze what, exactly, was going on between them. They were friends, of course. He genuinely liked her and respected her. But he had plenty of other women friends, and he hadn't been losing any sleep over them lately, remembering what it was like to kiss them or wondering what it would be like to do more. He hadn't lain awake staring at his ceiling and making mental lists of all the reasons he should stay away from them.

He wanted her. That wasn't such a shock in itself. After all, she was an attractive and desirable woman, and it had been a while since he'd been intimately involved with anyone. He was a normal, red-blooded, young, single male, and it would be more surprising if he *didn't* want Teresa.

But he didn't date women with children. That had always been his rule and one he'd never been tempted to break—until now.

Her kids were cute. Well behaved. Bright. But he had no more interest in becoming a stepparent to them now than he had when he'd first met them. Now that he knew them better, now that he'd seen firsthand what a good mother Teresa was to them, he was even more aware of his own deficiencies when it came to parenting material.

Parents were patient and organized and dependable and unselfish. They knew how to handle childhood tears and tantrums, traumas and temperatures. Did any of that description apply to him? he asked the reflection in his mirror. Of course not.

And yet he still found himself drawn to Teresa. She'd been a great help to him during the past week. He might have been close to frantic about Bud by now if she hadn't been so calmly reassuring. She'd convinced him that Bud probably knew what he was doing and that he wouldn't stay away forever. When he was ready to talk, he'd call or show up on Riley's doorstep. He always had before.

He studied his reflection in the mirror, checking to make sure he was presentable. He'd finally gotten around to having his hair trimmed, so it didn't look as shaggy as it had lately. He wore a long-sleeve black-and-oatmeal checked shirt unbuttoned over a black pullover and khakis. After a brief mental debate, he'd donned a pair of socks before sliding his feet into brown leather slip-ons. Because he liked the look, he fastened a short necklace made of shells in shades of brown and black around his neck. Fastening the brass buckle of his braided brown leather belt, he decided he looked fine for a casual evening out in Edstown.

He liked clothes, but he didn't usually obsess about them quite as much as he had for this date. Which only proved that there was something different about his responses to Teresa Scott.

Even though he was ten minutes early, Jenny's little car was already parked in Teresa's driveway when Riley stepped outside. He rapped on Teresa's door, hoping she was ready. Mark opened it.

"Hi, Riley. Cool necklace."

"Thanks. I got it in Hawaii last summer."

The boy's eyes widened. "Hawaii? Really?"

"I picked up several while I was there. Sort of got carried away. Maybe you and Maggie would each like to have one?"

"*I* would. All the guys at school are wearing shell necklaces, but I don't think any of theirs came all the way from Hawaii. Bobby got his at Wal-Mart."

Smiling as he moved past the boy, Riley nodded toward Teresa and Jenny, who were standing in the center of the living room. "Ladies."

Jenny grinned. "Hey, Riley."

"How's your family?"

"Everyone's great, thanks. I'll tell them you asked about them."

"Do that." Riley couldn't keep his attention away from Teresa any longer. She looked beautiful. As he'd suggested, she'd kept her outfit casual—a royal-blue-and-black color-block sweater with black slacks—but she still looked like the regal princess he always compared her to. She'd left her hair down, which she rarely did. It fell in a soft, shiny golden curtain around her shoulders, perfectly framing her delicately oval face.

"You look very nice," he said, vividly aware of the three pairs of eyes watching them. "Are you ready to go?"

"Yes." She picked up a black leather purse. "Mark and Maggie, you behave yourselves tonight. Do what Jenny says, you hear?"

"Yes, ma'am," they chorused dutifully.

"Jenny, you have my cell phone number. I'll have the phone on all evening if you need me."

"Don't worry, we'll be fine. You and Riley just go have a good time."

Teresa hesitated for a moment, then moved to Riley's side. He might have wished she looked a bit more enthusiastic about the outing, but maybe she was a little nervous about leaving the kids with Jenny for the evening. He held the door for her, and she stepped past without meeting his eyes.

She was definitely having second thoughts, he decided, closing the door behind them. He supposed he couldn't blame her.

She waited until they were in his car before breaking the silence between them. "I forgot to ask where we're going tonight."

He chuckled. "There aren't a whole lot of choices unless we leave town. Have you ever been to Gaylord's?"

"The Cajun place on the outskirts of town? I've heard of it, but I've never been there."

"I think you'll like it—unless you'd rather go somewhere else?"

"No. I want to get to know my new hometown, and Gaylord's is certainly a local landmark."

"I don't think you'll regret it. The service is lousy, but the music's good and the food is great."

"That sounds promising. I only had a salad for lunch, and now I'm hungry."

"Do you like spicy food?"

"Yes."

"Wait until you try Gaylord's gumbo. It's the best I've ever had. And the jambalaya—oh, man, that's good."

"Now you're *really* making me hungry."

He was pleased that she seemed to be relaxing a bit. Maybe they could have fun tonight, after all. And maybe by the time the evening ended, they would be friends again, those increasing moments of awkwardness put firmly behind them. He'd always found that the more time he spent with a woman, the more the initial attraction faded, and the easier it was for them to be friends.

He was sure that would be especially true with Teresa. Since they were such a mismatch, anyway, the differences between them would probably be magnified during the next few hours. So dating her tonight was a very clever way of getting past this awkward obsession he'd had about her lately.

At least it sounded good in theory. He knew full well that what he was really doing was clutching at any rationalization he could find to spend more time with her.

Gaylord's was noisy, crowded and smoky, and so familiar to Riley it was almost like a second home. It had been several weeks since he'd dropped in, and he realized now that he'd missed it. He was greeted by nearly everyone there, including barrel-chested Chuck, the owner who did double duty as bartender. Intimate conversation wasn't an option because of the loud zydeco music pouring out of numerous overhead speakers. The patrons didn't seem to mind. They didn't come here to talk; they came to relax and party.

There weren't many open tables, but Riley found a tiny booth in a relatively secluded corner. It was so cramped their knees touched beneath the table, but at least they could converse without risking permanent vocal cord damage. Because he knew it would be a while before one of the servers made it to them, he went to the bar to place their orders, knowing Chuck would make sure the food would get to them eventually.

"Who's the lady friend, Riley?" Chuck asked in his booming drawl. "Don't think I've seen her before."

"Her name is Teresa. She's only been in town a couple of months."

"And you moved in fast, hey? I can see why. She's pretty. You know who she looks like?"

"I know. Princess Grace."

Chuck frowned and shook his head. "She looks like Margaret St. John."

"Who?"

"My seventh grade English teacher." Chuck sighed nostalgically. "Oh, she was fine, you bet. All us boys were in love with her."

Riley laughed, then said, "You want to take our orders?"

"I'll send over some of tonight's specialties. You'll like what you get."

"Just make sure we get gumbo."

"Sure you get gumbo. You think I don't know what you like by now? What does the pretty lady want to drink?"

"White wine. And I'll have—"

"A beer," Chuck finished with him, setting the already filled mug on the counter. "When's that uncle of yours going to come back in? Haven't seen him in a while."

Picking up the beer and the filled wineglass Chuck had set beside it, Riley shrugged. "I'm sure he won't stay away too long. He'd go into gumbo withdrawal."

Laughing as if Riley had just said something incredibly clever, Chuck turned to his work, and Riley made his way to the booth where Teresa waited for him.

Dragging his gaze away from the action on the crowded dance floor, Teresa accepted her wineglass with a smile. "It looks like things are getting interesting over there."

Following her gaze, Riley grinned. A curvaceous, copper-haired woman in a skimpy halter top and low-riding tight jeans was dancing with two men, making sure she stayed in the prime spotlight. "Lorrie does love being the center of attention."

"Lorrie?" Teresa repeated, her eyes on him.

He lifted one shoulder. "An old friend. Sort of."

"Oh." She looked at her wineglass, running one fingertip slowly around the rim. "You seem to have a lot of friends."

"I suppose I do, considering I have some basic loner tendencies."

"I don't think of you as a loner."

"Only when I choose to be." He paused to let a sudden burst of laughter from the other side of the room die down.

"I read your column in yesterday's newspaper," Teresa said when he could hear her again. "You were actually quite complimentary about the high school administrators."

"I believe in giving credit where it's due. That new student outreach program is a good idea. Keeping kids involved in their community is one way to keep them engaged and out of trouble."

"One of the at-risk students is working at the diner before school, serving the early breakfast crowd. She's doing very well—and Marjorie, of course, has really taken her under her wing. Every paycheck is accompanied by a grandmotherly pep talk."

"Marjorie would mentor every kid in town, if she could. She's a compulsive do-gooder."

Teresa frowned at him as if she were trying to decide if he was poking fun at her employer. "Marjorie has the biggest heart of anyone I know."

"She's one of the finest people I've ever met," he assured her. "I'm crazy about her."

"So am I. She's been so good to me during the years I've been lucky enough to know her."

A young waiter brought a tray with two big bowls of gumbo and a basket of corn fritters. Filling their water glasses, he told them he'd back shortly with their next course, then ambled off at the usual leisurely speed of the staff here.

"You're right," Teresa told him a few minutes later. "This *is* good gumbo."

She had tasted the spicy stew without even blinking. When she reached for the Louisiana Hot Sauce and added a few drops for extra heat, Riley almost sighed. A woman after his own heart, he thought—a heart he'd spent most of his adult life protecting.

Chapter Thirteen

Riley and Teresa took their time with the meal. They talked about her children, about the high school program he'd researched for his column, about the upcoming holidays. "I usually join my parents in Florida for Thanksgiving," Riley said in answer to a question she had asked him. "But this year I'm staying here."

"Because of Bud?"

"Partly."

"Surely you'll have heard from him by Thanksgiving. That's still more than a week away."

He looked at the almost-finished jambalaya the waiter had finally brought him. "I hope so."

"And if he hasn't?"

"Then I'm going to keep looking for him."

"What have you found out so far?"

"Not much," he admitted. "I've been searching the newspaper archives, looking for any old stories that might have had anything to do with Bud and R.L. They've led pretty uneventful lives, actually."

"I find that hard to believe."

"Let's just say their exploits didn't make headlines. What I know about their past is that they graduated from the local high school with a close-knit group of about a half dozen friends. A couple of them moved away shortly after graduation. Since then, another died of a heart attack, one got on the wrong side of the law and ended up in prison, and only Truman, Bud and R.L. remained together over the years. They all married in their twenties, but Truman's was the only union that lasted until death parted them. His wife died of cancer ten years ago. R.L. was divorced once, Bud twice.

"They each started their own businesses, and all did well, though none of them got rich. Truman retired a couple of years ago, Bud a year later, and R.L. retired after our friendly hometown firebug burned his business down. They spent their free time fishing, hunting, bowling—just having a good time—until Truman died in that fire earlier this year and someone tried to kill R.L. just weeks ago. As far as I know, Bud received no threats and had no close calls or anything else to send him on the run. The only specific incident I can point to is spotting that van outside your house."

"He left the next day."

Riley nodded grimly. "Without a word of warning."

Resting her elbows on the table, she leaned slightly toward him, obviously giving her full attention to their conversation. "You're still assuming there's a connection between the fire that killed Truman and the shooting at Mr. Hightower's house?"

"I still think it's a possibility."

"Murder." She shivered slightly as she whispered the word.

"Maybe," he agreed reluctantly.

As if her appetite had suddenly vanished, she set down her fork and drew a deep breath. "Okay, what are the usual motives for murder?"

He'd been over the list a dozen times in his mind. "Money."

"But you said none of them were rich."

"Right. Comfortable, but not rich. And even if they had money, the only people who would stand to gain are members of their own separate families."

"What else?"

"Revenge."

She frowned. "You said they led quiet, uneventful lives. What would they have done to drive someone to want that kind of revenge against them?"

"Nothing that I could find."

"So...what else?"

"Jealousy."

"I don't suppose they all courted the same woman at some point?"

He smiled, but it felt crooked. "Not that I'm aware of."

"There's always the possibility that we're getting completely carried away here. Truman Kellogg could have died in an accidental fire, or one started by that boy who admitted setting all the others. And it's very likely that R.L. has a personal enemy who isn't out to get anyone else. And that the van in front of our house was full of carousing teenagers who had no interest in any of us."

"You're probably right. So where's Bud?"

"Obviously with his friend. Maybe just keeping him company until they believe it's safe to come home."

Now it was Riley's time to pose questions. "If R.L., and presumably Bud, knew who fired those shots, why wouldn't they have told Dan?"

"Maybe they aren't sure."

"Then why wouldn't they have at least shared their suspicions?"

"Maybe they're looking for answers on their own?"

"Doubtful."

"Or maybe—"

"What?" he prodded when she suddenly fell silent.

"Never mind. I'm probably getting carried away again."

"I'd still like to hear what you were going to say."

"What if Bud and R.L. not only knew who fired those shots, but why? And what if that's what they don't want to share with Chief Meadows?"

Riley went still. "You're suggesting they're hiding something. Something…illegal?"

"Embarrassing, at the least. I told you it was probably far-fetched."

"No." He sighed. "Actually, it makes a lot of sense. And it's a possibility I've already considered. The way Bud was acting, sort of guilty and evasive—well, I knew he was hiding something."

Her expression turned sympathetic. "He'll call you when he's ready."

He tried to smile for her again. "That's what you keep telling me."

"He will."

A heavy hand fell on Riley's shoulder. "Hey, Riley. How's that food?"

Dragging his attention to their surroundings, Riley

nodded. "As good as you promised. Teresa, this is Chuck, our host."

Teresa smiled warmly at the establishment's owner. "The food was delicious. I haven't had jambalaya like this since I spent a week in New Orleans five years ago."

While Chuck responded to her compliments and swapped stories about their favorite restaurants in New Orleans, Riley reflected that Teresa had probably made that trip with her husband. A romantic getaway, perhaps. He didn't like thinking about it.

Chuck examined the nearly empty plates in front of them. "You haven't had dessert? Let me get you some beignets out here."

"I'm too full," Teresa protested. "I ate too much already."

"Then you should dance up an appetite, hey? Have dessert later."

"Sounds like a good idea to me," Riley said promptly. "Would you like to dance, Teresa?"

He had been fully prepared for her to decline. Instead, she said, "I wondered if you were ever going to ask."

Chuck laughed and thumped Riley's shoulder again. "Our Riley, he's pretty slow sometimes. Dance with the lady, boy. Your dessert will be ready when you're finished."

Teresa could dance. Maybe Riley shouldn't have been surprised by that, but he was. She moved with a grace he expected and a sensuality that caught him unaware. Watching her, he almost forgot how to dance himself. He would have been perfectly content to stand there watching her.

He reached out to take her hands, pulling her closer

so they were moving together. "You're sure you only spent a week in New Orleans?" he asked.

She laughed softly. "I said I last spent a week in New Orleans five years ago. I never said it was my first visit there."

"You spent a lot of time there?"

"My husband was raised in New Orleans until he was a senior in high school. He went back every chance he got. It was where we spent our honeymoon and nearly every vacation after that."

Great. Riley had brought her on a date that couldn't help but remind her of her late husband. Deciding that he didn't want her thinking about anyone but him just then, he pulled her even closer, so that his body brushed hers as they danced. She blinked a couple of times, but she didn't pull away. The music swelled around them, and she stayed with it beat for beat.

She loved to dance, he realized with a sudden flash, studying the pleasure on her face. Absolutely loved it. How long had it been since she'd had the opportunity?

"You dance very well," he told her, speaking into her ear so that she could hear him over the music.

Turning her head, she smiled at him. "Thank you. I enjoy dancing."

He didn't tell her he'd already figured that out.

The fast number ended and a slower one began. Aaron Neville's sultry voice poured through the speakers, and the colorful lights, programmed to flash and dim with the music, pulsed seductively. Riley laid his cheek against Teresa's soft hair, letting one hand slide down her back to rest very close to the swell of her hips.

So much for his theory that spending an evening with her would lessen his fascination with her. He wanted her so badly he ached. And it wasn't only a physical attraction. Everything about her appealed to him. Except for the complications she brought with her, of course.

But it was hard to think of those complications when she was in his arms. When he could feel her hair beneath his cheek and smell the faint scent of a floral perfume. When they swayed with the music and her breasts brushed his chest, her thighs moving against his. He had no doubt that she could feel his reaction to her. If it shocked her, it didn't show in her dancing, and she made no effort to move away.

He was almost relieved that the next song was a fast dance again. Had it been another slow one, he could not have predicted what he might have done. Throwing her over his shoulder and hauling her off somewhere private was only one of the improbable scenarios that crossed his mind. Funny, he didn't usually think of himself as the primitive, macho type. He wondered how Teresa would feel if she knew she brought out that side of him.

He wondered if it would make her as nervous as it did him.

They danced until they were both flushed and winded. The dance floor was growing more crowded as the evening wore on, and several acquaintances spoke to him, but he answered in little more than monosyllables, all his attention focused on Teresa. Lorrie approached him at one point, blatantly trying to entice him to ask her to dance. He wasn't interested, and because he had never had the patience for social niceties, he wasn't particularly tactful about it.

"Feel free to dance with your friend if you want to," Teresa urged when Lorrie flounced away.

Riley pulled her into his arms again for another slow dance. "I don't want to. I want to dance with you."

She looped her arms around his neck and smiled at him. "I haven't danced this much in years."

"I'm glad you're having a good time."

"I'm having a wonderful time." She sighed a little. "But it's going to have to end soon. I don't want to keep Jenny out too late."

Those complications were intruding again. Resting his cheek against her hair, Riley closed his eyes for a moment and tried to pretend that she was as free as he was. Free to spend the entire night dancing in his arms. Free to take off to the islands for the weekend if they wanted. Or to lock themselves in his bedroom and not come out for a week.

The song ended, and so did the fantasy. It was time to take Teresa home to her children.

Teresa was a bit confused when Riley turned the car in the opposite direction from the duplex after leaving Gaylord's. "Where are we going?"

"A sight-seeing detour," he replied vaguely. "You said you want to experience all of Edstown, didn't you?"

"Well, yes—but I didn't necessarily mean I wanted to do it all tonight."

He chuckled. "We won't be too long. I'm just not quite ready for the night to be over."

That argument silenced her. She wasn't ready for the evening to end, either.

She'd had such a good time tonight. With the exception of the somber discussion about Bud, she and Riley had kept their conversation light and entertaining. The food had been so good, the atmosphere so festive and the dancing so much fun.

The dancing. Oh, it had been so long since she'd

danced. Since she'd let the music sweep through her and move her body. Riley was a wonderful partner, almost instinctively matching her steps. And when they had slow danced and she'd known that he wanted her—

She swallowed hard, knowing she'd better put those thoughts out of her mind right now. This date had been a one-time event. She'd accepted his invitation by rationalizing that he needed a diversion to help him stop worrying about his uncle for a few hours. Yet she'd known all along that she really wanted to accept. She had known that Riley would show her a good time. He always did.

She recognized the road he eventually turned onto. It wasn't far from Serena's house. "This road leads to the lake, doesn't it?"

She saw the flash of his grin in the shadowy interior of the little sports car. "Yeah. There's a nice view at night, with the moon shining on the water."

Trying to keep her voice stern, she said, "I've lived here long enough to know that the lake is where the local teenagers come to make out on weekends."

"Mmm. But they all park on the other side of the lake. I know a nice spot the kids don't come to."

She moistened her lips. "I definitely don't think this is a good idea."

"I only want to show you a pretty spot. There's nothing wrong with that, is there?"

"That depends on what else you want to do while we're admiring the view."

He laughed softly. "We're in a two-seater with a stick shift between us. I'm in pretty good shape, but I'm no contortionist."

Maybe he just wanted to talk a bit more, she thought as he made another turn, this time onto a hard-packed gravel road. But somehow she didn't think that was his only purpose in bringing her here.

As he'd promised, the view was lovely from the spot where he parked. They were at the top of a hill, in a clearing surrounded by big trees that were rapidly going bald for the winter. The moon's reflection laid a bright silver path across the metallic black surface of the lake that stretched ahead of them. Lights from houses and security lamps were visible in the distance, but the spot Riley had brought her to felt very private and secluded.

He released his seat belt and twisted in his seat to face her. "Was I lying? Isn't this a great view?"

"It's lovely," she admitted with a smile. "Very peaceful."

"I'm going to build a house here someday."

She tilted her head in surprise. "Do you own this land?"

"An acre of it. My parents bought it for me when they sold their house here and moved to a retirement RV park in Florida. I think they felt guilty for abandoning me here, even though I was basically grown and on my own."

"That was a very nice gesture on their part."

"Yeah. I come up here sometimes just to listen to the radio and clear my mind. In the summer, I turn off the radio, open the windows and listen to the frogs and crickets."

"That must be nice. I love to be outside on summer nights."

"I should have guessed that. It surprises me sometimes how much we have in common."

A bit uncomfortable with that observation, Teresa reached up to tuck a lock of hair behind her ear. "Somehow I doubt we're that much alike."

"Oh, I don't know. The differences seem to be more circumstances than personalities."

She shook her head. "We both like summer nights, Cajun food and zydeco music. That hardly makes us soul mates."

"No. But it certainly gives us a good foundation for a friendship."

Friendship, she thought wistfully. She knew they should settle for that. It was more than she had initially expected to develop between them—but less than they might have had, had things been different.

Riley reached out to smooth another strand of hair from her face. The car was so small that he didn't have to reach far. The moon was so bright through the windshield that she had no trouble seeing him. "I think I mentioned once before that I think you look beautiful in moonlight," he murmured.

"Riley—"

He leaned closer. "It's been such a great evening. A kiss would finish it off nicely, don't you think?"

She supposed a kiss or two in the moonlight wouldn't be such a terrible mistake. If this evening was a one-time event, a special night to indulge in fantasies or what-might-have-beens, a kiss would actually be a very fitting way for it to end.

She unsnapped her seat belt and leaned toward him in implicit invitation. He took her up on the offer without hesitating, his lips settling swiftly, unerringly on hers.

Her arms went around his neck, her head tilting back to give him better access to her mouth. He took full advantage of the freedom she offered him, delving deep with his tongue for a more thorough taste than he'd sampled previously. And Teresa found herself thinking again that Riley did everything well.

She couldn't say how much time passed before she returned to her senses. It happened between one long, drugging kiss and the next. It seemed as if she blinked and suddenly became aware that she was half sprawled beneath him, entwined in a position she would have sworn was impossible in a two-seater.

And he had denied being a contortionist.

She untangled her fingers from his hair and dragged her mouth from his. "We have to stop this now," she managed to say, her voice hoarse.

He groaned. "Are you sure?"

She looked wistfully at his so-talented mouth and removed his hand from beneath her sweater. "Very sure."

He sighed but levered himself into his own seat.

Her face flaming, Teresa made an effort to straighten her clothes. She resisted an illogical impulse to check her body for handprints. Waves of heat were still coursing through her when she sat taller in her seat and reached up to run her hands through her tumbled hair.

Riley sat very still in his own seat, staring out the windshield at the shimmering lake ahead of them. He was quiet for so long that Teresa finally felt compelled to ask, "What are you thinking?"

"I was just thinking about taking a quick dip in the lake," he said, his tone almost whimsical even though his voice was still rather strained. "It's the closest semblance to a cold shower I have available."

"We, um, sort of got carried away, I guess."

"A bit, perhaps."

"It must have been the wine. And the dancing."

"Or maybe the moonlight?"

"Maybe."

"Or maybe," he said, still not looking at her, "it's more than that."

"It can't be more. You know that as well as I do."

He was quiet for a moment, and then he nodded. "You're probably right."

She glanced at the lighted clock on his dashboard and gasped. "It's getting so late. We have to go home."

He reached down to start the engine. "It was a nice fantasy…while it lasted."

"Yes," she agreed evenly. "But that's all tonight was. A fantasy. A temporary lapse in judgment. I had a wonderful time, I can't deny that. It's been years since I've danced…or since I've been carried away by passion," she added, trying to keep her tone light.

Riley focused on the road ahead, but she knew she had his full attention. "Carried away by passion? Is that what just happened between us?"

"Something like that."

"Whatever you call it, it was fantastic."

"I can't argue with that," she murmured, remembering.

The car swerved almost imperceptibly on the narrow road. Riley spoke in a near growl. "Unless you want me to turn this car around and take up where we left off, you'd better get back to the topic of why we had to stop."

"I don't think it's really necessary for me to spell it out again."

"You're really content to go back now to the way you've been living? Concentrating only on your kids and your job?"

"It's a good life. A comfortable life. The children are happy and healthy. I enjoy working for Marjorie, and I'm making new friends in town. I really can't ask for more."

"And what about your own needs? Don't try to convince me you don't have any. I know better now."

Her cheeks warmed again, but she managed to speak evenly. "My needs can wait until the children are older. They require all my time and attention now."

"Which is exactly why I'm still single and childless," Riley muttered. "I'm much too selfish to change."

He wasn't selfish, of course, Teresa mused as she gazed out the side window without responding. Riley had broken his rules to rent to her. He'd changed her tire and sat with her sick child without protest when she had needed him. He was so good to his uncle, so patient with her children.

The cynical, tough, loner reporter act of his was mostly facade, maintained for reasons of his own—possibly just habit—but that was something Riley would have to acknowledge before he could make a decision to change. If, in fact, he ever found anyone who made him want to change.

Chapter Fourteen

It was close to lunchtime Friday morning and the streets of downtown were already busy. People who worked in the banks and other businesses still located in the aging business district were leaving their offices for their lunch hours, quite a few headed for the popular Rainbow Café.

Standing on a sidewalk only a few short blocks from that dining destination, Riley resisted an urge to follow them. Except in passing, he hadn't seen Teresa since he'd taken her to her door last Saturday evening. He needed a bit more time before he saw her again for an extended period.

On an impulse, he entered the corner candy store, located in an oddly shaped old stone building that had been renovated only a couple of years earlier. The candy store owners had struggled for the first year after they opened, but the addition of a line of gift items such as specialty teas and coffees, porcelain teapots and fruit-scented candles had been a clever and profitable idea. Riley stopped by whenever he was in the area because he had a fondness for gourmet flavored jelly beans, and Sweets 'n' Treats had the biggest selection around.

The store's owner, Angelina Santiago, looked up from her work with a smile when he entered. *"Hóla,* Riley. *¿Cómo estás?"*

"Bien, gracias, Angelina." Having just exhausted his Spanish vocabulary, he switched to English. "How's your family?"

Her English was much better than his Spanish. "All well, thank you. Tomas is coming home from college next week for Thanksgiving weekend. I can't wait to see him."

Riley was already reaching for a plastic bag to fill with jelly beans. "And how are the wedding plans coming along?"

Angelina's broad face beamed. "My daughter is going to have a beautiful wedding. It will be December twenty-second. Her attendants are going to wear dark green dresses and carry red and white flowers—very Christmasy."

"Sounds nice." Riley dumped a scoop of sour apple jelly beans in the bag, then added scoops of watermelon and peach flavors.

"So when are you going to be a groom, hmm? I've heard you've been dating the new waitress from the Rainbow Café. I have seen her. She's *muy bonita.*"

He nearly dumped a scoopful of strawberry-cheesecake flavored candies on the floor. He just managed to get them into the bag. "I'm not dating anyone. And I'm certainly not planning a wedding."

"Mmm. We'll see. I'm a little psychic, you know."

"So you've always claimed."

"I feel big changes coming on for you."

He added cappuccino, cinnamon, chocolate malt and piña colada jelly beans to his already bulging bag. "You know I don't believe in psychic powers, Angelina."

"But do you believe in the power of love?" she retorted whimsically.

"I believe in the power of root-beer flavored jelly beans," he said, dumping yet another scoopful into his bag.

"You fight all you want, Riley O'Neal. Love usually wins in the end."

He set the bag on the counter to be weighed. "You just concentrate on your daughter's wedding and let the rest of us happy bachelors be. Do you have any of those chocolate pecan patties I like so much?"

"Of course." She turned to a shelf behind the counter, selecting a box from the assortment arranged there.

Riley's attention was caught by a display of lollipops in battery-powered musical holders. They were colorfully decorated with instantly recognizable figures—Disney characters, comic book superheroes and perennial kid favorites like unicorns and dinosaurs. He picked up one of the unicorn figures, pressing the button and listening to the high-pitched electronic melody that resulted. Maggie would like this, he thought. And Mark would probably get a kick out of the one that looked like...

He quickly set the trinket back in the display. He'd come into this store to buy candy for himself, not for Teresa's kids.

Angelina set the box of chocolate pecan patties next to the bag of jelly beans. She glanced at the display he'd been studying. "Will there be anything else?"

"No," he said, a bit more firmly than he'd intended. "What do I owe you?"

Her dark eyes glittered with amusement he suspected was at his expense, but she rang up his purchases without commenting further on his personal life.

He left the candy store and headed straight for his car. He had a column to write that afternoon, and he planned to lock himself into his apartment until it was finished. He didn't even glance at the diner as he passed it.

Two hours later, he was sitting in front of his computer, his mind as blank as the monitor in front of him. A sizable dent had been made in his bag of jelly beans. He was beginning to feel a little queasy from his sugar lunch.

He'd heard Teresa arrive home five minutes or so ago. She was early; he hoped nothing was wrong. Any hope he'd had of coming up with a clever column idea had vanished with the sound of her car pulling into the driveway. All his energy was turned toward keeping himself from going to her.

No matter how hard he tried, he hadn't been able to put her out of his mind since Saturday night. He kept remembering things. Like the unexpectedly sensual way she danced. And the heat of her response to his kisses. Even now he could feel a responsive warmth coursing through him.

So much fire. So much passion. And she kept it all so deeply banked.

Frustrated with his lack of progress—in work and in putting Teresa out of his mind—he stood and walked downstairs, thinking he would make a pot of coffee. Maybe the bite of caffeine would counteract the sweetness of the jelly beans.

He didn't know how he ended up at the front door

when he'd intended to go to the kitchen. Even as he stepped outside into the breezy afternoon air, he asked himself what on earth he was doing.

This was no way to get over her.

Teresa had been sitting in her living room, trying to read but finding it very difficult to concentrate. She was home a little earlier than usual. The lunch rush had fizzled to just a few lingering customers, and Marjorie had urged her to go home.

"You look tired," she had said. "Go spend a little quiet time before the children get home. Take a bubble bath. Read a good book. Rest."

Rest. Something Teresa hadn't gotten enough of lately. She'd spent entirely too many hours lying wide-eyed in bed, replaying every minute of Saturday night.

The hour and a half before her children were due home stretched in front of her. Maybe she should have stayed at the diner and helped Marjorie set up for breakfast in the morning. At least that would have kept her too busy to think.

The knock on her door almost made her heart stop, because she knew who was on the other side. He'd been staying away since their date—whether to give her some space or because he'd finally accepted there was no chance of anything happening between them, she couldn't say.

Wiping her hands down the front of her khaki slacks, she drew a deep breath and opened the door.

Riley stood on the stoop, one hand resting on the doorjamb. The brisk breeze tossed his longish brown hair around his lean face and into his silvery-gray eyes. He wore a long-sleeve black T-shirt and faded jeans, and he looked young and lean—and, for the first time since she'd met him, just a little bit intimidating. Maybe it was his brooding expression. The hard set of his jaw. Or the glint of what might have been anger in his eyes.

Afraid that he'd heard bad news, she asked with her heart in her throat, "What's wrong?"

"It isn't working."

"*What* isn't working?"

"I've been trying to convince myself to stay away from you. But I keep remembering how good we are together. Thinking about how good we could be."

Her knees threatened to go weak. "I thought we agreed—"

"*This* is what we agree on," he muttered, pulling her somewhat roughly into his arms.

Without giving herself time to think about it, she met the kiss halfway, her hands going to his shoulders.

She heard him kick the door closed behind him. Felt the bunching of muscles in his arms and torso as he gathered her closer. The tension in him was palpable, the hunger unmistakable. She couldn't have resisted him just then if she'd tried.

She didn't try.

He rained kisses over her face, nuzzled her throat, nipped at the lobe of her ear. "How long do we have?" he asked in a mutter.

"Just over an hour," she whispered.

"It's not enough." He kissed her mouth again, a long, deep, drugging kiss. "But I'll take what I can get."

They barely made it up the stairs. They stopped every few feet to kiss, to explore, to pleasure. By the time they reached her bed, they were both panting, their clothes already half off. Riley swept the spread out of the way, then tumbled her onto the sheets, falling on top of her. She'd already lost the clip that had held her hair; he buried his fingers in the soft waves and crushed her mouth beneath his.

She got rid of his pullover, baring his chest to her eager hands. His skin was warm and smooth, stretched tautly over muscles that were rather surprisingly well-defined, considering his sleek physique. He wasn't exactly the indolent couch potato he liked to pretend to be.

There were a lot of things about Riley that weren't quite what they seemed.

Having dispensed with her shirt, he skillfully released the clasp of her bra. There wasn't time to be self-conscious about her nudity; his hands and mouth were already covering her, driving inhibitions out of her mind. Her back arched, her fingers clenching in his hair. His teeth closed lightly around her nipple and she gasped, sensations shooting through her to sensitize every inch of her body.

Still paying exquisite attention to her breast, he ran a hand down her stomach and inside the unsnapped front of her jeans, his fingertips sliding beneath the elastic top of her panties. When he reached the damp heat between her legs, she nearly erupted from the bed.

"Easy," he murmured, raising his head to kiss her lips again.

It didn't seem quite fair that he was still coherent while she was losing her mind. She reached deliberately between them, her fingers closing around him through the tightly stretched fabric of his jeans. He jerked as if he'd been shocked.

To her great satisfaction, his movements grew less practiced, more urgent. Rolling across the bed, they struggled out of the remainder of their clothes, tossing them recklessly aside, ignoring the thud of the overturned brass lamp on her nightstand. Teresa didn't hear anything break—and wouldn't have cared at that point if she had.

Riley had enough presence of mind to take care of protection—and she was too grateful to wonder whether he made a habit of carrying the little packet in his pocket or had brought it specifically for this. They'd have been in trouble if he hadn't thought of it; condoms weren't something she'd had reason to buy during the past few years.

A thin cry escaped her when he surged into her. Her legs locked around him, and she moved with him in an almost desperate pursuit of release. She peaked quickly, hard pulses of pleasure racking her body. Through the sensual haze that blurred her vision, she saw a rather feral flash of satisfaction cross Riley's face, and then he, too, allowed himself to climax with a deep, raw groan.

Murmuring her name, he kissed her lingeringly, then collapsed on the bed beside her.

Teresa lay motionless for a long time, trying to re-member how to breathe normally, letting her pulse return to something close to a steady rate. Her entire body still thrummed with an occasional vibration, faint aftershocks from the earthquake they'd created between them.

She was finding it hard to believe she'd just had wild, steamy sex with Riley O'Neal. That he was even now lying damp and naked in her bed, one strong arm stretched beneath her.

She didn't have to ask herself if she'd lost her mind. She had. No doubt about it.

Having accepted that premise, what truly amazed her was that she had absolutely no regrets. Concerns, yes. She knew she had just risked complications that could only lead to heartache on her part—but she wasn't sorry. How could she be? It had been fabulous.

She felt him drop a kiss on the top of her head. "Are you okay?"

Her smile felt shaky. "I think so."

"I think we just blew our professional landlord-tenant arrangement."

She laughed softly. "I think you're right."

"I really did try to stay away."

"I really tried to *want* you to stay away."

"It was inevitable, I guess. We were an explosion waiting to happen."

"I suppose you're right." Even when she'd first met him, her reactions to him had been strong. She'd tried to convince herself then that she didn't like him. She hadn't wanted to admit that she had been drawn to him from the first time he'd looked at her and smiled.

She still wasn't free to admit that.

Reminded of her obligations, she lifted her head to check the clock on the nightstand. The numerals were covered by a pair of white briefs. Her lamp lay drunkenly on its side, and piles of clothes—hers and his—were tangled together on the floor, along with the spread from her bed. Definitely a scene of debauchery, she thought with a slight wince.

"Where are you going?" he asked, tightening his arm around her when she moved to rise. "We have a little time yet."

"It's going to take me a while to put everything back in order," she replied, and lifted a hand to her tumbled hair. "Myself included."

Lifting himself to one elbow, he watched as she righted the lamp and gathered her clothes. She was a bit self-conscious now that the haze of passion had receded.

She was thirty-one and the mother of two. Her workout routine consisted of doing housework, waiting tables and trying to keep up with the kids. She wasn't model thin or athletically muscled—but Riley hadn't seemed to mind a few minutes earlier.

He didn't seem to mind now, either. His expression was appreciative when she risked a quick look at him. "Come back to bed," he urged.

"I can't. And you need to get dressed."

The smile he gave her should have been illegal. He patted the bed. "Just for a few more minutes?"

"No. My children will be home soon. I need to get ready for them."

He sighed.

She paused in the doorway to look at him steadily. "You knew when you came to my door that this is who I am."

"Yeah." He swung his legs over the side of the bed and reached for his clothes. "I knew."

With a sigh of her own, she stepped into the bathroom and closed the door behind her.

He was a rat. Selfish, greedy and overindulged. Maybe his parents should have had more kids—just so he could have learned to share.

Riley was sitting in front of his computer again, and the monitor was as empty as it had been before. There was silence in his home, but if he listened very closely he could almost hear the sounds of laughter coming from the adjoining apartment. Teresa was probably having a great time over there with her kids. She'd probably forgotten all about him.

He was a jerk.

He had finally found a woman he couldn't put out of

his mind when he wasn't with her. A woman he wanted so badly he couldn't even remember his own iron-clad rules when he thought of her. A woman whose love-making had taken him higher, deeper, further than he'd ever been before—and he thought he'd experienced it all.

He'd been wrong.

Damn it, he'd fallen in love for the first time in his life, and he couldn't have chosen anybody more wrong for him.

Love. The word made him break out in a sweat. It wasn't really love he felt for Teresa, of course. Not the always-and-forever type of love, anyway. It was more like lust—with a whole lot of liking thrown in. Teresa was...special.

And he was a selfish, greedy rat.

He hadn't wanted to leave her after they'd made love. All he'd wanted was to make love to her again until neither of them had enough strength left to move a limb. And then he'd wanted to sleep with her in his arms, wake up and start all over again.

But she had had to get ready to welcome her kids home from school. And then to feed them and bathe them and help them with their homework and whatever else a mom did, leaving very little time for herself—or for him.

Which was exactly why he'd always made it a practice not to get involved with women with children, he reminded himself irritably. He never had gotten very good at that sharing thing.

Maybe he should have accepted her invitation to join them for dinner. But even as that thought crossed his mind, he knew it would have been a mistake. It would be prolonging the inevitable and adding the children to the list of people who were probably going to be disappointed when this attraction faded—as he was sure it would. They all did, eventually.

Maybe he should have bought those fancy candy things for the kids.

Muttering a curse, he shoved himself away from the computer. This was ridiculous. Riley O'Neal didn't sit around moping over a woman. And he sure as hell didn't want to spend a Friday evening watching television with her and her kids. There were parties going on out there, people who knew how to have a good time without expecting the festivities to last forever.

He was tired of sitting here alone in his rooms, worrying about his uncle, brooding about Teresa, telling himself what a louse he was. His uncle was old enough to take care of himself, Teresa had her children to occupy her time, and his character flaws were probably too deeply ingrained to change at this point.

He was going out to have a good time—and to remind himself of why he liked being footloose and free to do whatever he wanted, whenever he wanted.

Except, of course, for the one thing he wanted most— which was to be alone with Teresa again.

It was almost noon Saturday when Teresa heard a knock on her front door.

"I'll get it," Maggie said, starting to rise from the table where she and her brother were having lunch.

Teresa closed the washer she'd just finished loading. "*I'll* get it," she said. "You finish your lunch."

She mentally appraised her appearance as she approached the front door. Ponytail, little makeup, unbuttoned denim shirt over a white T-shirt and khakis. She most assuredly looked like a soccer mom today—and perhaps that was for the best. She'd seen Riley's face yesterday when she'd reminded him of her obligations to her children. She thought she had made it clear that they would always come first to her. She was all they had.

She needn't have worried about her appearance, she decided a moment later. Riley looked as though he'd just climbed out of bed. His hair was rumpled; his eyes were heavy-lidded. He hadn't shaved, and his shirt and jeans looked like he might have slept in them. He'd shoved his bare feet into a pair of sneakers but hadn't bothered to tie them.

"Um, just get up?" she asked, trying to read his somewhat glazed expression.

"Why is your phone off the hook?"

"It's not—is it?"

"According to the operator it is."

She grimaced. "Maggie," she called. "Did you leave the phone off the hook when you were talking to Samantha this morning?"

"Oops," Maggie yelped from the other room. "I'll go check."

Teresa turned apologetically to Riley. "She was talking to a friend earlier. I guess she didn't get the receiver back in the cradle completely. Were you trying to call?"

"No. Serena was. She said to tell you it wasn't important, but she was starting to get worried that something was wrong, so she called me to come check on you."

"And she woke you up," Teresa guessed. "I'm sorry."

"Not your fault." Riley shoved a hand through his hair. "Do you have any coffee?"

"I can make a fresh—" She suddenly stopped, staring at his left ear. "What is that?"

"What—oh." He lifted a hand to the small gold hoop in his earlobe and grimaced sheepishly. "I guess I got my ear pierced. Damn, that's sore."

"You got your ear pierced," she repeated slowly, staring at him. "After you left here yesterday?"

"Last night. There was this group of guys at Gaylord's, and everybody decided to go to the twenty-four-hour tattoo and piercing parlor next door, and someone said I'd look like a younger version of Harrison Ford if I... Oh, hell, mark it up to temporary insanity. I don't know what I was thinking."

What he was *drinking* was probably more accurate, Teresa thought with a shake of her head. "Come in and have some coffee. You look like you could use some. Oh, and by the way, you don't look at all like Harrison Ford—with or without the earring."

"Just start a coffee IV line in my arm," he muttered, following her into the kitchen. "You can mock me later."

Maggie had returned from the other room, her expression guilty. "Sorry, Mommy. The phone wasn't hung up right."

"Whoa, Riley. You look hungover," Mark observed with the typical tact of a ten-year-old boy. "Like Bruce Willis in that movie I saw at Jacob's house last week."

"Mark!" Teresa frowned at her son in disapproval. "You know better than to say things like that."

She was definitely going to be more vigilant about monitoring what movies her son was watching with his friends.

Riley pulled out a chair and dropped into it. "I'm just

sort of tired," he said a bit awkwardly to the boy. "I guess I stayed up too late last night."

Teresa started a pot of coffee, then opened the refrigerator. "We're having tuna salad sandwiches and raw vegetables for lunch, Riley. Are you hungry?"

He swallowed. "I think I'll just start with the coffee, thanks."

Ignoring the remains of her lunch, Maggie had been staring at Riley with a frown. "Are you wearing an earring, Riley?"

"He's not—hey. Yes, he is. Why did you do that, Riley?" Mark asked curiously.

Teresa thought Riley looked as though he'd rather like to disappear beneath the table. Served him right, she thought, taking a coffee mug out of the cabinet. She didn't appreciate him showing up in front of her kids sporting the evidence of a night of carousing.

If he was trying to prove that she shouldn't be thinking of him as a potential stepparent for her children, he could have spared himself a headache and a sore ear. How dense did he think she was?

She thought she saw an apology in his eyes when she set his coffee in front of him. He accepted it with a murmur of thanks, lifting it to his lips as if it were a lifesaving elixir.

"If you two are finished with your lunches, why don't you go play upstairs for a little while," she suggested, glancing at the children's nearly empty plates. "Riley and I need to talk about something."

As usual, Maggie jumped up to obey, while Mark looked as though he wanted to linger. The look Teresa gave him made him reluctantly leave the room, saying over his shoulder, "Don't leave without saying goodbye, okay, Riley?"

"I won't." Riley waited until they were out of hearing before saying, "Sorry. I guess I shouldn't have come in. I wanted to talk to you, but I should have waited until later."

Cradling her coffee mug between her hands, she sat in a chair close to his and looked at him. "You're always welcome here," she said rather primly. "I'll back up your story that you aren't feeling well today."

"You shouldn't have to lie to your kids for my sake. Damn it, I *am* hungover—for the first time in at least a decade."

"Maybe I'm a bad influence on you," she murmured, studying the disgusted look on his face.

He sighed. "I was trying to prove something last night. To myself, not to you."

"And did you?"

"Oh, yeah," he muttered. "But it wasn't what I expected."

He looked so somber that she couldn't help taking pity on him. A little. "If it makes you feel any better, I rather like the earring."

He winced. "I'm just glad I didn't let them talk me into a tattoo."

So was she, actually.

She started to say something else but was interrupted by another knock on her door. "That's probably Serena or Marjorie, or both, here to check on me," she said. "I should have called to let them know I'm fine."

"I told them I'd call if there was a problem."

"I'll go see who it is."

She nearly collided in the entryway with her children, who had dashed down the stairs to see who was calling. "Would you two stay back?" she asked in exasperation.

"Honestly, you would think no one ever came to our door."

"They don't very often," Maggie said as Teresa opened the door.

The man on her stoop was a stranger. Somewhere in his late thirties, perhaps, he had thinning brown hair, a ruddy broad face and narrowed brown eyes. His expression was bland, but something about him gave her an odd feeling. "May I help you?"

"Would you mind if I come in?" His tone was polite, his voice gruff. "I have some information about Bud O'Neal that might interest you."

Riley moved behind Teresa. She hadn't realized he'd followed her from the kitchen. "I'm Riley O'Neal, Bud's nephew. Who are you? And what do you know about Bud?" he demanded of the newcomer.

The man stepped inside, closing the door behind him. Mark, curious as always about someone new, stepped closer to study him, though Teresa motioned him to stay back.

"My name is Carl Brannon Jr." The visitor kept his eyes on Riley as he spoke. "Does that mean anything to you?"

Riley frowned. "There used to be a guy who lived here in town named Carl Brannon. He was a schoolmate of my uncle's. You're his son?"

"Yes. He's dead now. He died last Christmas."

Teresa's eyes widened. Another friend of Bud's who had recently died? Was it possible that this man knew something about what was going on?

Judging from Riley's sudden tension, she suspected his thoughts mirrored hers. "I'm sorry to hear that," he said. "But why are you here?"

"I need to talk to your uncle. I was hoping you could tell me where he is."

"Uncle Bud's on vacation," Mark volunteered. "He's going to take me fishing when he gets home."

"Mark, please," Teresa said. This was no time for her chatty son to try to get in on the conversation.

"My uncle is out of town," Riley said evenly. "If you'd like to go next door to my place and talk to me, I'd be happy to try to get a message to Bud."

"I'd rather talk to your uncle personally. So if you could just tell me where he is…"

"I'm sorry, I'm not at liberty to say."

A dark flush came from beneath Brannon's shirt collar and spread up his already reddened face. "I want to know where he is. Hightower, too. I think you'd better tell me."

Teresa's heart jumped into her throat in response to the man's tone. This guy was dangerous, she realized abruptly. Belatedly. Why had she allowed herself to be so distracted with her other problems that she'd permitted him to come inside her home?

"Mark, Maggie, go upstairs," she said quietly. "Now."

Maggie ran upstairs, and Mark started to follow. He didn't even argue. Perhaps he, too, realized something was wrong. He had taken only a step when Brannon reached out to grab his shoulder, jerking the boy against him.

"Hey!" Mark protested.

Teresa and Riley both moved instinctively to intercede, Teresa's face flushing with anger that someone had dared touch her child.

The gun seemed to appear from out of nowhere. Teresa went still, her heart seeming to freeze in her chest.

Brannon held the weapon in his right hand as he gripped Mark with his left. He wasn't pointing the gun at Mark, but he got his point across.

"Where are O'Neal and Hightower?" he asked Riley quietly. Menacingly. "Tell me now, and no one here gets hurt."

Chapter Fifteen

Riley had never considered himself a violent person. But seeing Carl Brannon's hands on young Mark and the fear in the boy's eyes and on Teresa's stricken face made a surge of fury go through him. If—when—he managed to get his hands on this guy, he wasn't sure what he would do to him.

"Please," Teresa said, her voice shaking. "Let my son go upstairs with his sister. He's just a little boy."

"I'm not going to hurt him," Brannon said. "Not if your friend here tells me what I want to know."

"I don't know where Bud is," Riley insisted, trying to keep his tone mollifying. "He didn't tell me where he was going. I assume he and R.L. are together, but no one around here knows where they went."

"I don't believe you. They wouldn't leave without telling someone. Their families, their friends. The cops."

Riley shook his head. "I'm the only family Bud has

in this town. If he'd told anyone, it would have been me.''

''I don't believe you!'' the other man shouted. ''They wouldn't just disappear. I've looked everywhere for them, waited hours outside Hightower's house and your uncle's crappy trailer. I kept figuring they had to come back. They live here, damn it.''

Riley help up both hands in a gesture meant to calm the guy. ''What do you want with them?''

''That's none of your business. Just tell me where they are.''

Mark tried to move toward his mother, who hadn't taken her eyes off him since Brannon grabbed him.

Brannon tightened his grip, making Mark wince in pain. ''Be still!''

Teresa reached out instinctively toward her son. ''Please let him go,'' she begged. ''You're frightening him.''

''Let the boy go,'' Riley added. ''You won't get anything this way.''

''Tell me where they are!''

He was facing a man who had gone over an edge, Riley realized sickly. Dan would have known how to handle this situation. But Riley didn't have a clue. He knew only that Mark was on the verge of tears, Teresa was terrified, and it was up to him to do something.

''Let the boy go,'' he repeated. ''I'll go with you to my apartment, and we'll talk. You can keep the gun.''

Teresa tore her eyes from her son to glance at Riley, violently shaking her head. He made a motion with his hand, assuring her he knew what he was doing. Which was, of course, a blatant lie.

Brannon's hand was starting to shake—not a good sign. Riley balanced his weight on both feet, ready to spring forward at the first opportunity. His heart was beating so fast he thought it might burst. There was nothing he wouldn't do to get Mark away from this guy—but he was petrified that he would do something wrong and somehow make everything worse.

He moved experimentally, and the barrel of the gun was suddenly pointed directly at his chest. He took another step forward, his eyes locked with Brannon's.

Reacting to the determination he must have seen on Riley's face, Brannon tightened his grip on the weapon, his hold on Mark loosening. "Stay where you are."

Riley moved a step closer. He heard Teresa gasp, but he kept his full attention focused on the other man. He was close enough that he could dive forward and grab the gun before Brannon could turn it on Mark. What he couldn't guarantee was that he could grab it before Brannon pulled the trigger.

If only he could make sure Mark and Teresa were out of the way. "Let's talk, Brannon."

"You're the only one who's going to talk," Brannon insisted, extending his arm in Riley's direction. He seemed to have almost forgotten the boy. "Tell me where they are."

From the corner of his eye, Riley noted that Teresa had inched closer to her son, and he knew she was as poised to act as he was. "*Now,* Terry!" he snapped, and made his leap.

Teresa must have grabbed the boy and jerked him out of Brannon's grasp, because suddenly Brannon was fighting Riley with both hands. Riley clutched the other man's wrist, struggling to keep the gun pointed upward. Brannon was bigger, but their strength seemed to be about equally matched.

At least Riley hoped so.

The gun went off, so loud in Riley's ear that the sound seemed to echo inside his skull. An oddly detached part of his mind seemed to observe the details of the desperate scene in the little entryway—the screams from Teresa and Mark, the rain of plaster from the broken ceiling, his and Brannon's grunts and growls as they fought for control of the weapon. And then the crash of the front door opening.

He hoped that sound meant Teresa was getting her son outside to safety, and he prayed Maggie was hiding somewhere equally safe. And that his own strength would hold out until help arrived.

Other hands joined unexpectedly with his, overpowering Brannon. Riley was suddenly surrounded by people.

Still shaken and disoriented by the events of the past few minutes, it took an effort on his part to identify everyone. Dan was there, holding Brannon facedown on the floor while he cuffed his hands behind his back. And Bud and R.L., standing on either side of Riley to support him when he swayed, his limbs shaking from exertion and fear.

He shook them off. "What the hell is going on?" he demanded of his uncle.

"I'll tell you everything," Bud promised. "As soon as things settle down."

Teresa and Mark were there suddenly, both of them determined to make sure Riley was unharmed. "I can't believe you threw yourself at him like that," Teresa scolded, her face still unnaturally colorless. "You could have been killed."

"I had to do something." Riley wrapped his arms around Mark as the boy hid his face in Riley's chest. He felt the heavy shudders going through the little body, and he held him closer, his eyes meeting Teresa's over Mark's head. "Find Maggie."

She was already moving toward the stairs, calling her daughter's name.

The sound of sirens—something not often heard in this usually quite little cul-de-sac—grew louder as Dan's officers arrived to take Brannon away. Through the open door, Riley could see curious neighbors gathering on the sidewalk. Lindsey would be here soon, and Cameron and Serena and Marjorie, most likely. He could have used a few minutes to sit quietly and recuperate—preferably with Teresa—but he had a feeling he wasn't going to have that luxury for a while.

Teresa returned with Maggie, who also threw herself at Riley, so that he had two trembling children clinging to him. Maybe he should have felt trapped, suffocated. But all he could seem to do was hold them more tightly, his eyes locked with their mother's.

"Your mouth is bleeding," Bud said, staring intently at his nephew's face.

Riley could feel the throbbing of a split lip. He must have been too numb from shock to feel it earlier. He remembered Brannon getting in a couple of wild blows while they had wrestled for the gun. "I'm okay."

"And what the hell is that? An earring?" Bud demanded, taking a step closer. "What possessed you to—"

"Riley would probably like to sit down, Bud." Teresa interceded quickly, placing a hand on the older man's arm. "Let's get him into the kitchen where I can put some ice on his poor mouth."

"All right. But I still want to hear about that earring," Bud added darkly.

It was going to be a very long day, Riley decided in

resignation. And heaven only knew when he was going to be alone with Teresa again. He had a few things to tell her when that opportunity finally arrived.

It seemed to Teresa that there was a great mob of people in her little kitchen. She could hardly move without bumping into someone. The six wooden kitchen chairs were all filled. Riley sat in one, holding an ice bag to his mouth and talking to Dan, who sat in the chair on his left side, taking notes. R.L. and Bud took up two of the other chairs, Bud holding Maggie in his lap while Mark, still unnaturally quiet from his ordeal, leaned against his side. Marjorie and Serena, who had just arrived after being called by someone, occupied the final two chairs, Marjorie on Riley's right.

Cameron North leaned against a counter, sipping coffee and quietly watching the proceedings. Lindsey Meadows, who'd been working at the newspaper office and had hurried over as soon as she'd heard what was happening, stayed close enough to her husband to hear what he and Riley were saying but was careful not to interrupt as she scribbled in her reporter's notebook.

Teresa had refused to sit, needing to stay busy to calm herself. She'd made coffee and sandwiches and filled plates with cookies and chips. No one seemed to be eating, but that didn't matter. Setting out the food gave her something to do with her hands. The others must have sensed what she needed, because no one tried to discourage her actions.

Riley had already told Dan everything that had happened after Carl Brannon arrived at the door. Now he wanted to know the rest of the story, as did Teresa. "I want details," he said, addressing the comment equally to Bud, R.L. and Dan.

"Your uncle and R.L. and I were on our way to meet here when I got the call that Maggie had called nine-one-one," Dan explained.

Teresa felt her eyes go wide. She turned from the counter to stare at her daughter. "You called nine-one-one?"

Maggie nodded. "When that man grabbed Mark and you sent me upstairs, I knew I'd better call the police," she said matter-of-factly.

"Good thinking," Riley complimented her. "You really kept your head."

"I was scared," Maggie admitted. "But I didn't know how else to help."

"You did exactly the right thing," Bud assured her, tightening his arm around her. "That's my brave, smart girl."

She beamed under his approval, responding to him as the surrogate grandfather Bud had become to Teresa's children despite her efforts to keep them from getting too involved with Riley and his uncle.

"Anyway," Dan continued, "Bud had called me a short while earlier and asked me to meet him and R.L. here at Riley's place. They said they had some information I would want to hear, but they wanted to tell me in front of Riley. As I said, I was on my way to meet them here when Maggie's call came in. I requested backup and got here as quickly as I could. Brannon's van was parked in Teresa's driveway. Bud and R.L. pulled in right behind me. We were running toward the front door when we heard the gunshot."

Bud swallowed audibly. "That sound took a few years off my life, I can tell you."

Teresa could identify with that sentiment. She had just taken advantage of Brannon's distraction to pull Mark into her arms and into a corner behind the stairs when she'd heard the gun go off. She had been terrified that Riley had been shot. Torn between protecting her child and rushing to Riley's aid, she'd been paralyzed with a crippling fear that she prayed she would never have to experience again.

She was glad when Riley spoke, distracting her from the painful replay. "Why were you coming here, Bud? Did you know Brannon was here? And what the he—heck did the guy want with you, anyway?"

He'd looked at the kids when he'd changed his words. Trying to be a better influence on them? Teresa wondered.

Bud kissed Maggie's cheek, then said, "Marjorie, darlin', have you seen the kids' rooms lately? They have some very interesting collections."

"Of course." Smiling sweetly, Marjorie stood and reached out a hand to Maggie. "Will you show me your toys, children?"

"They want us to leave the room," Mark told his little sister with a resigned sigh.

"I know," Maggie answered in a stage whisper. And then she smiled at Marjorie and took the offered hand. "But that's okay. Mommy will tell us about it later, won't you, Mommy?"

She nodded. She would tell them what she thought they needed to know. She knew Serena and Cameron would make sure Marjorie learned all the details.

Bud waited only until the children were out of the room before responding to his nephew's obvious impatience. He looked at Dan, then at Lindsey and Cameron. "You decide how much of this you want in the papers, Dan. I guess there's no way we can keep it quiet with the owner and the whole staff of the newspaper right here with us.''

"Just talk," Dan advised a bit gruffly. "I want to know everything you know about Brannon and what he's been up to.''

Bud and R.L. exchanged glances. R.L. gestured for Bud to speak.

Drawing a deep breath, Bud began. "It started more than thirty-five years ago. R.L., Truman and I were still in our twenties, old enough to be working but still young enough that we spent most of our weekends partying. I already had one divorce behind me. Truman was engaged but still sowing some wild oats. He started hanging around quite a bit with an old friend from high school. Carl Brannon.''

"The father of the guy I just arrested?" Dan clarified.

Bud nodded. "Carl was trouble. Always had been. R.L. and I didn't like to be around him much, but Truman kind of hero-worshiped him. He thought Carl was cool and tough, wouldn't take any guff off anybody. You know the type. Anyway, Carl started getting into trouble with the law, and R.L. and I warned Truman he was going to get caught up in it if he wasn't careful.''

"Told him Carl was a loser," R.L. muttered.

Bud continued. "So Truman comes to us one night all upset and he says he's in trouble. Real trouble. Carl just knocked over a liquor store and shot the clerk. Truman was with him.''

Teresa looked at Riley, who was suddenly frowning, the ice pack long since discarded as he listened to the story. "Carl Brannon went to prison for killing that liquor store clerk. I remember reading about it in the newspaper archives. But there was no mention of Truman being involved.''

"Bud and I covered for him," R.L. explained, casting a quick, guilty look at Dan. "We all went to the chief of police at that time and told him we had reason to believe Carl was the shooter. We implied that we'd overheard him telling someone else about it. Bud and I swore that Truman was with us that night, and his fiancée said she was there, too. Carl tried to convince the cops Truman was involved, but there was never enough evidence to implicate him. The cops just assumed he was trying to get back at us for turning him in."

Dan's face had gone hard. "You knew Truman had been involved in a murder and you protected him?"

"He wasn't involved in the way you mean," Bud said quickly. "He and Carl had been out drinking, driving around in Carl's car. Carl said he was too drunk to drive, so he gave Truman his keys and told him he was in better shape. He asked Truman to stop at the liquor store. Truman told us he didn't want to stop, but Carl talked him into it. Truman waited outside while Carl went inside. The next thing he knew, Carl was running out of the store, stuffing a gun and a handful of cash in his jacket and telling Truman to step on the gas. There were no witnesses, so there was never any proof that Carl didn't work alone."

Bud took up the tale again. "Truman drove back to Carl's place, and the two of them got into a big fight. Carl offered Truman half the money, but he refused. Said he didn't want anything to do with it. Carl threatened to kill Truman if he said anything and told Truman he would take him down with him if he was caught. He convinced Truman they'd both do life—Carl for murder, Truman for being an accessory. Truman came to us damn near hysterical. That's when we convinced him we could protect him but we wouldn't protect Carl."

"Acting on our tip, the cops raided Carl's place," R.L. said. "They found the cash and a gold watch the clerk had been wearing. The clerk's mother identified it, said it had belonged to his late father. Carl went to prison, and Truman became a model citizen. Married his sweetheart, never caused anyone a day's trouble in this town."

"There was a confidential reward for information leading to Carl's arrest," Bud added heavily. "Ten thousand dollars. R.L. and I split it. That's the money we used to start our businesses a few years later. Truman wouldn't touch a penny of it. He never fully recovered from that night. He was never the same guy afterward."

"You shouldn't have protected him," Dan argued. "Doing so made both of you accessories after the fact."

"The statute of limitations on that has long passed," Serena said, using what Teresa had always considered her attorney's voice. "Even at the time it would have been debatable whether Bud and R.L. could have been charged with much more than interfering with an official investigation. There is no statute of limitations on murder, so Truman could, perhaps, still face charges if he were living. Since he's not, I'm not sure there would be any purpose in the details of this story getting out."

"We'll decide that when we've heard everything," Cameron said, speaking as the managing editor of her newspaper. "Go on, Bud. Tell us the rest."

"We knew Carl had a son, though he never married the boy's mother. She moved away from the area after Carl went to prison. None of us heard anything from any of them since. Then Truman died in that fire earlier this year. R.L. and I were upset, of course. The three of us had been together a long time, been through a lot together. We didn't expect to lose one of us so soon."

"We thought that Stamps boy had something to do with it," R.L. said. "We never thought of Carl, though Bud and I talked a lot about what had happened all those years ago after Truman died. About how he'd never gotten over it and all."

"Then R.L.'s place burned." Bud took up the tale. "It seemed strange to us that the Stamps kid would hit two of us, but we still didn't think of Carl. Until someone tried to shoot R.L. in his bed. That's when we started to put it all together. R.L. left town to do some research. I stayed in touch with him, of course. Knew where he was the whole time. It turned out Carl died in prison last Christmas."

"Yes, his son told us that," Riley murmured.

"We were pretty confused for a while. I started getting the feeling that someone was watching me," Bud confessed. "One night a van followed me down Snake Hill, then passed me so close I damned near ran off the road and into the ravine. It was all I could do to keep from it."

"Damn it, Bud, you should have told me!" Riley exploded, obviously having listened patiently for as long as he could.

"I was going to," Bud answered apologetically. "I really was. After you brought Teresa home from that fancy dinner. I thought everything would be okay until then. I didn't think whoever was after me would know I was at Teresa's place with the kids. If I'd thought I could be putting them—or anyone else—in danger I'd have stayed far away from them. When I saw the van that had nearly run me off the road sitting outside the house that night—well, that's when I decided to get out of town before someone was hurt."

It was R.L.'s turn to speak. "He came to me. We kept

looking for answers. It was pretty obvious to us that our problems had something to do with Carl Brannon. That was the only trouble any of us had ever been in. We found out Carl's son used to visit him in prison real often and that Carl filled the boy full of bull about what a hard life he'd led. How everything and everyone had conspired against him—including a bunch of guys who had set him up for murder. He told his son he had nothing to do with that liquor store robbery, that he was framed. By us.''

''Turned out Carl Junior was just as big a loser as his father,'' Bud said. ''Everything he tried failed. He'd been dumped by his second wife and been fired from a dead-end job just before his father died. He needed someone besides himself to blame his failures on. He decided to follow his father's example and blame us.''

''He told his ex-wife that we'd profited from framing his father,'' R.L. said. ''That we'd taken the reward money and started businesses and lived comfortable lives while Carl Senior rotted in prison. He decided to take revenge.''

''You found all this out since you left town?'' Dan asked skeptically.

R.L. lifted a shoulder. ''I had to do something. All it took was a few phone calls. I was in business for a lot of years, you know. I had some resources.''

''I helped him when I joined him,'' Bud added. ''It didn't take us long to figure out who had a grudge against us, but we weren't sure we could prove it. When we'd gathered all the information we could find, we came back to town to turn everything over to Dan. I knew Riley would be worried, so R.L. and I decided to have Dan join us at Riley's place where we'd only have to tell the story once. We had no idea Brannon would show up at the same time. I didn't think he would dare come out in the open. I thought he'd either wait for us to return, look for us elsewhere or give up."

"When he couldn't find either of you, he lost patience," Riley explained. "The man I faced this afternoon had gone over the edge. I don't know if his father was crazy or just criminal, but Junior's nuts."

Teresa shivered, remembering the look in Carl Brannon Junior's eyes. She agreed with Riley's assessment. The man had been out of control. And he'd had his hands on her son.

"Teresa, sit down," Lindsey urged, suddenly appearing at her side. "You've gone pale."

"I'm fine," she protested, but allowed herself to be guided into the seat Marjorie had vacated, the one next to Riley.

He reached out to cover her icy hands with one of his own. "Are you okay?"

"Still a little shaky," she admitted. "But okay."

He squeezed her hand. "I know the feeling," he murmured.

Dan had a great many more questions for Bud and R.L., of course. Lindsey, Serena and Cameron had some questions, as well. Oddly enough, Teresa and Riley had the least to say. She suspected it was because they were both still too dazed to think of anything to ask.

He was still holding her hand, and she didn't pull away. For now, she needed to cling to him. She would be strong and independent again later, when she had to be.

Dan eventually turned to Riley. "I do have one more question for you."

Teresa thought Riley sounded weary when he responded. "What is it?"

"When the hell did you start wearing an earring?"

* * *

It seemed like hours later when things had settled down and Teresa and her children were alone again. To her great relief, Mark seemed to have recovered almost completely from his scare. She talked to him for quite a while after Maggie went to sleep and then, reassured that he was all right, she left a night-light burning in his room and urged him to call her any time during the night if he needed her.

She placed a soft kiss on his forehead after she tucked him in. "You were so brave today," she murmured. "I'm so proud of you. And so very glad you're safe."

"I'm glad Riley and Uncle Bud are okay," he murmured, his eyelids already growing heavy. "I don't suppose you'd let me get my ear pierced, would you, Mom?"

"Not anytime soon," she answered firmly. "Go to sleep, sweetie. We'll talk more tomorrow."

She walked downstairs knowing it would be several hours before she would sleep. She was afraid to close her eyes for fear of replaying the entire episode. She could almost hear the echo of that gunshot, could feel the fear that had gripped her when she'd thought Riley could be hurt—or worse.

She seemed to have a great talent for falling in love with the wrong men.

The tap on her door was so quiet she barely heard it. Even though she knew who it would be, she checked the security viewer before she released the lock. After today, she wasn't sure she would ever open her door again without a lingering uneasiness.

"I just wanted to make sure you and the kids are okay," Riley said when she let him in. "How is Mark?"

"He's okay. He was so exhausted he fell asleep almost before I turned off his light."

"And Maggie?"

"Also sound asleep. I'll listen for nightmares tonight, but they both seem to be okay."

He glanced at the ugly, ragged hole in her entryway ceiling. "I can almost guarantee that I'm going to be having nightmares for a while. When Brannon grabbed Mark..."

He didn't have to finish the sentence. Clasping her arms, Teresa swallowed hard and nodded. "I know. I was so scared. And then when you jumped at him...and I heard that gun go off..."

"I didn't know what else to do. The way his face was flushing and his hands were beginning to shake, I could tell he was starting to lose whatever control he had. I knew I had to do something before he completely lost it."

"I thought he had shot you." She heard the starkness of her own voice.

He pulled her into his arms, laying his cheek on her hair. "I'm okay. We all are. It's over."

Burying her face in his throat, she drew a shuddering breath. "I know. It's just going to take me a while to recover."

"We'll recover together."

That brought her head up. He hadn't meant that the way it sounded, she assured herself. He was only offering comfort. She wouldn't let either of them get carried away by the aftereffects of terror. "I'm fine now, and so are the children," she assured him, stepping out of his arms. "Thanks for checking on us, but we'll be okay."

"Just the three of you, right?"

She couldn't quite read his tone, but she nodded. "Of course."

"Sometimes I wonder if there's any room for anyone else in the cozy family you've created."

She had her arms wrapped around herself again, a purely defensive gesture. "I'm not sure what you mean."

"Maybe I should be a bit more specific. Is there room for *me*, Teresa?"

Self-protective instincts drove her to take another step backward. "You don't want to be a part of a family," she reminded him, her throat tight. "You want to be completely unattached. Free to spend your evenings hanging out at Gaylord's, having fun drinking and doing crazy, impulsive things."

With a slight wince, he touched his left ear. "Have you once heard me say that I had fun last night? I had a miserable time. I spent the entire evening thinking about you and trying to pretend I wasn't."

"I can't leave my children with sitters every night to go play with you. That's not something I would be willing to do even once a week."

"Nor would I ask you to," he replied evenly. "Your kids deserve better than that."

"Exactly. They deserve to come first with me."

"No argument there. I'm asking if you think there's a chance that I could come second with you, after the kids."

She shook her head. "You don't want to be talking about this now. You aren't thinking clearly tonight. You're getting carried away by everything that happened earlier—"

"What happened earlier scared the stuffing out of me," he interrupted. "I would have willingly given my life to protect Mark and Maggie—and you. But that didn't come as a complete surprise to me. I'd already decided how much you all meant to me.''

''When did you decide that?'' she asked skeptically. ''Before or after you pierced your ear?''

''Would you forget my ear?'' he asked, sounding irritable and more like the Riley she knew so well. ''That was an impulse. A souvenir, in a way.''

''A souvenir of what?''

He shrugged. ''The last night of my old life, I suppose.''

''Now you're not even making sense.'' She half turned away from him, convinced that he would be sorry he said these things after he'd gotten a good night's sleep.

''I love you, Terry.''

She gasped. ''Please don't...''

''You love me, too.''

She stiffened. ''I didn't say that.''

''Yes, you did. When you made love with me. Not in so many words—but I know you well enough to understand that you wouldn't have taken me into your bed if you didn't love me.''

Her throat was so tight she could barely speak, but she managed to say, ''You're a conceited and arrogant man, Riley O'Neal.''

''I know. But no one's ever accused me of being stupid. You're the best thing that ever came into my life, Teresa Scott.''

She closed her eyes, thinking that he'd come to know her too well. He was right, of course. She wouldn't have made love with him had she not loved him. ''I can't talk about this tonight,'' she said. ''It's too much.''

''I'm sorry. I guess my timing's lousy. I was going to

tell you these things earlier, after I had my coffee this morning—but we were interrupted. If you need more time, you've got it. Now that we've found each other, we have all the time in the world.''

All the time in the world. She'd come to understand all too well how unpredictable life was, how quickly things could change.

She'd been only a breath away from losing her son that day. From losing Riley. She was afraid to take any more chances today.

''I was married to a charming, fun-loving man who couldn't follow through on his commitments,'' she murmured. ''Not to a job. Not to his wife. Not even to his children. I think he really wanted to keep his promises, but it just wasn't in him. Schedules suffocated him. Obligations weighed too heavily on him. I tried to be responsible enough for both of us, but it was too much. I can't go through that again.''

She heard Riley release a long, deep breath behind her. ''Looks like I've got my work cut out for me,'' he murmured. ''I'm going to have to prove to you that I'm not your ex-husband. I've had a good time being single and footloose, but I have no doubt that I'll find just as many challenges and just as much satisfaction with you and the kids. However long it takes for me to convince you of that, I'll make you believe me eventually.''

''It could take a very long time,'' she whispered.

His hands fell gently on her shoulders. ''We have all the time in the world.''

Epilogue

Teresa had underestimated Riley's powers of persuasion. They were married on Valentine's Day.

It was a festive occasion, and it seemed that almost everyone in Edstown was in attendance. There were several who said they'd had to see it with their own eyes. Riley O'Neal, a family man. Who would have believed it?

Teresa did. Now.

Smiling at her husband during a brief lull at the crowded reception, she marveled at how handsome he looked in his evening clothes. He'd worn socks for respectability—and the small gold earring to prove that he was still Riley.

She had worn a simple but elegant white suit. In honor of the holiday, she had carried red roses. Her two attendants, Serena and Maggie, had worn red dresses, Serena's cut to accommodate her expanding waistline. Bud and Mark had served as groomsmen. Riley's parents were in attendance, of course, almost humorously delighted that he was getting married and providing them with grandchildren all at once. Teresa was already quite fond of them and believed the feeling was mutual.

It had been a simple wedding, but beautiful. Perfect, in her opinion.

"So how much longer do we have to stay at this thing?" Riley murmured in her ear, sounding impatient to get away.

"We can leave soon," she promised. "I just want to make sure Serena has everything she needs for the children while we're gone."

"You've already checked twice," he reminded her patiently. "You've left her the numbers where we can be reached for the next four days and the kids' schedules mapped out to the minute. And you've given her our keys so she has access to everything the kids own if she needs anything. They'll be fine."

"I know," she admitted. "It's just the first time I've spent so much time away from them."

"If it bothers you that much, we'll cancel the trip. Take a honeymoon later—or take the kids with us."

Though she was touched by his offer, she shook her head. "We deserve a honeymoon. The children understand that. And it's only four days. But thank you for offering."

"To be perfectly honest, I was hoping you would turn me down," he admitted with one of his crooked smiles.

She laughed. "I know. But I know also that the offer was sincere."

"We're going to have a great honeymoon," he said, his eyes gleaming in anticipation.

"I know that, too." She was already tingling in anticipation.

They had so many plans. They were going to build a house by the lake on the property Riley's parents had bought for him. Riley was trying to talk Teresa into enrolling in the local college for summer classes to finish her education and obtain her teaching degree. She was giving it serious consideration.

She'd finally read Riley's novel and she thought it was wonderful. He'd promised to start trying to find a publisher for it as soon as they returned from the honeymoon. In the meantime, he still had his job with the newspaper.

Money would not be a problem. She'd been stunned to learn that Riley had an impressive financial portfolio, a legacy from his mother's parents who'd had no other grandchildren to leave their accumulated assets to. Even the duplex had originally belonged to his parents, the previous owners he'd told her he bought it from.

Because material possessions weren't all that important to him, there had been no way for her to know when she'd met him that he wasn't living paycheck to paycheck. She'd told him since that she was glad he'd waited until after he'd convinced her to marry him to share that information with her. She wouldn't have wanted him to have any doubts that she was marrying him for love, not money.

Just as she knew he had married her for exactly the same reason. As she had acknowledged earlier, he was a very persuasive man. He had made her believe that when he finally made a commitment, he dedicated himself completely to fulfilling it.

She was taking the greatest risk of her life to accept that Riley would always keep his promises to love her, to be faithful to her, to be a loving and devoted step-parent to her children. But somehow she knew that her faith wasn't misplaced this time.

Love had given her the courage to believe in him.

Some of her thoughts must have been reflected in the smile she gave him. His eyes gleamed, and he pulled her close to his side. "When can we leave?" he asked again.

She reached up to kiss him lingeringly. "What's your hurry?" she asked. "We have all the time in the world."

* * * * *

Beloved author
Sherryl Woods
is back with a brand-new miniseries

THE CALAMITY JANES

Five women. Five Dreams.
A lifetime of friendship....

On Sale May 2001—DO YOU TAKE THIS REBEL?
Silhouette Special Edition

On Sale August 2001—COURTING THE ENEMY
Silhouette Special Edition

On Sale September 2001—TO CATCH A THIEF
Silhouette Special Edition

On Sale October 2001—THE CALAMITY JANES
Silhouette Single Title

On Sale November 2001—WRANGLING THE REDHEAD
Silhouette Special Edition

"Sherryl Woods is an author who writes with
a very special warmth, wit, charm and intelligence."
—*New York Times* bestselling author
Heather Graham Pozzessere

Available at your favorite retail outlet.

Where love comes alive™

Visit Silhouette at www.eHarlequin.com   SSETCJR

Celebrate the season with

Midnight Clear

A holiday anthology featuring
a classic Christmas story from
New York Times bestselling author

Debbie Macomber

Plus a brand-new *Morgan's Mercenaries* story
from *USA Today* bestselling author

Lindsay McKenna

And a brand-new *Twins on the Doorstep* story
from national bestselling author

Stella Bagwell

Available at your favorite retail outlets in November 2001!

Silhouette®
Where love comes alive™

Visit Silhouette at www.eHarlequin.com   PSMC

where love comes alive—online...

eHARLEQUIN.com

shop eHarlequin

- ♥ Find all the new Silhouette releases at everyday great discounts.
- ♥ Try before you buy! Read an excerpt from the latest Silhouette novels.
- ♥ Write an online review and share your thoughts with others.

reading room

- ♥ Read our Internet exclusive daily and weekly online serials, or vote in our interactive novel.
- ♥ Talk to other readers about your favorite novels in our Reading Groups.
- ♥ Take our Choose-a-Book quiz to find the series that matches you!

authors' alcove

- ♥ Find out interesting tidbits and details about your favorite authors' lives, interests and writing habits.
- ♥ Ever dreamed of being an author? Enter our Writing Round Robin. The Winning Chapter will be published online! Or review our writing guidelines for submitting your novel.

All this and more available at
www.eHarlequin.com
on Women.com Networks

SINTB1R

Silhouette Books cordially invites you to come
on down to Jacobsville, Texas, for

DIANA PALMER's
LONG, TALL TEXAN
Weddings

(On sale November 2001)

The LONG, TALL TEXANS series from international
bestselling author Diana Palmer is cherished around the
world. Now three sensuous, charming love stories from
this blockbuster series—*Coltrain's Proposal, Beloved* and
"Paper Husband"—are available in one special volume!

*As free as wild mustangs, Jeb, Simon and Hank vowed
never to submit to the reins of marriage. Until, of course,
a certain trio of provocative beauties tempt these Lone Star
lovers off the range...and into a tender, timeless embrace!*

You won't want to miss
LONG, TALL TEXAN WEDDINGS
by Diana Palmer, featuring two
full-length novels and one short story!

Available only from Silhouette Books at your favorite retail outlet.

Where love comes alive™

Visit Silhouette at www.eHarlequin.com

PSLTTW

**Coming soon from
Silhouette Special Edition**

The continuation of a popular miniseries
from bestselling author

SUSAN MALLERY

**DESERT
ROGUES**

**Escape to The City of Thieves—
a secret jewel in the desert where
seduction rules and romantic
fantasies come alive....**

THE SHEIK AND THE RUNAWAY PRINCESS
(SE #1430, on sale November 2001)

**Passions flare between a tempestuous
princess and a seductive sheik....
How hot will it get?**

Available at your favorite retail outlet.

Silhouette®

Where love comes alive™

Visit Silhouette at www.eHarlequin.com   SSEDR01

Revitalize!

With help from
Silhouette's *New York Times*
bestselling authors
and receive a

FREE

Refresher Kit!
Retail Value of $25.00 U.S.

LUCIA IN LOVE by Heather Graham
and LION ON THE PROWL by Kasey Michaels

LOVE SONG FOR A RAVEN by Elizabeth Lowel
and THE FIVE-MINUTE BRIDE by Leanne Bank

MACKENZIE'S PLEASURE by Linda Howard
and DEFENDING HIS OWN by Beverly Barton

DARING MOVES by Linda Lael Miller
and MARRIAGE ON DEMAND by Susan Mallery

Don't miss out!

*Look for this exciting promotion, on sale i
October 2001 at your favorite retail outle.
See inside books for details.*

Only from

Where love comes alive™

Visit Silhouette at www.eHarlequin.com   PSNCP-POPR